Paula's Way

By Anna Jacobs

THE LARCH TREE LANE SERIES

Larch Tree Lane

THE PENNY LAKE SERIES

Changing Lara • Finding Cassie

Marrying Simone

THE PEPPERCORN SERIES

Peppercorn Street • Cinnamon Gardens

Saffron Lane • Bay Tree Cottage

Christmas in Peppercorn Street

THE HONEYFIELD SERIES

The Honeyfield Bequest • A Stranger in Honeyfield

Peace Comes to Honeyfield

THE HOPE TRILOGY

A Place of Hope • In Search of Hope

A Time for Hope

THE GREYLADIES SERIES

Heir to Greyladies • Mistress of Greyladies

Legacy of Greyladies

THE WILTS HIRE GIRLS SERIES

Cherry Tree Lane • Elm Tree Road

Yew Tree Gardens

THE WATERFRONT SERIES

Mara's Choice • Sarah's Gift

Paula's Way

Winds of Change • Moving On

Change of Season • Tomorrow's Path • Chestnut Lane

In Focus • The Corrigan Legacy • A Very Special Christmas

Kirsty's Vineyard • The Cotton Lass and Other Stories

The Best Valentine's Day Ever and Other Stories

a&b

Paula's Way

ANNA JACOBS

Allison & Busby Limited
11 Wardour Mews
London W1F 8AN
allisonandbusby.com

First published in Great Britain by Allison & Busby in 2023.

A CIP catalogue record for this book is available from the British Library.

First Edition

ISBN 978-0-7490-2956-2

Typeset in 11/16 pt Sabon LT Pro by
Allison & Busby Ltd

Printed and bound by
CPI Group (UK) Ltd, Croydon, CR0 4YY

Prologue

Wiltshire, England

Richard Crawford's heart sank when he saw who'd sent the email that had just pinged into his mailbox. It was from the private investigators he'd hired and he'd thought he'd finished with them now. They were only going to contact him if they discovered something new.

He felt such a strong sense of impending disaster he hesitated even to open it.

When he'd finished reading the message, he sat frozen for a moment, then swore and thumped his clenched fist on the desk several times. As the anger subsided, he forced himself to re-read the email and its attachments, paying close attention to every detail. But there could be no doubt what this meant, no hope that it was a mistake.

He'd rearranged his whole life to deal with the situation and it had all been in vain.

The stupid thing was that this last-minute disaster was his own fault entirely. The family lawyers had been quite satisfied with the situation and who should inherit: as grand-nephew of Roy's fourth son, he was the closest relative they'd found alive because it was not the most prolific family. It was he who'd called in another team of private investigators because he'd thought the first lot rather slapdash.

After a while, he telephoned the family lawyer to discuss how best to sort this new situation out. Even there he disagreed with Mr Perett. Such important news ought to be delivered to the new heir personally, not sent by letter. Besides, he needed to get away for a while and rearrange his life all over again. What better excuse could he have than this?

Putting the phone down, he went back online, checking flight times and making a booking.

Only when he could put it off no longer did he go and tell his aunt, who did the weeping for him, and some shouting and thumping of tables as well.

Chapter One

Mandurah, Western Australia

Paula Grey stood behind the bar on her thirty-second birthday, sipping a glass of champagne and smiling round her small domain. Her life was coming together nicely now and that felt good.

When her cheating husband had been killed two years ago in a car accident just a few days after he'd left her, she'd hit an all-time low. She'd had to reluctantly agree to sell their house because she'd not been earning enough to take over the mortgage on their jointly owned house, which had water frontage. She'd wept into her pillow several times over that.

Then it turned out that Phil hadn't got round to changing the beneficiary on his life insurance policy and since his new woman had also been killed in the accident, Paula had inherited it all. That had been enough to pay off most of the mortgage and let her stay there.

It had also made her think good and hard about how she wanted to face life from now on. She'd given in to her ex too often and wasn't going to put up with any unfair treatment from now on, not from anyone.

By sheer hard work she was well on the way to owning

her own business, something Phil had taunted her about and said she'd never manage.

She'd done this with a partner who had also become a dear friend. She called him Uncle Nick, because he was as near an uncle as she'd ever got. Then, to top it all, after two years of leasing the building which housed their popular little bar, they'd bought it and now had a joint mortgage on it.

Well, he had seventy per cent of the mortgage and she had thirty per cent, and it had been hard even to find that much of the deposit. She'd had to rent out her lovely home and move into the granny flat attached to it for the time being in order to make up the rest of the monthly payment.

Nick came into the bar from the back room. 'Happy birthday, love!' He poured himself a red wine and raised the glass in a toast, merely wetting his lips with its contents. The same glass would be raised twenty times that evening, but the last mouthful would not be swallowed until after they closed.

'No, let's drink to mortgages and making your dreams come true. They're much more important than birthdays.'

He clinked glasses again, then stepped back to study her appearance. 'May I say how lovely you look tonight, young lady? You may have just turned thirty-two, but you're wearing well and I absolutely love that outfit.'

She chuckled. 'Not exactly a young lady now, but *merci du compliment*, kind sir.' Dipping a curtsey, she spread out the long Indian print skirt and let her bangles clink. A hot pink peasant blouse completed the ensemble and its brightness, together with the rows of sequins on her red bolero, had made one customer blink as he entered the bar.

Well, Paula didn't care. She loved bright colours and retro clothes, and bought hers mostly from charity shops. That supported people in need, saved money and got her the genuine articles, which was a triple bonus as far as she was concerned. Her husband had hated her wearing them, saying they should be kept for parties.

Well, she'd hated his navy business suits and white shirts. After his last promotion, he'd tried to get her to iron his white office shirts because she was better at it. She'd refused point blank. She'd given up ironing years ago, didn't believe it was a worthwhile human activity because the minute you put a garment on, it started acquiring wrinkles.

'What treat are you planning for your birthday, Paula love? You should at least take a day off.'

Her happiness slipped for a moment or two because her best friend had just moved across to the other side of Australia and it was no fun wandering round shops on her own. 'I don't need time off. I enjoy my work. Thanks anyway.'

She gave him a quick hug then took another sip of champagne.

'No luck with your latest search?'

'No. I think I must have been created in a vacuum.' She didn't understand why, but a few years ago she had started longing to know where she came from, but her search hadn't ended in success. She couldn't find her birth family because her father hadn't kept any relevant information or documents and Tony, as he'd preferred her to call him, had insisted he had no close relatives. He'd passed away over two decades ago.

Her birth mother was still alive but rarely came near

her and she too said they had no close relatives left.

Paula checked the bar. No customers needed attention, so she raised her glass in a silent toast to her beloved stepmother, who had been a wonderful mother. Jenny had always made a big fuss over her birthday. Sadly she'd died eighteen months ago.

Nick finished checking the shelves. 'I'd better fetch some more bottles of that fancy new craft beer from the storeroom, Paula love. It's selling far better than I'd expected. I'll only be a couple of minutes.'

The street door opened and she set down her glass at once. A guy stood there, letting in a blast of hot air and the faint sounds of voices and traffic from the street. He frowned and stared round as if searching for someone.

Nick always said how important it was to keep an eye on the customers so Paula studied him, as she did everyone who came in. He was about her age, with exhaustion radiating from him, dimming the personality behind the attractive face. It was more than mere tiredness, she decided as she continued to study him; he looked sad, too.

He let the door swing shut behind him, rubbing one temple absent-mindedly. His head must be aching, his dark business suit was badly creased and he definitely didn't look like a man out for a good time. Perhaps he was meeting someone here? Last business appointment of a long, hard day? She loved to guess about the customers' backgrounds.

As if he could feel her eyes on him, he turned to stare in her direction then walked towards the bar.

'May I help you, sir?'

'I hope so. I'm looking for Paul Grey. I was told he worked here.'

'Paula.'

'I beg your pardon?'

She smiled. He was a Pom with an upper-class English accent. 'It's Paula – not Paul. I'm a she.' She struck a pose and added, 'Ta-dah!'

He remained unimpressed, so she stifled a sigh and unstruck the pose. 'May I get you something to drink, sir?'

He was staring at her as if she'd just fallen out of a tree. 'There must be some mistake. The Paul Grey I'm looking for is thirty-one and was born in America—'

'Thirty-two today, actually. It's my birthday. But the America part is right.'

He continued as if she hadn't interrupted. '—and he's the son of a guy who called himself Tony Grey, who left England and moved to America thirty-five years ago.'

How the hell did he know all that? 'Look, there is no Paul, but I am the daughter of Tony Grey.'

'Oh, hell!' He goggled at her as if she'd suddenly grown a second head so she waited for him to speak.

What did he mean by 'called himself Tony Grey'? What other mess had her father left behind? He'd been a poor husband and parent, more absent than present in her life, a con man rather than the sales director he always claimed his occupation to be. He'd only taken charge of her when her American mother remarried and dumped Paula on him, telling him she'd looked after their daughter for five years and Tony could take her for the next five.

Give him his due: he'd kept her, though it had been his second wife, Jenny, who had looked after her from then on.

It hadn't surprised either Paula or Jenny when Tony crashed his car and made his final exit while trying to escape from an angry victim of one of his scams.

At nine, Paula had been terrified about what was going to happen to her then but Jenny had adopted her, with her mother's permission, secured through a lawyer.

Jenny had then taken her to live in her own country of birth, Australia, and Paula had felt instantly at home there. She had become an Australian citizen on her twenty-first birthday.

She shook her head to banish the memories and watched as the guy set his briefcase down on the bar stool and began to fumble through its contents, muttering to himself. 'It says in this document that . . .' He put some papers down on the counter.

Was he doubting her word? Feeling annoyed, she slapped her hand down on top of the documents, fingers splayed. 'I don't care what it says on your pieces of paper. I'm the *only* child of Tony Grey and I'm Paula, not Paul.'

He closed his eyes, muttering, 'Oh, hell! What next?' and sagged down on a bar stool, rubbing his forehead again.

He definitely had a headache, she thought. 'So, what can I get you to drink, sir?'

'What? Oh, I don't want anything, thank you. Look, if you really are the only child of Tony Grey, I need to talk to you.'

He was staring at her so disapprovingly, she shot a quick glance sideways to check her appearance in the wall mirror behind the bar. No, her hair was as tidy as the rampant curls ever allowed and she didn't have a smut on her nose. 'Just get to the point, will you? The main rush of customers will be upon me soon.'

'Very well. I've come to tell you that, subject to your being able to prove that you are who you claim, you've inherited a house in England.' He still sounded dubious about her identity.

As what he'd said sank in, the world spun round her for a moment. Even the murmurs of the customers chatting seemed to recede into the distance. *Inherited a house!*

Then she guessed what was happening and grinned at him. 'Yeah! And the Queen of England is waiting for me to go to Buckingham Palace and take tea with her. Right?'

He blinked at her, his mouth falling open in shock.

She chuckled. 'You do it well. You had me sucked right in for a few minutes. This is a new one, isn't it? I've had Strippseygrams and parrotgrams in here before, but—'

'What in hell's name are you talking about?'

'Your act. You do it well. You look exactly like a tired lawyer, even to the conservative tie and worn briefcase.' She tapped him lightly in the chest with her forefinger. 'But I wasn't born yesterday, mate, and I'm on to you.'

'You're – on to me?'

'Yes. But go on. Finish your spiel. Then I'll shout you a drink and you can tell me who paid you to play this birthday trick on me.' She chuckled. 'They'll get theirs one day. Inherited a house in England, indeed. I should be so lucky. What will people think of next?'

His voice became a lot louder. 'Look here, Miss Grey—'

'If this fellow's giving you a hard time, Paula,' one of the regulars called, 'you've only to say the word and we'll get rid of him for you.'

'No. He's one of those – you know – birthday jokes, like Strippseygrams.' She turned back to the guy, who looked as if he'd just swallowed a garden rake. 'Unless you *are* going to strip for us.' She studied him, head on one side, and couldn't resist teasing him. 'I wouldn't mind that, actually. You look as if you're nicely built.' She blew him a kiss and winked.

His gulp was audible and though the lighting was subdued, she could see his cheeks turn red, which made her chuckle again.

He closed his eyes for a minute before pulling himself upright and eyeballing her as if she had just escaped from custody. 'I am *not* a Strippseygram, nor am I delivering a joke message from a friend. I've come all the way from England to tell you that you've inherited a house.'

Nick came in from the back. 'Sorry to be so long, Paula my pet. I dropped a bottle of beer. I think I've got all the broken glass cleared up now, but watch how you tread when you go in there and—'

The stranger uttered a noise like a cow in labour and hammered on the bar suddenly, 'Look, will you damned well listen to what I'm saying, woman!'

Nick stiffened, immediately ready for trouble. No one could sort out a drunk as quickly as him. Though he was a big man and innately gentle, when he got that look on his face, few would care to challenge him.

Behind her back, she made a hand gesture to let him know she didn't need help, then turned again to the guy. 'Sorry. Go on. You're clearly determined to do the whole act.' She was getting rather tired of it now, though.

'As I keep trying to tell you, Miss Grey, you've inherited a house in Wiltshire and – why the devil are you laughing?'

'Because I love your posh English accent. Oh, hell, I

can't keep a straight face, never could. Look, you've done your bit and earned your fee. Let me shout you a beer. It is my birthday, after all.'

He started thumping the counter again. 'I don't – want – a beer! I just want you to take me seriously.'

Nick was there beside her. 'Keep your voice down, son.'

'You keep out of this. I'm trying to tell this crazy female that—'

As he slipped out from behind the bar to stand beside the man, Nick jerked his head to one of his friends who'd lent a hand before. 'I think Paula's had enough of your little games now, mate. Please leave this bar.'

The man shoved Nick's hand away from his arm. 'Are you *all* stark raving mad? This is *not* a game!'

Everyone in the bar had stopped talking to stare. It took a lot to make Paula angry, but she was feeling steamed up now. This fellow must have been born ten cents short of a dollar. Couldn't he see when a joke had gone far enough?

'You'd better leave now, sir. You're upsetting the other customers.' Nick and his friend linked arms with the offender, one on either side, and walked him swiftly to the door. He looked so shocked and surprised, he didn't struggle till they were standing on the pavement outside. When he wriggled out of their grasp, Nick let him go but stayed between him and the entrance.

Paula followed them with the briefcase, winking at a table of customers as she passed.

Nick said slowly and clearly, 'If you try to come back inside, sir, I'll call the police.' The skin of his shaven head gleamed under the row of lights over their sign and his voice was deep, rumbling in his broad chest. It was a rare customer who argued with him in this mood.

Paula tossed the briefcase down at the fellow's feet and went back to work, joking with the nearest customer about the tricks people play on your birthdays. In a few minutes it was as if the man had never been there.

Except that she kept remembering him. Poor sap. Only trying to do his job, really. And he'd looked genuinely tired. Pity he hadn't been able to let the joke go. She hadn't met a man she fancied this much for ages. Not since she and Nick had started this bar, in fact.

She made coffee, served alcoholic drinks, handed out the small snacks they sold – packets of cheese and biscuits, olives, nuts and the like – and of course she chatted. Some customers liked to talk more than they liked to drink, especially the lonely older ones, and she enjoyed cheering them up and seeing them leave with smiles on their faces.

Things stayed quietly busy for the rest of the evening. Which was exactly what they and their sort of customers preferred. She loved this job, could still remember how unhappy she'd been working in an office, dressing conservatively, going to stupid meetings where everyone except her was trying to show off how with it and eager beaver they were about the project in hand.

Ugh! She wasn't cut out for the formal life. Or for bureaucracies. No way!

On the pavement outside the bar, Richard Crawford straightened his clothes. People sitting at tables in front of the next-door café were staring at him. On the other side of the road, beyond a car park and stretch of grass, lights were reflected in the water of the estuary.

He'd never felt as embarrassed in his whole life.

Within a few minutes, the spectators had dispersed and he'd calmed down somewhat. He picked up his briefcase from the gutter, angry at himself. He had been too tired to think straight when he got off the plane from England. After the taxi dropped him at his hotel here in Mandurah, he should have waited till morning to find the heir.

Instead, when he'd learnt that the bar was only a short stroll away, he'd decided to see whether he could find this Paul Grey because he was desperate to get this unpleasant task over and done with.

The private investigators had told him the heir knew nothing about it. There would be questions and explanations to make about what Stovell Abbey was like, photos to show. He could do it, but once he'd handed over the estate, he had to figure out what he wanted to do with his life from now on. That would be far more difficult.

He planned to take a little holiday in Western Australia because he'd only ever visited Sydney and the east coast before. He liked Australia. It was a friendly place – usually.

As a neat little sign over the entrance saying *Nick's Bar* slowly changed from red to blue, someone went inside. Before the door closed, he saw her standing laughing with two of the customers. She was lovely in a weirdo sort of way, if you liked bright colours, which he didn't usually. But they looked OK, well, actually, more than OK with that sun-tanned skin and the dark curly hair. She had a bit of a bohemian air and was tall, too. He didn't like tiny, pale women.

But, he reminded himself firmly, she was also crazy, the sort of person who jumped to stupid conclusions and wouldn't listen to reason. If she really was the long-lost heir to Stovell Abbey, there was going to be trouble ahead for them all. She might have a lot of difficulty fitting in.

As he turned and walked away, his embarrassment gave way to enjoyment of the warm evening. He'd be back, he'd *have* to come back, but he'd make sure he kept his temper under control next time.

He wiped his forehead. If this was the West Australian summer, it was hotter by far than he'd expected and he felt sweaty and uncomfortable in a suit. He really should have changed into something lighter for the flight, but he'd had a meeting with the lawyers in London to sort out the final paperwork he needed to give the heir, and it had taken longer than he'd expected.

He'd only just got to the airport in time for the flight and there hadn't been any chance to change his clothes before his suitcase had been whipped away and he'd been hurried onto the plane to endure the tedium of a seventeen-hour journey to Perth.

He sighed as he went into his hotel room and took a long shower. He'd made a complete ass of himself tonight. What had she compared him to? A Strippseygram, for heaven's sake! She'd also told him he was nicely built.

He chuckled as he towelled himself dry, beginning to see the humour in the incident now. No woman had ever said anything like that to him before, certainly not one as gorgeous as her.

Well, she would be gorgeous if she didn't dress like a neon street sign.

He didn't feel sleepy now. The argument had well and truly woken him up even though he'd felt deep-down exhausted before. He'd been working damned hard over the past year. Too hard. And for what? For nothing.

But that wasn't her fault. He'd go back to the bar in the morning and apologise, then convince her that he wasn't joking and she really had inherited Stovell Abbey.

He'd escort her back to the UK, help her to take possession of it, then leave. But he still hadn't worked out what he'd do.

He'd once thought of emigrating to Australia and while he was here he'd have a good look round. He had a few ideas about his future, and the west might be the sort of place he was looking for.

He rang his aunt Marian in the morning. 'Just letting you know that I arrived safely.'

'Good. We had a storm pass through last night. The stable roof's leaking again.'

'It's at the top of the list of major repairs needed.'

'*If* the new owner lets you spend the money. *If* you're still around to see to that sort of thing. Have you met him yet, Richard?'

'*He* turns out to be a she, Paula not Paul.'

Silence, then, 'You'd better marry her, then. It'd be the perfect solution. If you did, we could both stay here.'

He felt indignant at the mere thought of that. 'I'd not marry someone for that reason. It'd be dishonest and a recipe for disaster. Anyway, I doubt anyone's going to turn you out. You're the perfect housekeeper for a large home and the only one who understands the vagaries of that particular place.'

Silence, then, 'I was joking but actually, it might be a good idea to cosy up to her, Richard. Not if she's horrible, of course.'

He changed the subject. Since his aunt's divorce a few years ago, she'd been very cynical about love. If he ever married, it would be because he cared about someone so much he didn't want to live without her. He hadn't been lucky enough to find a woman who affected him like that so far, though he'd had a couple of near misses, but he hadn't given up hope.

Marry someone for what they owned, indeed! His own Stovell ancestors might have done that in the past, but he would never, ever consider doing such a thing.

His aunt was only joking, surely?

Chapter Two

Marian put down the phone. So the heir was a woman! Did she know how lucky she was? This was such a wonderful old house. Marian would sell her soul to live out her days here and continue caring for it.

It was all very well Richard saying the new owner wouldn't be able to manage without her but that wasn't true. Anyone could learn to do what was needed in a minimal way, though they'd have to be able to run the place economically, given the state of its finances. There were extras you could contribute, though, if you knew and loved a place. She felt she understood the house's soul.

She didn't need or want to go job-hunting at her age. She had enough money to live on because Roy Stovell, the former owner, had left her an adequate income and a brilliant reference, which would get her another job easily.

Since she'd been housekeeper here she'd lived in the housekeeper's quarters, renting out her own little cottage in the village. She didn't want to go back to the small rooms and living cheek by jowl with neighbours, whether she liked them or not. She loved the spaciousness of Stovell

Abbey's interior. She could give notice to the tenants and get her home back but even more important to her was the need for some meaningful sort of occupation.

She'd made enquiries after Roy died and found that there was a demand for short-term housekeepers, where agencies moved people into and out of jobs, chopping and changing, taking shortcuts, skimping on what they did and serving what she thought of as the Great God Money.

She'd enjoyed being her own boss for over a decade and managing the house she loved properly. She even had a list of minor renovations she had planned to put into place at minimal cost. Richard had told her she had an eye for that sort of thing and if she'd been born now she'd have been able to train as an architect.

She didn't have any Stovell blood in her veins. Her half-brother had married one of Roy's nieces.

Roy had been a recluse, a charming man but not sociable. The one thing she'd missed about her marriage was the social entertaining that had been necessary for her husband's job. She'd been good at that. Even *he* had admitted as much. He shouldn't have been unfaithful then, should he?

It was sunny today, even if it was cold, so she decided to cheer herself up by going for a long walk and to hell with everything else. Anyway, it was one of Joan's days to clean the house, and there was no need to supervise a woman she'd grown up with, a woman who seemed to regard dirt as a personal enemy.

When she went to tell her she was going out, Joan switched off the vacuum cleaner to have a chat. 'Do you good. Any news from Richard?'

'Only that he's arrived safely in Australia.'

'Good. Did you hear the latest in the village? Dan Peverill's back. Buried his wife last year in America, it seems. He's the one who bought the old hall, so perhaps he's come back to stay.'

'Yes, I had heard.' Of course she had. At least three people had gone to the trouble of phoning her with the news, knowing she'd had a fling with Dan when she was young. That had been over two decades ago, for heaven's sake. She'd been married and divorced since then, not to mention starting to show signs of ageing like turning grey and putting on a little weight.

Dan would no doubt have changed too. She'd probably walk straight past him in the street. But it puzzled her why a widowed man, who'd spent the last two decades in America, would want to buy a big house like Beechley Hall in a village he'd said he never wanted to see again.

He was up to something, must be. He had never done anything without a very good financial reason and she doubted that would have changed.

She put on a hooded coat and a scarf, and went out the back way, taking her favourite path through the woods. Lost in memories, she didn't see him till she was quite close then she stopped dead and debated briefly fleeing down a side path. But he saw her before she could do anything and pride alone kept her walking steadily forward towards him.

At first glance he hadn't changed all that much. He was still lean and looked fit. But when she studied his face she did see changes – well, she thought she did. His once luxuriant hair was thinner, the light brown faded to pepper and salt, and there were lines round his eyes.

Like her, he'd been lost in thought but she saw the exact

moment when he noticed her and realised who she was. To her surprise the cool expression gave way to a genuine smile.

'Marian! How delightful to see you again!' He strode forward, taking her shoulders in a light grip and kissing her cheeks, one after the other, the way strangers often did these days. She always wished they wouldn't because it meant nothing, only this kiss might perhaps have meant a little more than usual, a reminder of her youth at the very least.

She didn't know what to say so simply smiled back at him till she realised that he hadn't let go of her, was studying her face intently.

'Something's worrying you, Marian.'

'That's a fine greeting after all these years!'

'I've done the kissy-kissy routine. What else do you need as a greeting? Or do you want me to pretend I don't know you and discuss the weather?'

She felt her own stiffness melting a little. 'No, of course not.'

'I know you well enough to read the expression on your face still and it's not a happy one.'

She sighed, wondering how best to respond.

'Going for a walk?'

'Yes.'

He turned to face in the same direction as her. 'Good. We'll walk down to the lake together and catch each other up on our news. You can tell me what's worrying you or if you don't want to do that, you can bring me up to date on your precious Abbey. Is it as beautiful as ever? Do you love it as much? You must have put down deep roots in Wiltshire because you've never moved away.'

'Yes, I do still love the Abbey. My nephew's been doing some renovating and it hasn't looked as good for years.'

'He's wasted his time, though, hasn't he? Someone else will benefit from it now. He must be disappointed not to have inherited after all.'

She was startled. 'Word of that's got out already, even to a visitor like you?'

'Of course it has. This is Stovell Magna. Rumours breed like rabbits on speed in our village, always have done. Though I don't exactly count myself as a visitor.'

'Well, to tell the truth, Richard and I are both disappointed about the new heir. If anyone was perfect as custodian of the Abbey, it was him.'

'I heard that he once had other plans.'

'He shelved those.' She shook her head in a vain attempt to banish her worries about her nephew. 'Don't let's talk about that. I'm sick of answering questions about the new heir. All I know is the latest news is that it's a she, not a he. You're the first to hear that.'

He let out a long, low whistle.

'Now, tell me about America. I was sorry to hear you'd lost your wife so young.'

'Yes. And cancer can be a difficult way to die. You'd have liked JoBeth and she'd have liked you.'

'And your children?'

'Off my hands now – if children ever are totally off your hands. Kelly's working in IT and got married recently, and Brandon's struggling to make his name as an actor. He's good, but so are a lot of other young men his age and it's a chancy profession.'

'Goodness! How can he be the son of someone like

you, who never liked to be the focus of attention, and want to be an actor?'

He shrugged. 'I've got over that attitude now. Had to. But I still don't approve of his choice of job. It has no financial security whatsoever.'

He offered no further information so she didn't pursue the point, just asked the main question that interested her. 'Are you back for good or only visiting?'

'Surely they told you I'd bought Beechley Hall?'

'I assumed it was for an investment. You swore you'd never come back to live here permanently.'

'Well, I've unsworn it. I'm here to stay.' He caught her cynical expression and added, 'For a while, at least. I'm just waiting to do the final handover for a job in the Middle East, which will only take me a few days, then I'll take full possession of the Hall.'

'What are you going to do with yourself?'

'Update the hall and its grounds. I have a few other plans brewing.'

Which probably meant it offered him some business opportunities, she thought. She'd have cared what they were once; now, she was only mildly interested.

They'd reached the lake so stopped in unspoken agreement and stared at it.

'It's as pretty as I remembered. Do you still go boating?' he asked.

'No. The boats got too old and unsafe and no one cared enough to buy new ones. The lake is still suitable for boating, of course, if you want to put a boat or two on your end, that is.' She caught sight of her watch. 'Is it that time already? I've got to get back now and lock up after Joan. It was nice catching up with you, Dan.'

He took her hand but didn't let go immediately. 'Come and have a meal with me tonight. I'm at the King's Head in the village and they have a pretty reasonable cook. Evenings can be lonely when you're in a hotel room, and I never did like sitting around on my own in public bars.'

'I don't think—'

He didn't let go of her hand. 'Please, Marian.'

She hesitated and was lost. Evenings could be lonely when you were the only person living in a big house, too. That had been the main downside of her job working for a recluse like Roy. 'You come and have a meal with me instead, Dan. At least that way, people won't be staring at us and trying to listen in on what we're saying.'

'All right. I'll be interested to see what the interior of the Abbey is like these days.' He gave her hand a squeeze and let go at last. 'I'll bring some wine. Still like Merlot best?'

'Yes. Come about four o'clock and I'll show you round the main rooms before it gets dark.'

'The library has gained quite a reputation. I'll look forward to it.' With a wave, he turned and strode away.

She stood and watched him as she had done when they were going out together. He was still attractive. Too attractive for a sensible woman like her. She preferred men who weren't so charismatic. They were much easier to live with.

Still, it'd be nice to have some company.

Chapter Three

The morning after the incident, Paula looked up from putting away the clean glasses and froze. Oh, no! That lunatic was back again. Only he didn't look like a stuffed shirt this morning, not when he was wearing jeans and a short-sleeved top. He was smiling tentatively, as if unsure of his welcome, as he entered the bar.

When he took out a white handkerchief and waved it in the air in a gesture of surrender, she couldn't help smiling. 'It's all right. I won't have you thrown out again – unless you start shouting at me, of course.'

'I'm really sorry about last night.'

She shrugged. 'We'll forget about it. You not working today?'

'I wasn't working last night, not at being a lawyergram, anyway, or whatever you thought I was. Look, can you come and sit down for a few minutes? I really do need to talk to you and I can show you proof of my identity. In fact, I ought to do that before we even begin our conversation.'

He gestured to a table by the window and she hesitated, then joined him there, feeling puzzled by this talk of proving who he was. But he was speaking calmly and quietly so deserved a hearing.

'I'm really sorry for shouting at you last night, Miss Grey. I didn't handle things very well at all, did I?'

He gave her another of those crooked, rueful smiles as she sat down opposite him and her heart gave a little twitch. He was a very attractive man. 'No, you didn't.'

He offered her a business card and then showed her his passport to prove the card wasn't a fake.

She handed them back with a nod, feeling more puzzled by the minute. Why was he going to these lengths? If he hadn't been delivering a birthday message, what had he come to see her for last night?

He was still hesitating so she prompted, 'You didn't handle what well exactly?'

'Telling you some important news.' He took a deep breath. 'You see, Miss Grey—'

'Paula. We use first names in Australia.'

'Right, Paula it is. And I'm Richard.' He held out his hand.

As she shook it, she froze, startled by the warmth that seemed to be running through her from it. She pulled hers away hastily. You read about this sort of thing in romance novels, but she'd always laughed at the idea of such a sudden attraction. And what's more, she didn't want to be attracted to someone who was just passing through, didn't want to be strongly attracted to any man ever again, actually. Been there, done that, didn't win a medal.

He had been avoiding her eyes, fiddling with one of the new beer mats, but now he looked up and took a deep breath. 'I was telling the truth about one thing last night, you know.'

'What?'

'You really have inherited a house in England, Paula.'

It was a moment before she found enough breath to reply. 'You can't be serious?'

'I am. You've inherited a house in Wiltshire.'

She opened her mouth to protest then closed it again, because she'd never been to Wiltshire or as far as she knew had any connections with someone from there. Her father had always joked that he came from here, there and everywhere, and her mother came from Texas, though she hadn't stayed there, was living in France these days with her third husband.

Only, if Paula had ever seen sincerity, it was painted across the face opposite her. You learnt to judge people fairly accurately when you were running a bar. 'Who's left me a house? It must be a mistake. I was born in America and we came to Australia when I was nine. I've never even been to England.'

'It's not been left to *you*, exactly, you're just – well, the next in line, as it were. The heir. The house belonged to your great-uncle Roy Stovell, but he had only the one child, a daughter who died before him. He was one of seven children, though. He lived to be ninety-five but died early last year. He was a nice guy, but he'd never talk about the succession, only said someone else could sort it out after he'd gone. And that has taken a while.'

When he looked at her, she nodded to encourage him to continue.

'After he died, we had to check out all Roy's brothers and sisters, looking for offspring. He left us with a list of their names and ages, only all six of them were dead.

They'd scattered across the face of the globe, so it took a while to trace their offspring.'

'I'm sure there's a mistake. Tony, my father, always said he didn't have any relatives left and was an only child.'

'I wonder why he said that. Roy's generation was the largest number of surviving children ever produced by the Stovell family, and the archives go back to the early eighteenth century. It took the lawyers over a year to trace them all, because Roy hadn't kept in touch. We nearly gave up on your branch of the family. Your father covered his tracks pretty well when he went off to America, probably because he took a few pieces of family silver with him.'

It wasn't the first time her father had embarrassed her. Would she never be free of him? 'He was a con man but I never thought he'd be a thief as well. I'm sorry, but I never saw him with any old pieces of silver so I can't give them back or even hint at where they might be.'

'We're not expecting you to do that. It's water under the bridge.'

'How did you settle on me as heir, then?'

'The private investigator had a bit of luck and discovered your mother, who told us you existed.'

'I don't see much of her. When I was little I didn't see her for years, though she sent me the occasional birthday or Christmas cards.' When she remembered, which wasn't every year.

'She knew you'd come to Australia but not exactly where, so we set a private investigator onto it. And voilà! Here I am. It turns out you're the next in line so you inherit the house.'

She began to feel excited. She might be able to sell it and

pay off the mortgage on her canal house, not to mention getting rid of her tenants. Now, that would make a very nice birthday present indeed.

'What's the house like?' she asked eagerly.

'It's very old—'

Disappointment made her sigh. 'Oh, only worth block value, eh? How much would that be on the present market?'

'Block value?' He looked puzzled.

'You know, as in house falling down so only worth the price of the land.'

'You've never even seen the place and you want to sell it! My goodness, you're quick off the mark!'

He scowled and turned into an instant stuffed shirt again, positively bristling at her. She felt a matching anger begin to rise. 'Look, a house in England is no use to me. Apart from anything else, I have a home and business here.'

'Well, you have a house in England now as well.'

She gestured around them. 'I love running the bar and I also love my home here. It's on a canal development here in Mandurah with water frontage. Fortunately it has a granny flat built along one side that I was able to move into and put tenants in, but I still have some views and one day I'm going to get my home back.'

She let that sink in before adding, 'So I'm not trudging off with sentimental tears in my eyes to find my family's English roots, thank you very much. As far as I'm concerned, my roots are here and have been since I was nine years old. So *if* you don't mind, I'd like some idea of the market value of this old shack I've been left.'

'It isn't an old shack.'

'You're the one who said it was old.'

'Yes, it is. But it's not a shack. It's, well, I suppose you'd call it a stately home. Smallish, but definitely part of the national heritage of England. The oldest part is early eighteenth century, with the ruins of the original thirteenth century abbey in the grounds. It was destroyed during the dissolution of the monasteries under Henry VIII. Oh, and there's a small modern wing at the rear added in the nineteenth century, which is where the housekeeper lives nowadays.'

The bar seemed to spin round and his voice echo down from the far end of a very long tunnel. 'Say that again,' she croaked.

'You've inherited a small manor house called Stovell Abbey in Wiltshire.'

She hadn't a clue where Wiltshire was. She'd thought vaguely about travelling the world for a year or so after she finished uni, because other people seemed to think that was a wonderful thing to do. However, a holiday in Hong Kong had made her instantly homesick, so she'd not made any more attempts to travel abroad. And what with a marriage that failed rapidly and her stepmother's long final illness, she'd not done any real travelling even in Australia for the past few years.

Richard continued to scowl at her. 'The Abbey isn't the sort of place you can sell. In fact, you aren't allowed to sell it. There's a family trust and the estate has to be passed on intact to the next legal heir. It can't be split up at all and it's heritage listed.'

She didn't know what to say, felt utterly knocked for six by what he'd said.

'Are you all right?'

She sucked in a couple of lungfuls of air but it didn't seem to help. 'No, I'm not – not at all.'

She gasped in more air and before she knew it, he was forcing her head between her knees and then Nick was trying to drag him off her and they were both shouting and . . .

It took a few minutes for her to calm the two men down again.

'Couldn't you just go away and pretend you couldn't find me,' she begged as Richard brushed dust off his rumpled clothing from where Nick had forced him away from her onto the floor.

'Certainly not. You're the heir and you have to come to England to claim your inheritance and . . . I suppose it'll be up to you to decide what you're going to do with it from then onwards if you don't intend to live there. No one has ever done that before so there's no precedent.' He stared at her disapprovingly.

She groaned and buried her head in her hands for a moment, then lifted it to glare at him. 'Well, I didn't ask for it and I don't want it, so I'm not coming.'

'Paula!' Nick said warningly. 'You really shouldn't take any hasty decisions about something so important.'

She glared at them both. 'I mean it. I'm *not* going to England.' And she did mean it. Definitely.

'It won't hurt to listen to him and think about it,' Nick said quietly.

He had what she thought of as his kindly but stern uncle look on his face so she folded her arms and waited. She realised after a moment that he was staring at her foot, which was tapping impatiently, and she forced herself to sit still and pay attention as Richard explained all over again about this stupid inheritance, giving even more details this time.

'Stovell Abbey was built in the early eighteenth century. It's a neat, well-preserved manor house with about twenty internal rooms and several outbuildings. It stands on just under thirty acres of land in Wiltshire.'

'Where in England is this Wiltshire?'

He looked surprised but said, 'Near Bristol. Know where that is?'

'I've seen it on maps.'

'Well, if you drive to Bristol from London, Wiltshire is the county on the left, so to speak, just before you get there.'

'Right. Got it. I'll look it up properly on a map later. Go on.'

'The Stovell family has lived in the house continuously for over two hundred years. The last owner was Roy Stovell. He was both eccentric and reclusive, and didn't produce an heir. He lived there mainly alone, except for a series of housekeepers. He was only interested in restoring and extending the library, and did that so well that it's heritage listed. But he didn't care about looking after the land and the interior of the house. He only looked after the exterior because of protecting his precious library. When it became in need of serious renovation a couple of years ago, he hired me to start the most urgent repairs. I trained as an architect and I specialised in restoration of older properties, you see.'

Paula held up one hand in a stop sign. 'Give me a minute to digest this.' She frowned for a moment or two then said slowly, 'It means Tony wasn't lying about his family background. Which must be the only time on record for him to have been telling the truth about his past!'

'Why do you call your father Tony?'

'He said calling him Father made him feel old and he refused to answer to any version of it.'

'Oh. I see. Didn't he tell you any other details at all about his family?'

'Nothing specific. He used to say his father came from the upper classes and his grandfather grew up in a stately home. We thought – my stepmother and I – that he was just spinning another of his tales. He changed his life story as needed for each scam he organised, you see. He was very clever, managed to avoid being arrested, though there were one or two close calls. We had to move house a lot, sometimes twice in a year.'

'Well, your father was definitely telling the truth about his background.'

Nick was sitting astride a chair now, leaning on his folded arms on the top of its back and listening intently. He grinned suddenly. 'And you weren't lying last night, either. Sorry about chucking you out of the bar, Richard. We thought you'd had a few too many drinks.'

'I was more jet-lagged than I realised.'

The two men nodded to one another as if making peace, then both turned to look at her, so Paula stated her case again, speaking loudly, clearly and slowly, on the principle of water dripping on a stone.

'What you've said doesn't really alter things. If I can't sell it, this Stovell Abbey is no good to me. I definitely do *not* want to go and live in England. Apart from the fact that I loathe cold weather and it's winter there, I've bought into this bar, I have a home I love and I don't know anyone in the UK.'

As the two men continued to simply stare, she added,

'Anyway, I'm Australian and proud of it. I was born in America, for heaven's sake, so I don't feel at all English, even though for some stupid reason my father made Jenny promise to maintain my British passport. He said that was a valuable commodity in its own right.'

Richard frowned at her. 'Whatever you decide to do about the house, you'll still have to go over there and sort out all the legal stuff. I can't do that for you.'

She waved one hand dismissively. 'They can send the documents here and I'll find a lawyer to deal with them.'

'Don't you even want to see the house? It's a little gem. Well, I think it is.'

'If this had happened at another time, yes, I might have gone to see it, though I'm not really into travelling overseas. But not only is this make or break time for Nick and me, I don't have the money to spare for an overseas trip.'

'Presumably the estate will pay her expenses?' Nick looked at their visitor.

'Yes, of course.'

She transferred her glare to Nick. 'Whose side are you on?

He gave her the smug smile he always used when determined to ignore her wishes and her heart sank. 'I'm on the side of doing the right thing. You really ought at least to go and look at the place, Paula my pet. See exactly where your family comes from.'

'You of all people know I can't do that at the moment, Nick. We're both needed to run this place.'

'I'm not so sure. It'd have been hard for you to go last year, but this year the bar is doing quite nicely. I could get my friend Jonno to come back and work here. He and I are becoming rather good friends, so I'll enjoy his company.'

He winked at her in a way that spoke volumes about his new relationship, then patted her shoulder and added, 'Anyway, you're more than due a break, my pet. You've been looking distinctly peaky since you had flu a few weeks ago. So go and take a health break at somebody else's expense.'

'But Nick, I don't want to go overseas. You know it's not my thing.'

He ignored that. 'Are you going straight back to England, Richard? It'll take me a few days to make arrangements to replace Paula temporarily because Jonno is in Sydney at the moment.'

'Well, I wouldn't mind seeing a bit of Western Australia while I'm here. Especially the old colonial architecture. I specialised in heritage work and would love to have a proper look at some of the older Australian homes. I could hang around here for . . . oh, ten days, maybe even a couple of weeks if I push it. Paula isn't the only one who's more than due a holiday.'

'Fine. That'll give us plenty of time to make arrangements for staffing the bar.'

She banged on the table. 'If you two have quite finished rearranging my life, I want to repeat what I just said. Watch my mouth carefully, Nick. *I do not wish to go to England.*'

She gave him a dirty look but he only shrugged, so she turned to the man opposite her and repeated the message. 'Richard, I'm definitely *not* going to England with you. There has to be some way to sort this mess out from here.'

'There isn't, actually. And if you don't take up residence, you'll be the first owner in nearly more than two centuries to abandon the Abbey.' He gave her another of those reproachful looks.

She covered her eyes with both hands, muttering, 'This is a nightmare. Why can't I wake up?'

Letting her hands drop, she caught Richard's eye and made one last stand. 'Go back and tell them thank you very much, but I refuse the bequest. I'll give you a signed and witnessed letter to that effect.'

To emphasise that the discussion was closed, she left the table and went into the back, where she pretended to tidy up some shelves, making plenty of noise.

She half expected Nick to follow her, but he didn't. She peeped out of the half-open door when she heard low voices but it was nearly fifteen minutes before Richard left the bar.

That worried her. What had the two of them been talking about?

If Nick was plotting something, as he did sometimes, he was going to be very disappointed. Whatever they were cooking up, she wasn't giving in to him this time.

Definitely not.

A few minutes later, someone came into the back room. 'It's only me.'

She turned round. 'Has he gone away for good now, Nick?'

'Of course not. Only for the moment. And I'm hoping you've cooled down. Come and have a cappuccino with me before we open.'

She looked at him warily. 'You won't make me change my mind.'

'You can't ignore the facts, love. Let me get the coffees, then we can talk about the situation.'

'I still can't believe it,' she said when Nick came back. She picked up the spoon and scooped up some of the froth. 'I really don't want that house, Nick.'

'Do you think you have a choice?'

She was silent.

'Paula love, you're not your father, to skip out on your responsibilities.'

She didn't look up as she muttered, 'You know exactly which buttons to press, don't you?'

'I know you. You've been closed as tightly as a clam to any emotions since your husband skipped off with that woman. And it didn't help that they were killed.'

'You're trying to shame me into doing this and it won't work.'

'Well, why not treat it as a holiday? No one can force you to stay there. But from the photos Richard left with me, it looks to be a beautiful old house.' He waited a moment and added, 'You know you enjoy historical stuff.'

He leant sideways and picked up some photos from the next table, slapping them down in front of her. 'This is Stovell Abbey.'

She pushed them hastily away.

He pushed them straight back. 'You should at least see where your family came from.' He picked up the top photo and set it down in front of her.

As she looked down at it, she felt the weight of responsibility settle on her shoulders. Heavy. Implacable. But she wasn't ready yet to admit that she'd have to go there. Not nearly ready.

She made Nick and Richard wait three more days for that.

Chapter Four

As she finished preparing dinner that afternoon, Marian admitted to herself that she felt nervous and wished she hadn't invited Dan for a meal. When she heard the car drive round the house to the rear and saw it through the kitchen window pulling up next to hers, she took a deep breath and told herself not to be so stupid.

He was just an old friend, well, sort of. Hardly even a friend these days because she hadn't seen him for years. And actually they hadn't parted all that amicably. He'd been determinedly friendly this afternoon, though. Which had made her wonder what he wanted. She was a lot more cynical about her fellow human beings these days – and about him.

She watched him get out of the luxury car, get something out and walk towards the kitchen door. As she went to open the door, she took a deep breath and prepared herself mentally.

He presented her with a huge bunch of flowers.

'How beautiful!' She buried her nose in them.

'There's no smell, I'm afraid. They've been bred for

beauty. If I remember rightly you have some wonderful old-fashioned roses here at Stovell Abbey. I hope you'll let me take some cuttings for the gardens at the Hall.'

'Of course. But I shall enjoy looking at these flowers. Beauty is its own reward where flowers are concerned.'

She realised she was barring the way in and stepped back. 'Do come in. I'll – um – just put these in water.'

He followed her into the kitchen and stood in the middle, staring round, as she got a vase out in the scullery. 'It hasn't changed much.'

'No. I like that. Though we do have some new appliances, thank goodness. And a new heating system in this part of the house, too. That old coal-burning stove was a contrary devil. Unfortunately, Roy drew the line at replacing the system for the whole house.'

He came to the doorway of the scullery just as she was pressing her hands to her hot cheeks in a vain attempt to reduce their colour. 'Don't get your knickers in a twist, Marian. We're such old friends.'

'It's because of what happened all those years ago, *old friend*, that I'm nervous. I was so . . . naïve.'

'While I was too certain of myself. And of you.'

She turned to look at him, vase in hand. 'And did it all work as you expected? Are you now rich?'

'As comfortable as I need to be. I have no aspirations to become a billionaire. JoBeth's family showed me how to make money, but I'm not greedy for more and more these days. What I enjoy is creating systems that function well.'

'You must have spent a sizeable chunk on your new home.'

'It was worth it. I've always liked the Hall.'

He stood back to let her past and she went to set the flowers on the dresser. 'I'll keep them in here, then I can enjoy them as I work.'

'Are you the chief cook and bottle washer as well as housekeeper these days, then?'

'I am, rather. But most of the time there's no one to cook and clean for except myself and Richard.'

'You didn't have any children? I heard you'd married – and divorced.'

'No. I couldn't. We divorced partly because of that.'

'I'm sorry.'

'I was too. But I had Richard staying here quite often. That made up for a lot.'

'I gather he's gone to Australia to fetch back the newest heir.'

'Yes. But she couldn't leave for a few days.'

'I'm glad of that.'

She looked at him in puzzlement.

'It'll give you and me time to get reacquainted without interruptions. Your nephew never did like me. I'm not all that proud of some aspects of the old me now, either.'

'Why is getting reacquainted with me so important to you?'

He didn't pretend. 'Because when I saw you, my pulse speeded up. It surprised me, I must admit. But I haven't reacted strongly to another woman since JoBeth, so I guess it means something. I'd like to find out what, if that's all right with you.'

She'd been going to get him a drink but she spun round, angered by that. 'I'm not something you can pick up and put down as convenient.'

'I'm sorry. I didn't mean to sound arrogant. I've been a bit . . . adrift. Without JoBeth, America seemed rather alien sometimes.'

'But you have children there. Don't you have grandchildren as well?'

'No, there are no grandchildren so far.'

'Well, just so you know where you stand, I'm not looking for another man in my life.' And she suddenly realised that he wasn't the sort who would interest her in that way nowadays anyway.

'What are you looking for, Marian? To go on working here as a posh housekeeper if the new heir keeps you on?'

'I don't know. It's been my home for so long and I love it, so I'll have to see what happens. If Richard had inherited I'd definitely have stayed. When this woman takes over, well, I'll have to find out what she's like and whether I want to work with her. She might not want me to anyway. Now, would you like a drink? Then I'll show you round the rest of the house before it gets dark.'

'I'd love a drink. And a tour.'

She was surprised at how closely he studied the Abbey. What was behind that? Something, she was sure.

Afterwards, she was pleased to see him enjoy the meal and they discussed food while they ate. He seemed very knowledgeable about it.

He didn't stay late because he was leaving for London early the following morning to attend a business meeting.

'I've not been inside the Hall for years,' she said. 'The last owners didn't live there full time and when he died, she simply went back to their other house and locked the Hall up, except for a grumpy caretaker.'

'Well, she kept the roof watertight, that's the main thing, but it's dreadfully old-fashioned inside, not to mention full of dust and cobwebs. And I've given the old caretaker notice. He was a grumpy old sod who didn't want to change anything.'

'Bad tactics.'

'Yes. I shall bring in a firm of professional cleaners before I do anything, so that I can see the potential of what I've got in more detail. I bought the furniture as well, which means I can move straight in.'

'Sounds like a plan.'

'We'll catch up again once I get back,' he promised, kissing her cheek and holding her right hand in both his for a moment.

Only when he'd left did she realise how skilfully he'd steered the conversation away from business matters. She didn't even know what he'd been doing with himself in the States during the last few years, apart from 'working in JoBeth's family business'.

She'd enjoyed his company – dangerous, that – but he hadn't made her heart race in the same way as when she was young. And she would never fully trust him again.

When they were young, Dan had assumed she'd go to America with him after he landed a job there without consulting her, and they'd argued for days. She'd ended up shrieking at him to go on his own and leave her in peace because she was never leaving Wiltshire.

He had done just that and not even written her a letter, not one.

Oh, why was she thinking about him? He was yesterday's news. She smiled at the thought. He'd not like her calling him that. It was obvious that he still liked to be centre stage and he'd been the one to manage the conversation for most of the evening.

She waved one hand as if to push him literally out of her thoughts, only it didn't work. As she finished clearing up, she found herself wondering why he was really here. Daniel Peverill wanting to settle peacefully into the English countryside? She didn't think so.

Anyway, she was more concerned at the moment with what the future might bring to Stovell Abbey than what Dan was plotting and scheming about. Her situation here was uncertain now and she found that surprisingly stressful.

She hadn't realised till recently how deeply her roots went here.

Chapter Five

Once she'd agreed to go to England, Paula decided she might as well get it over with as quickly as possible and worked at a frenetic pace to get everything ready to leave, putting a proper security system into her house and arranging to have it monitored while she was away.

Richard popped into the bar a couple of times and she could tell that he was lonely. She could imagine how it felt to be alone in a foreign country, would soon be in the same position herself, so invited him over to her home for lunch the next day.

'Are you sure?' he asked bluntly.

'Yes. It's not your fault I turned out to be the heir and I never hold grudges. Besides, where I live is – well, rather special. I think you might enjoy seeing it and it'll help you understand why I don't want to move to a big, draughty stately home in a cold and rainy country.'

'It's not always cold and rainy.'

'I've been looking at the UK weather reports online and it's been very cold and rainy lately. So are you coming?'

'Yes, I'd love to see this house of yours if it's as special as you believe.'

'Do you want me to pick you up from the hotel?'

'No need. I've hired a little run-around and it's got a satnav. Thank goodness they drive on the same side of the road here, though. I always have trouble adjusting to driving on the right in France.'

She scribbled down her address and gave it to him. 'See you there tomorrow around noon.'

She shook her head as she went back to work. He name-dropped countries like she name-dropped wines.

The next morning she went into work as usual, buying some food from the café next door to form the basis of the lunch. She left the bar just after eleven and sang along to some music as she drove. When she was approaching her granny flat, she broke off abruptly because there was a removal van parked outside the main house and two men were carrying furniture out and loading it in the van. *Her* furniture!

What the hell was going on? Her tenants hadn't given notice and anyway, that was one of her antique chests of drawers being carried into the van.

It had been standing in her bedroom in the granny flat when she left for work, so how had anyone got it outside today? The connecting door was always very carefully locked.

She parked so that she was preventing the removal van from getting out of the drive and phoned triple zero to report a burglary in progress. The police mustn't have been busy because they said they'd be there in a few minutes.

She was about to march into the house and give the thieves what for when Richard drove up.

She beckoned to him and pointed to the space behind her tenants' car, and he twigged on quickly that she wanted him to park there. When he got out and came to join her, she explained what she thought was going on.

She took a photo of the two removal men starting to carry out another of her pieces of antique furniture and before they could ask what she was doing, she marched inside, fury sizzling through her. She wasn't waiting for the police to arrive.

When she walked into the big living-room-cum-kitchen, she saw the shock on the two tenants' faces. Before they could do anything, she took a photograph of them packing some of her appliances into big cardboard boxes.

'What the hell do you think you're doing stealing my furniture?' she yelled.

Her tenants came towards her and one of them tried to shove her aside. 'Get out of the way! We're leaving.'

She shoved the woman right back. 'Not with my furniture, you're not,' she yelled.

The two removal men stared open-mouthed from her to the women who'd rented the part-furnished house from her and immediately put down the antique sideboard, backing off, arms spread in a gesture of surrender.

'We didn't know they were stealing this!' one of them called.

'Well, you know now.'

The tenants tried to push past her but Richard blocked the doorway and refused to move. As the two women struggled to get past him, she went to join him there.

There was the sound of a siren and another car stopped outside.

'It's the police,' one of the removal men called unnecessarily.

'Good.'

The two tenants hesitated, then stopped trying to escape and moved back into the room.

One of the police officers smiled at the two women. 'Up to your old tricks, are you, Sandy?'

It took them nearly two hours to sort things out and Paula had to go round the house with one of the officers and check what was missing as the removal men unloaded their vehicle. Two antique chairs were not to be found and the big garage was completely empty, with all her tools missing, which made her furious all over again.

'They're not only the tools I use, but the historic ones I've been collecting for over a decade, which were quite valuable,' she told one officer.

'The chairs will probably be in one of the pawn shops. We'll send a warning out.'

To her relief, they found the tools in the boot of the would-be thieves' car, then the police took the two women away.

The removal men were only too eager to help Paula and spent a further hour putting the furniture back in place. After that, she shoved the tenants' clothes and other possessions into bin liners and piled them up in the empty part of the triple garage.

When the big van had throbbed away into the distance, she flopped down on a chair. 'What next?'

Richard sat on the next chair, smiling now.

'What's so funny?'

'You are. Life is certainly not boring when you're around.'

She shrugged. 'That incident was hardly my fault.'

'No. Definitely not. And I'm very glad you got your things back.'

'So am I. Some of them have high sentimental value to me. But there are two antique hall chairs still missing. I know a few shops they might have sold the chairs to. I'm going round them after we've eaten.' She stood up. 'I don't know about you but I'm ravenously hungry now. Good thing the food was in an eskie. It'll have kept cool even out in my car boot on a sunny day. And since I love the view from this patio and I've got my house back again, let's eat outside.'

'Shall you have to find new tenants before we go?'

'I'll leave it till I get back from England. I won't be away for all that long, couple of weeks at most.' She stared at him challengingly as she said that and he rolled his eyes, but didn't contradict her.

They had a lovely late lunch and she saw him relax as they stayed out on the patio, watching boats and birds pass by.

He looked across the table at her at one stage and said quietly, 'You're right, Paula. It is beautiful here.'

She nodded.

Then he spoilt it by adding, 'But it's beautiful at Stovell Abbey too. Please give it a chance.'

She changed the subject, not wanting to spoil the pleasant afternoon. 'The water views are one of the reasons I bought this property after my husband was killed, so that I could live here and rent the granny flat out.'

That caught his attention and he looked shocked. 'You've been married?'

'Why are you so surprised?'

'You don't seem like a grieving widow.'

'I'm not. Phil had just left me for someone else, but luckily for me he hadn't transferred the life insurance benefits to her. He wasn't the most practical of men. Anyway, they were both killed in a car crash, so I wasn't depriving her of anything. I reckon I earned the money because I was left to pick up the pieces of both our lives.'

She grimaced at the memory and added, 'Which included clearing her underclothing out of their drawers. Ugh.'

'Do I say tough luck, then?'

She shrugged. 'You can say what you like. I'm well over it now. I was upset at the time, of course I was, but we hadn't been happy together for a while, so I got on with my life and bought this house with the money.'

'No one else around at the moment?'

She shrugged again, wondering why he was asking that. 'I'm not interested in getting into another relationship. No way, Narelle.'

'It always amuses me when Aussies say that. Do you know where the Narelle comes from? It's not a common name, after all.'

'Not the foggiest.'

'Sorry, go on.'

'I've been too busy running the bar to miss having a man around, and I'm with people all day so I'm not lonely. In fact, it makes for a very pleasant life. I really like working in hospitality. I'd not want to work in a bar for ever, nothing is for ever, but for the next few years till I can save some more money.'

'For some other project?'

'It's still gestating so I don't talk about it yet.'

He was too easy to chat to. She'd end up telling him about her ambitions and hopes if she didn't watch out. She changed the subject hastily. 'Fair exchange: have you ever been married?'

'No.'

'Are you involved with anyone?'

'Not now. I've had a couple of longer relationships but they didn't work out. Luckily I have several childhood friends, people I met when visiting my aunt as a kid, and they're still living near the Abbey. We go out together sometimes.' She saw him grimace as if the memories weren't all pleasant, but didn't pursue the point because a tourist boat came past along the canal just then and people waved to them. He waved back but she didn't bother doing it. Boats came past all the time.

She was feeling sad at the prospect of leaving here, not to mention nervous about going to the other side of the world from the lovely summer sun into a cold English winter. Nick said she was an archetypal Mrs Stay-At-Home. Not hard when you had a home as lovely as this one.

She had a sudden horrible thought. 'Is it likely to snow at this time of year in England?'

'What on earth made you ask that?'

'I went for a skiing holiday once in Thredbo in New South Wales and I absolutely hated snow. I didn't enjoy feeling frozen to the marrow and I fell a few times so abandoned any attempt to learn to ski because I didn't want to risk a broken leg. Then it snowed some more. Ugh! So I stayed in the bar at the hotel instead, reading or chatting to people.'

'You get used to snow.'

'Thanks for that thought but I don't intend to try. You can have my share.'

He grinned and changed the subject. 'I might go on one of those night tours of the canals. Which one would you recommend?'

She glanced at her watch. 'We could go on the sunset cruise tonight, if you like. I'm not going into the bar this evening. Nick wants to see how things go with just him and his friend Jonno working there.'

'I'd love to go on a cruise with you. If you're sure you don't mind, that is.'

'I wouldn't have offered if I did mind. I can't afford either the time or the money to run a boat of my own, so I go out with the tourists two or three times a year. I like to see how many new houses have been built. They started by building a few watery canals in Mandurah several years ago, but the houses with water frontage have been so popular they've continued to create more of them.'

As they got ready, she wondered if she'd been wise to offer to go with him on a boat trip. She'd have to take care to steer the conversation away from his precious Stovell Abbey. But she couldn't really settle to anything at the moment with a trip to the other side of the world looming, so she might as well chill out a bit. Anyway, she could hardly back out now.

In fact, she enjoyed herself far more than she'd expected. It was perfect weather, still warm enough in the evenings for short sleeves, and tonight there was a glorious sunset to enjoy.

A glass of fizzy wine came with the cruise and as they sipped somehow they got talking about houses and how they had changed in style over the centuries. She found he had a wealth of knowledge about that because he'd specialised in restoring older heritage properties till he went to work at Stovell Abbey as land agent and manager.

They both commented on the houses they passed, agreeing that some of them looked like nothing more than huge boxes with glass walls. A boring architectural style compared to the elegant heritage properties in both their countries.

The evening passed quickly but after she'd dropped him at his hotel, she couldn't resist driving to the bar and parking in a place from which she could see inside it. She sighed at the sight of everything looking fine without her. Jonno was talking animatedly to a group of customers and Nick was watching his friend fondly. There was definitely something going on between the two of them, and good luck to them, but she didn't want anyone taking her place in the café.

She itched to go in and join them but Nick had strictly forbidden her to come in that evening.

She hadn't changed her mind about going to England, didn't want to do it, but she felt she had been trapped into it. When she went to bed, she shed a few tears at the prospect then grew angry with herself for giving way to her emotions.

Only, she felt uneasy as she had in her childhood with their constant moves. This inheritance was unsettling her more than she'd expected. Why did things have to change?

Well, no one was going to trap her into staying there. Definitely not. She loved life here in Australia, had done from the start. Jenny had loved it here too, though she'd had to work hard to support them. Paula owed so much to her stepmother, had such happy memories of life with her.

She hadn't seen or heard from her birth mother for years, didn't care if she never saw her again.

Two days later, Richard asked her if she'd like to go with him to the Bunbury area south of Perth to see some older buildings and, since Nick wanted another day working with only Jonno, she said yes.

They set off very early and were shown round some larger old homesteads by one local estate agent in the morning and another in the afternoon. Both of them were very knowledgeable about the various eras in which they'd been built.

Richard had warned her not to give away the fact that he wasn't really looking to buy a property here for a country hotel, but that he might buy one somewhere one day.

'What? Leave your precious abbey?' she teased.

'When the time is right. I don't want to work for other people all my life and I enjoy being in the hospitality industry. My last job before starting work at the abbey was to redesign an older country house that needed renovation so that it suited that sort of a business. I really enjoyed doing it.'

That surprised her. But she managed not to tell him that she too would like to run a country hotel. Only hers would have to be on a much smaller scale because she wasn't likely ever to be rich enough to purchase a large heritage property.

This time when they got back, he kissed her goodnight. 'I enjoyed your company today, Paula.'

'I enjoyed yours, too.' She'd been surprised how much. She'd better be careful. There was no future for the two of them because she was utterly certain that she wouldn't want to go and live permanently in the UK.

Pity.

They boarded the plane ten days after Richard had first come into her bar, and a flight attendant fussed them into the business-class seats.

She stared round at the more generous seating arrangements than there had been on her other flights, leaning her head back and letting out a long sigh. 'I must be crazy. Why did I let you and Nick persuade me into doing this?'

'You've been saying that for the last two days. Do you think you could accept the fait accompli now and cheer up a little? You might as well enjoy your trip to England.'

She'd said so many times that she didn't want to go that she simply stuck out her tongue at him. Then a flight attendant came along with a tray of glasses and she accepted a glass of champagne.

He reached out to clink his glass against hers. 'Here's to a peaceful trip. We can at least agree on that, surely?'

He touched his glass gently against hers a second time. 'And here's to the new lady of Stovell Abbey.'

She shook her head and didn't drink to that, so he raised his glass alone and took a sip. His expression was sad as he did this, but she couldn't lie to him or anyone else either. The thought of all that responsibility still gave her the shivers.

But he was right about one thing: she should stop

complaining. Her presence here wasn't his fault. She looked round and tried for a neutral topic. 'It's a lot more comfortable in business class.'

'I suppose so. I've never flown economy.'

She rolled her eyes. 'You poor little rich boy!'

But for some reason this seemed to upset him and he shook his head, staring blindly into some bleak personal landscape. She watched the pain on his face, wishing she knew what was causing it and that she could find a way to ease his unhappiness. For a moment she stretched out one hand, intending to take his, even opened her mouth to ask what was wrong, then she jerked the hand back before he saw it and filled her mouth with champagne instead of careless words.

She couldn't afford to get involved with this man, because their lives were set on different paths.

Her plan now was to settle all the legal stuff quick smart. Afterwards she'd give herself a further week or two to see some of the historic parts of England that she'd read about, then she'd return to Western Australia and get on with her real life. She wasn't interested in Buckingham Palace but she would like to walk on Hadrian's Wall and visit Bamburgh Castle, which she'd thought magnificent when she'd seen photos of it jutting up proudly on a headland looking out over the sea.

And from what Richard had said, Stonehenge was just down the road from the village of Stovell Magna, and Salisbury Cathedral wasn't too far away either. It apparently had a wonderful chapter house with magnificent stained-glass windows and there was a copy of the Magna Carta on display there. How cool was that?

The silence was going on for too long so she said the first thing that came into her head. 'Tell me more about the house itself, Richard.'

He shrugged. 'I've shown you the photographs of the exterior and the library. I don't think I can do the interior of Stovell Abbey justice with words. It's just – a lovely manor house with a lived-in feel.'

'What, no picture galleries full of gloomy ancestors in fancy-dress costumes?'

'Well, a small gallery and yes, it is full of portraits of ancestors, though they're a fairly friendly-looking bunch. You resemble some of them. That dark curly hair crops up here and there over the generations. The Abbey has always been more of a home than a show house. The family has never gone in for mere display and . . .'

He loves it, she thought as she listened to him. *It's not his but he can't help loving it.* Was that what was upsetting him so much? That he would have to leave Stovell and the changes he'd been superintending to others because of her inheriting it? It added another worry to her load. She didn't want to hurt anyone and he was a nice guy, very kind to everyone, which mattered far more to her than good looks.

Though he had those too, she added mentally. His kiss had sent her pulse skittering around her body in a frenzied reaction. She mustn't let him kiss her again. Unfortunately.

Her father had been good looking too but definitely not kind. He'd fooled poor Jenny that he loved her, had stolen most of her money and spent it, giving her very little in return, not even a child of her own. She'd made Paula hers, though, and they had been as close as a birth mother and daughter right until Jenny's sudden death last year.

Another worry wormed its way into Paula's thoughts. If the house was as charming as Richard said, there might be another danger, one Paula hadn't even thought of before: she liked old houses. She didn't want to fall in love with the place, thank you very much, definitely not. She didn't want uprooting.

Tony had several times done it to her and Jenny in a rush to avoid angry creditors or gambling companions who suspected they'd been cheated. Each time it had been to a different American state. She still had nightmares about moving house secretly in the middle of the night and being afraid someone would catch up with them.

Richard's breath fanned her ear. 'Penny for them.'

For some strange reason, she changed her mind and began to tell him about her long-term dreams, something only Nick knew about so far. If she kept the thought of these plans in mind during this trip, it would help counteract the effects of a beautiful house that could never be truly hers, surely?

'One day I want to run a country hotel, a small but exclusive place where people can come for a rest and a bit of pampering. The odd family reunions or wedding reception too, perhaps, just small groups, not mammoth productions. What do you think?'

'Sounds good to me. I don't think you could do that at Stovell, though. It'd cost too much to convert and put in en-suite bathrooms. The coffers aren't empty but we still have to make every penny count.'

'I want to do it in Australia, where we don't have to fight snow and ice – though I shall make sure I don't buy one somewhere that's prone to bushfires or floods. You have to be very careful about the location wherever you open up a business, it seems to me.'

He looked thoughtful as he replied. 'I've been reading about Western Australian history in the evenings. It's a part of the country that's not as well known in the UK as Sydney and the eastern states are. I found it an amazing place even on my short visit, very different from sleepy old Wiltshire. There feels to be more energy crackling in the air there. I only had time to see the parts near Perth, but I really liked it, and the colonial architecture.'

'Yes. I enjoyed our trip into the country together.'

He stared briefly into space than added, 'I'd like to go back and explore other parts of the state sometime. WA is so big. I'd seen it on maps but hadn't realised that it covers a third of the land surface of Australia, give or take.'

'You fitted in a lot in a short time. We Aussies aren't the only ones with energy.'

He shrugged. 'There are some advantages to not having to penny-pinch.'

Was he rich, then? Or was he charging all this to the estate? Even a tactless person like her knew better than to ask that outright, but she couldn't help wondering.

'The guy I hired to drive me round for a couple of days was very helpful and I really enjoyed seeing the older suburbs of Perth. I kept stopping him so that I could take photos of houses I found interesting. I love your architectural history.'

'That surprises me.'

'Many years ago as part of my studies, I did a university project on colonial Australia, but to see it in the flesh so to speak, well, that was great. I'd meant to visit it then, but my aunt Marian was ill and I couldn't leave my uncle Roy to deal with everything on his own. It took her a while to get better.'

'Didn't you ever want to design houses or buildings? Most architects do.'

'Occasionally, but once I realised what other options were available, I changed my focus. I'm really into heritage and renovation work these days. Which is what Stovell needs.'

'Good for you.'

His eyes were warm on her face. 'Good for you, don't you mean. I think you'll be surprised by the place, Paula, and don't set yourself against changing your mind about going to live there. An amazing woman like you can do anything.'

'Me? Amazing?' For some strange reason, his compliment threw her off balance. What a word to use about her! And he'd meant it, wasn't the sort to offer empty compliments. She could feel a blush stealing up her neck and warming her cheeks. 'I'm not amazing at all. I'm just a – well, a businesswoman. One who wears wacky clothes.'

'They suit your personality.'

'You mean I'm wacky?'

'Delightfully so.'

She tried to sip her champagne again to distract herself, but the glass was empty. When another one was offered by the stewardess after they'd taken off, she accepted it and slurped it down in a way that would have had Nick tutting in disapproval. She didn't have a good head for alcohol and it made her sleepy, but she'd had a busy few days, so why not relax a little, especially with an ordeal looming?

Some time later, she woke to find her head on Richard's

shoulder and her hand clasped trustingly in his. 'Oh, hell!' she said before she could stop herself. 'How did we get so cosy?' She yanked her hand away and sat bolt upright.

'You were the one who got cosy, actually.' He chuckled. 'Are you always such a cheap drunk?'

'I don't often indulge, well, not more than one glass, sipped very slowly over a whole evening. Booze makes me drowsy, as you saw. Sorry to fall asleep on you like that.'

'I enjoyed it. It's been a long time since a woman cuddled up to me.' He raised her hand to his lips and kissed it gently.

Reaction zipped through her and she dragged her hand hastily away and stood up abruptly. It might be cowardly to take refuge in the toilet cubicle, but she needed time away from him to pull herself together as well as a visit there for the usual reasons.

The trouble was, it had felt nice to her to wake up cuddling someone as well. It had been a while and she'd forgotten how pleasant it could be.

She splashed water on her face and patted it dry briskly, but her brain seemed to have turned to cotton wool. *You're in trouble, my girl*, she thought as she stared at her reflection. *You're attracted to him and it can go nowhere. He's an upper-class Brit and fixed in the UK, while you're a dinky-di Aussie who dresses like a weirdo. The two don't mix. Not permanently, anyway.*

Three loud tones sounded from the PA system and a tinny voice announced, 'Ladies and gentlemen, I'm afraid we're in for some turbulence, so will you please return to your seats immediately and keep your seatbelts buckled at all times until the sign goes off.'

Paula straightened her clothes, opened the door of the

cubicle and headed for her seat. But before she could get there, the aeroplane began to toss her about with such force it was a struggle to stay upright.

Another tone sounded and a voice called, 'Cabin staff to seats!'

She had trouble moving forward at all. The plane dropped suddenly just as she was reaching out to grab the back of her seat and . . .

When she regained consciousness, she was lying on the floor in the aisle with a damp cloth on her forehead and an attendant kneeling by her side. She tried to sit up, but the woman pressed her down again.

'Please lie completely still for a moment or two, madam.'

Richard was sitting in her aisle seat now, leaning down towards her. 'How do you feel, Paula?'

'Woozy.'

'You knocked yourself out. Try moving each arm and leg in turn really slowly. We don't think you've broken anything.'

She wiggled them. 'They're all there. None of them hurts.'

The flight attendant studied her. 'Could you please try sitting up now, madam? Move gently, though. I don't want you to try standing up till we're sure you're not dizzy.'

Unfortunately she was dizzy – quite disoriented, actually – but if she admitted it, they might try to keep her lying here like an idiot.

Richard offered his hand and she didn't dare try to stand up, so edged round to sit on the floor next to his seat.

'How does that feel, madam?'

'Er, OK.'

Richard looked down at her suspiciously. 'Paula?'

She rolled her eyes. 'Well, I'm still dizzy. What do you expect? But only a bit. I don't feel as if I'm going to pass out on you again.'

'We're going to land in a few minutes,' the flight attendant said. 'If you can manage to move onto the seat with our help, we'll get you buckled in, madam. Mr Crawford, could you move back to your own seat, please? Don't get out of your seat after we land, Ms Grey. We've called a doctor and he'll be boarding the plane to see you.'

Feeling extremely embarrassed, Paula let them both help her into her seat. And damn it, she couldn't have managed that on her own! Not yet anyway. The flight attendant insisted on buckling her in.

People nearby were staring. 'I feel a fool,' she muttered to Richard.

'You had me worried. You were unconscious.'

She turned towards him and groaned as a pain stabbed through her forehead.

'What's the matter?'

'My head hurts when I move it.' Closing her eyes, she leant back, more shaken than she cared to admit. Perhaps she had concussion. She moved incautiously and her surroundings seemed to waver about. She mentally amended that to yes, she probably did have concussion. She'd had it once before and remembered a similar feeling.

After the plane had landed, the other passengers stood up. Paula didn't need urging to stay in her seat. She had no desire to walk anywhere, not till she'd got her head together. She closed her eyes.

'How are you feeling, Ms Grey?' a strange voice said.

She opened her eyes to see a man bending over her.

'I'm a doctor,' he said. 'Let me just check a few things.'

He felt her pulse and peered into her eyes using a little light. Paula wanted to push him away, but her limbs felt strangely heavy.

He moved back and his voice seemed to come from a great distance. 'She's concussed. Not too badly, but enough to be careful. She can't fly on till we're sure she's fully recovered.'

The woman's voice said, 'We'll book you both into a hotel, Mr Crawford, compliments of the airline. You can resume your journey as soon as the doctor approves.'

Paula tried to tell them she'd rather get the journey over quickly, but her voice was still not obeying her. All that came out was, 'Richard?'

His hand was there, clasping hers. 'You'll be all right, Paula. You just need to lie down and rest for a while. We'll get you to the hotel as quickly as we can, then put you to bed.'

She didn't like feeling so helpless but as she swung her body round suddenly, intending to protest, the cabin seemed to whirl round her again. So she stilled and shut her mouth. The only thing she felt sure of at the moment was the strength in that firm hand still holding hers, the reassurance and kindness in his gaze. 'You won't leave me?'

'No. Of course not.'

'Good.'

The journey to the hotel was a jumble of impressions, like a jerky old movie stopping and starting. The attendants insisted on putting her in a wheelchair to get her through the airport. She couldn't even summon up the energy to protest against what she felt to be an indignity.

From time to time, voices conferred above her, but it was impossible to concentrate on what they were saying. The jolting of moving around hurt her head and at one point she couldn't hold back a groan.

But most of the time Richard was there – like a lifeline. It made her feel safe to have him nearby, she decided dreamily. He had lovely hands, warm and firm.

A nurse stayed in attendance all the way to the hotel and said she would see her to her room.

'I hate all this fuss,' Paula muttered. 'I just want to sleep.'

'We're nearly there now.'

When they got there, they were whisked straight up in a lift, with her still in the wheelchair. She shut her eyes and endured, longing for the jolting to be over.

The room was comfortable but best of all was the bed – large and well-sprung, with the softest of pillows. She sighed with relief as Richard and the nurse helped her to lie down on it.

When voices started talking above her head, she ignored them and closed her eyes.

Later, she was woken out of a deep sleep by someone asking her name.

'Go away.'

'What's your name?'

'You know damned well it's Paula. Now, go away and let me sleep, Richard.'

The second time this happened, she told him to go and bury himself somewhere deep and dark.

His chuckle seemed to echo in her dreams.

The next thing Paula knew, it was morning. She woke in a strange room to find a man's face on the pillow next to hers and yelped in shock before she could stop herself.

Richard opened his eyes, blinked drowsily then came fully awake. 'Sorry. I didn't mean to startle you, but I couldn't leave you alone or that bossy woman from the airline would have brought in a nurse.'

'Oh. Well, thank you.'

'I had strict instructions to wake you at regular intervals – and let me tell you, you have a mean mouth on you when you're annoyed, Paula Grey.'

What did you say to a man, almost a complete stranger, with whom you'd just shared a bed? She said the first thing that came into her mind. 'I feel stupid.'

'What for?'

'Getting knocked out like that.'

'It wasn't your fault. That was pretty bad turbulence, the worst I've ever experienced, and it hit us even more quickly than they'd expected.'

'Tell me about it!' Something else took her mind off the conversation. 'I need to use the bathroom.'

'It's that door.' He jumped out of bed and peeled the covers off her. She stared down in shock to find herself clad in her own nightdress, a semi-transparent creation in midnight blue with creamy lace round the neck and sleeves. She blushed and pulled the sheet back up again, croaking, 'Dressing gown.'

He stepped hastily away. 'There's a hotel robe hanging up behind the door. Just a minute.'

She had to know. 'Richard – did *you* undress me?'

'I had to help the nurse. She was a tiny woman and you were too big for her to lift, especially when you weren't co-operating.'

'Oh.'

'Here you are.' He brought the towelling robe across.

Paula grabbed it and tried to wriggle into it without exposing herself further to his gaze. For once, she wished she wore pyjamas to bed, like most of her friends did, but she'd never liked them, even if they were fashionable. During the hot weather, she slept naked.

When he reached out to help her, she smacked his hand away. 'I can manage on my own now.'

He laughed at her embarrassment, damn him!

'Oh, but you might fall over. I'd better keep hold of you.'

She scowled. 'You're enjoying this!'

'I am, rather. I know you're recovering when you protest so fluently. I was really worried about you yesterday, though.' He took the tangled dressing gown out of her hands and shook it out, holding it for her to put her arms into, one after the other.

Trying to look nonchalant, as if she often paraded in front of strangers clad only in filmy blue material, she reluctantly let the sheet drop and slipped her arms into the sleeves of the gown without looking at him. When she had it belted round her, she headed towards the bathroom, only to find him walking beside her.

She stopped dead. 'Oh, no! I'm going in there on my own.'

'Of course you are, but don't lock the door. If you fell over . . .'

'I'm not going to fall over. Why don't you do something useful like order coffee.'

'Breakfast, too?'

'Yes, please. Get what you like, but for heaven's sake, leave me in peace for a few minutes.'

Once inside the luxurious bathroom, she clasped both hands to her scarlet cheeks at the sight of herself in the mirror. None of her night things were exactly cover-ups and she had a weakness for lacy underwear.

His voice from outside the door made her jerk into action. 'Are you all right, Paula?'

'Of course I am. What are you, a voyeur or something?'

That made him laugh again. He could laugh his head off out there but he'd better not come in.

Richard wouldn't let her go anywhere or do anything until the doctor had been and pronounced her recovered.

When she tried to sneak her clothes into the bathroom to have a shower and get dressed, he took them off her forcibly, which led to a short, sharp exchange of uncomplimentary remarks.

So she had to wait, wrapped in the towelling robe, which made her feel too hot. She drank a cup of coffee, ate some fruit, following that with bacon and eggs. Then she watched the news on TV, still too annoyed with him to chat.

When the doctor arrived, he prodded her around some more, and addressed his remarks to her companion.

'Hey! I haven't lost my hearing!' she announced, glaring

at the stranger. 'Why are you talking to him?'

'Sorry, Miss Grey. I think you'll be fit to travel tomorrow.'

'I feel well enough to leave today.'

They both smiled at her kindly.

'Don't push it,' Richard said. 'You had concussion.'

After the doctor had left, she glared at Richard. 'Don't ever do that again.'

'What?'

'Decide things for me as if I were a child.'

'You're probably not thinking very clearly yet.' His expression was sympathetic. 'Got a headache too, haven't you?'

She shrugged, but refrained from nodding because it'd start the hammers pounding inside her skull again.

'I'll get you some water and you can take a couple of the painkillers the doctor left.'

She debated refusing, simply on principle, but at the memory of how those damned hammers kept attacking her skull, she accepted the tablets. 'Hadn't you better see about getting a room of your own for tonight? It was very kind of you to – to—'

'Sleep with you?'

'Don't say it like that. People will get the wrong impression.'

'Not used to sharing bedrooms?'

'I don't make a habit of it.' And not at all since her stupid husband had died.

'Well, just to relieve your mind . . .' He got up and walked over to a door in the other wall, which she'd thought was a walk-in wardrobe, throwing it open dramatically. 'Voilà!'

'You mean you've had a room of your own all along and yet you still slept in my bed?'

'You needed someone to stay with you. And anyway – you seemed determined to keep hold of my hand.'

He would have to bring that up, damn him! 'Well, I don't want to hold it any longer, thank you.' With one quick shove, she pushed him through the doorway and locked it on her side. 'There are times when a woman needs privacy!' she yelled through it.

His laugh was loud and hearty.

Half an hour later, the tablets had banished the headache and she was getting bored. She went to the door and tapped on it. 'Richard?'

'I'm not holding a conversation through a door. I like to see the face of the person I'm speaking to.'

When she unlocked it, he came to lean against the door frame, studying her face.

'I – um – feel a lot better now that the painkillers have kicked in and I quite fancy going out somewhere. I've never visited Singapore before.'

'We'll go out for a meal tonight, then, and maybe have a ride round.'

'I've got cabin fever now. Can't we go for a short walk?'

'Let me see you walk across the room.'

She did that and even managed to sweep a curtsey as she turned. 'See. No dizziness now.'

'OK. We'll stroll round the nearest shopping mall for an hour or so and see how you go.' He waited, one eyebrow raised, clearly expecting her to argue.

She wasn't going to admit that was probably all she felt up to. 'Great. Give me ten minutes to get ready.'

Once outside the hotel, they strolled along side by side through air that was so warm and steamy you could almost have sliced it. The streets were busy and, to her disappointment, this part of Singapore seemed to consist of little except a series of shopping centres linked by busy streams of traffic.

'Want to go inside this one?' he asked, gesturing to a busy entrance.

'Not really. I'm not big on shopping. I'd rather keep on walking. I need some exercise and I like watching people.'

After a while, she raised her face and sniffed. The wind was wafting a smell towards them that was different from anything she'd ever encountered before and she didn't like it. 'What's that smell? I can't decide whether it's decay or growing vegetation or what.'

He stopped and pointed to a pile of green lumpy fruits a street seller had on display. They were as big as melons and reeked of something strange and nasty. 'It's partly that. Durian fruit. They won't allow it on an aeroplane, for obvious reasons.'

'It can't be a fruit,' she gasped, moving past quickly to get away from the pungency.

'It is. The locals say it smells like hell and tastes like heaven.'

She could only shudder. 'Have you ever tried one?'

'No. I couldn't get past the smell. Come on. Let's go into that shopping centre and find somewhere to sit and have a coffee.'

She was relieved, though she didn't say so. Once they were seated, she studied the coffee shop with a rival's eye. 'I think our bar is much more welcoming than this place.'

But the coffee was good and so was the pastry.

When they left the café, he insisted on turning back.

Once again they were laughing together, pointing things out to one another, as comfortable as old friends. Now how did that keep happening? she wondered as they walked into the hotel. It was a long time since she'd met a guy this easy to talk to or enjoyed kissing as much.

He stopped at her bedroom door. 'I suggest we visit the food markets and eat there tonight. A friend told me they have wonderful and very varied things to eat. You ought to have a rest now, but would you feel up to going out again?'

'I'd love it. I've heard about the food markets, too.'

'Will you be all right till then?'

'Yes, of course I will. Actually, I feel like another nap.'

'How about leaving the connecting door unlocked so that I can keep an eye on you?'

'OK, but knock first before you come in. Only if I yell for help are you allowed in without knocking.' Pulling a face at him, laughing when he pulled one back, she went into her room.

As she closed the door, she wished he was still with her. How stupid was that? She went to lie on the bed and let herself doze off again.

Some time later, she woke with a start to find him kneeling on the floor by the bed, shaking her gently.

'Are you all right, Paula? And before you complain about my presence, you didn't answer my call.'

She blinked at him. 'I must have fallen asleep again. And heavily. I never sleep at all in the daytime normally.'

'You don't usually have the effects of concussion lingering in your system. I'm wondering if we should stay here for another day or two.'

She was tempted to agree because this was the first time she'd left Australia and not felt dreadfully homesick. Was that because of him? 'It might be nice to do that anyway,' she admitted.

He smiled. 'I'd like to do that, too, and it'll probably be better for you to postpone flying. You're sure?'

'Yes.'

'Then I'll change our departure.' He studied her face and added, 'You've got a much better colour now. I'll collect you as soon as I've sorted out our flight, shall I?'

That gave her time to improve her appearance. Not that she could improve the bruising much. She hated putting gunk on her skin, however expensive the gunk.

Half an hour later, the flight was changed and they left the hotel, strolling along the street. *So many people*, she thought in amazement.

She didn't like it when they were separated and he seemed to know that, because he reached out to take her hand and thread it in his arm.

'That better?'

'Yes, thank you.' *Much better*, she thought, as a little shiver ran through her.

Perth had its share of food markets, but this place was huge and Paula had never seen some of the ingredients offered. As they wandered along, looking at the wares, vendors kept making energetic efforts to entice them to buy, but they weren't ready to eat yet.

He stopped to point out one delicacy advertised as 'Pig's Organ Soup'.

'Which organ do you suppose it is?' she whispered.

'I'd never dare ask! Look, I'm ravenous now and the smell of food is driving me crazy. Let's stop and have a fistful of satays before we decide what else to eat.'

'Good idea.'

They found a table and ate tender spicy chicken and beef strips from long bamboo skewers, laughing as the peanut sauce dripped down their chins and fingers.

Moving on, they tried a dish here and a dish there, vegetables in black bean sauce, seafood with noodles, thinly sliced chicken with ginger.

'It's delicious, but I can't eat another thing.' She pushed the final bowl of food towards him after one taste.

'Are you sure?'

'Very.'

She watched as he cleared the lot, including every last spoonful of rice. 'I thought Nick could qualify for the eating Olympics, but you'd definitely get a gold medal.'

'What can I say? I have a fast metabolism. It infuriates my aunt because she has to watch her weight carefully.'

'Does she live close by?'

'She lives at the Abbey. She's the housekeeper-cum-manager there and has been for well over a decade. I grew up spending my holidays with her even before she went to live in the official housekeeper's suite. I was at boarding school, you see, and my mother did a lot of travelling on business.'

'So the Abbey's been your home for a while.'

His smile faded. 'No. I've mostly lived elsewhere, at university, for instance, and when I was working as a junior architect in London. But a couple of years ago I was, um, given the chance to run the estate and manage some necessary renovations and I jumped at it.'

'So your job is estate manager?'

'Um . . . Yes. I suppose that should be my official title these days.'

She wondered why he'd hesitated but didn't like to ask. She didn't want to upset him tonight, was enjoying his company too much.

'My training's come in very useful as I've been able to arrange quite a bit of necessary renovation to the house and outbuildings, and then supervise it all.'

'You're not going to leave now, are you, Richard? I mean, I know nothing about that sort of thing and anyway, I'll only be in England for a week or two.'

'I think it'll take you longer than that to settle things, Paula.'

'No way. We can do anything else that's needed digitally.'

The look he gave her was disapproving and he didn't say anything else as they walked back to the hotel.

When she sneaked a peek sideways as they went up in the lift, he had little frown-wrinkles across his forehead. Of course, her inheriting must be a touchy subject for him in some ways. She should have realised and not been so vehement. She'd never been famous for her tact!

'I didn't mean to upset you,' she offered.

He looked at her solemnly, then gave her a wry smile. 'It wasn't you who upset me. It's the situation that I'm not happy about and that's not your fault. We won't spoil our holiday with business matters but wait till we get back. Who knows? Maybe you'll fall in love with Stovell Abbey.'

And maybe pigs will fly, she thought, but didn't say that, contenting herself with, 'I've already fallen in love with Australia. Very deeply in love.' And if things were different, she might fall in love with him, too.

They both sighed at the same time and avoided that topic from then onwards.

They spent another two days sightseeing, and even doing some shopping. She couldn't resist buying a couple of tee shirts and a beautiful full skirt that shimmered slightly.

Daytimes were fine but on the first of those evenings, a lad ran out of a side street and bumped into her and she would have fallen if Richard hadn't caught her.

When he didn't let go of her, just stared, she took matters into her own hands. After all, she prided herself on being a modern woman, an equal partner. So she put her arms round his neck and kissed him.

He stiffened for a moment, then returned her kiss and the world vanished for a few moments.

'Let's go back to my room,' she said.

'We shouldn't.'

'Why not? We neither of us have a partner, so we're free to do as we please. Unless you don't fancy me.'

He half-closed his eyes. 'The trouble is, I fancy you too much. But I don't want to take advantage of you.'

She couldn't be less than truthful. 'I don't usually dive into kissing like that, because I don't believe in casual sex. But how is it taking advantage to share a few kisses?'

'Because it might not stop there.'

'It'll only go further by mutual consent.'

'Oh, hell!' He gave her another kiss and then stopped a taxi that was passing by.

They kissed again in the taxi and in the lift going up to her room.

When they got to her room, he stopped and said, 'Are you sure?'

'Very sure.' She didn't know why she fancied him so much, hadn't met a man for years who'd made her hormones twitch to attention like this. Only it wasn't just hormones, it was him. He was kind and intelligent and, well, she really liked him.

When they got inside it, he didn't spoil things by asking again if she were sure. It was only too obvious that they both were.

He stirred afterwards and said, 'Do you want me to go back to my room?'

'No. I shall take offence if you do. I like cuddling and you're rather good at it.'

So they fell asleep together.

The second day was equally wonderful. They didn't stop talking and they spent that night together as well.

Then it was time to leave and this flight went smoothly. It seemed to go on for a long time, though. And he sat there with the frown back on his face.

She'd expected to sleep on the plane but couldn't manage more than a light near-doze, even with the comfort of a seat that turned into a fully lie-down bed. So she read a book she'd picked up in Singapore and since their seats were on opposite sides of the aisle on this plane, at a difficult distance for chatting, Richard watched something on his seat's personal screen.

When they reached England, they got through customs quickly and then went out to pick up the hire car he'd arranged to have waiting for them.

'It's easier to drive back from here,' he said as he stowed their things in the boot, then gestured to her to get into the vehicle. But first she looked up at the early morning sky and enjoyed a few deep breaths of fresh, if chilly air.

As she settled into her seat, Paula noticed that his slight frown was back so didn't force a conversation. She was beginning to dread what they would find waiting for them at Stovell Abbey.

She stared out of the car window most of the time, wanting to see as much as she could while she was here. They drove towards Bristol on the M4 motorway and she found the scenery early on in their drive rather industrial.

'When do we get to the real countryside?' she asked after a while.

'After we turn off the motorway.'

And he was right. Once they turned off the busy road and started driving through the countryside, things improved rapidly. She had to admit that Wiltshire was a beautiful part of England, even with so many trees standing leafless.

'No flowers in the hedgerows,' she said, trying for a light tone and sounding instead as if she was competing for a Worst Actress of the Year award.

'Well, it is only a few weeks until Christmas.'

'I'll be home in the sunshine by then.' She could have

bitten her tongue off as soon as she'd said that, it sounded so ungracious.

He didn't comment on that, just shot her an irritated glance and didn't try to start any further conversations.

She went back to staring out but couldn't stop herself from glancing in his direction occasionally. There hadn't been a second of the whole journey from Perth to London that she hadn't been aware of him – well, except for when she'd been knocked out.

And he'd seemed as deeply attracted to her as she was to him. Only, now they'd arrived in England he seemed to have withdrawn, as if determined to keep his distance from her. What did that mean? She hadn't a clue. What did she know about upper-class Poms and their hang-ups? Not much. And she'd never win a gold medal for dealing with men.

'There it is!' he called suddenly in quite another tone of voice, stopping by the side of the road and pointing ahead with a fond smile on his face.

She stared across a field, eager to see the house he'd shown her photos of come to life. 'It's . . . very pretty,' was all she could manage. It was but it still rang no chord within her. It was like the pictures in her history textbooks at school, simply an old house in a foreign country.

She couldn't believe she owned that expanse of stone and windows. Didn't want it, however rich that might make her. She was quite certain of that, still hadn't changed her allegiance to Australia and to what she could only describe as life at an individual level.

They set off again, passing through a pair of wrought-iron gates, left open for the world to go in and out. The part of the drive near the house was edged with bare flower beds but although the sun was shining, everything looked cold and the thin, hazy winter daylight made the colours seem washed out.

She shivered. She'd already found when they stopped for coffee that her jacket was far too light for this time of year in the northern hemisphere. Well, if she had to buy another one just for a couple of weeks, it'd come from a charity shop and cost as little as she could manage.

They drove all the way round to the rear of the house, which made her feel even more diminished by the grandeur of the building.

When he stopped in an area covered in gravel, which crunched as the tyres rolled over it, he said, 'We don't often use the front door. I hope you don't mind going in this way.'

'Of course not.'

He opened the car door and icy air howled around them. She shivered. 'How do you stand it?'

'Stand what?'

'The cold.'

'This isn't real cold by our standards.'

'Well, it is by mine.' She slung her cabin luggage over her shoulder, then dug her hands into her pockets and made no attempt to help him get her suitcase out of the boot.

'It gets much colder later in the winter. Wait till it snows.'

'I'd rather not. I hate the stuff. I've only seen it once and I kept falling over all the time. That was more than enough. I'm hoping there won't be any while I'm here.'

'It's not usual so early in the season.' He studied her, not looking as if he approved of what he saw. 'I'm hoping you'll feel better about life here when you've had a proper sleep. You're being rather bad-tempered. I suppose you're still recovering from the accident.'

She smiled reluctantly. 'Sorry. I'm always grumpy when I haven't slept well. Why do you have to be so damned cheerful and understanding? You leave me with nothing to shout at you for.'

He laid one hand across his chest. 'I can't help it. I was born with a smile on my face.'

They were laughing together as a door opened and an older woman stood looking at them. The heavy feeling returned to Paula's chest because the woman didn't look at all pleased to see them.

'Paula, this is my aunt Marian, who is the housekeeper here.'

'How do you do, Mrs . . . um?' She stuck out her hand.

'My surname's Saunders, but please call me Marian.' She shook Paula's hand but let go almost immediately and her tone was cool as she added, 'Do come inside. There's a real bite in the wind today.'

Paula followed her. She wasn't the only grumpy person by the looks of it. The other woman's back was rigidly erect, and the staccato sound of her leather court shoes on the wooden floors seemed . . . well, angry.

'I've put you in the east wing, Miss Grey, in the Indian room,' Mrs Saunders said as she led the way into the house. 'It's where the owner of the house always sleeps. When Richard phoned to say he'd found you, I moved his things out at once.'

Paula stopped walking for a moment. 'You mean I'm taking Richard's room? But surely that isn't necessary?

There must be plenty of other bedrooms I could use.' A house this size must have at least a dozen.

'The Indian room is always used by the master of the house – or in this case, the mistress. It has a small sitting room and a dressing room attached, with its own bathroom.'

Paula was puzzled as to why Richard had been sleeping there but before she could ask, Marian flung open a door and gestured to her to go in first. 'The bed frame is eighteenth century, but the mattress is new, as is the bedding, of course. We try to keep the Abbey homelike. It's not a showplace and we haven't been reduced to opening it to the public yet.'

'Um, yes. Of course.' *We?* Marian sounded as if she owned the place – or did it own her?

Richard appeared behind them. 'Here's your suitcase, Paula.'

'Thank you.' She stood aside to let him pass.

'I'll go and make some tea.' Mrs Saunders was turning to leave even as she spoke.

Paula had had enough of this curt treatment. 'Just a minute!'

The other woman turned round, one eyebrow raised enquiringly. 'Yes?'

'Why don't you tell me straight out what the matter is? How can I have done something to upset you when I've only just arrived?'

Richard laid one hand on her arm. 'I'll explain later.'

Paula shook it off. 'I'd prefer to have it explained right now. I don't understand why I'm getting the cold-shoulder treatment from a woman I've never even met before.'

His voice was a growl. 'I said I'd explain later.'

'I'd rather hear it from your aunt.'

The older woman took a deep breath and shrugged. 'All right. You can hardly expect me to be pleased to see my nephew losing the inheritance he loves so much. If he'd given up searching two months ago when the lawyers said they were satisfied that he was the heir, he'd still have Stovell and we wouldn't have to move out. *That* is what I find upsetting. So does he. Only he's better at concealing his feelings than I am.'

Lips pressed tightly together, she made for the door and this time Paula let her go, closing her eyes for a moment. It hadn't even occurred to her that she might have displaced someone who'd thought he was the heir. She turned to stare accusingly at Richard.

'Why didn't you tell me you had thought you were the heir?'

He shrugged, his expression calm, like that of a polite stranger.

'Are we related, then?'

'Very distantly.'

'You really ought to have told me, Richard.'

'Yes. I suppose so.'

'Why didn't you?'

'I don't know. Still coming to terms with it myself, I suppose.'

She folded her arms around herself to keep the warmth in because the air inside the house seemed chilly to her. 'You really love this place, don't you?'

'Yes, but it's not mine now. I've accepted that.'

'Why aren't you angry with me like your aunt is? You've been nothing but kind.'

His tone was ironical. 'I was brought up mainly in a boarding school. Stiff upper lip is more than just a saying, it's a way of life. And anyway, it isn't your fault so why should I blame you?'

'Well, I'd be angry if it were me.' Paula stared round her in frustration. She didn't even want the place. It said absolutely nothing to her. The air outside was cool and damp, and it wasn't much warmer inside. She'd left brilliant sunshine back in Australia and since the age of nine she'd experienced nothing like today's icy wind, sucking the warmth from her body.

Richard's voice brought her attention back to the present. 'Do you want to rest now, Paula? Or shall I show you round?'

'What I'd really like is a cup of strong coffee, black, no sugar. And a couple of cinnamon doughnuts. They make good ones at the café down the road from our bar.' Homesickness surged through her but she pushed it back. She could keep her upper lip fairly stiff, too, if circumstances demanded it.

'I'll ask my aunt to make you some coffee, then.'

'Oh, hell, don't do that. She's upset enough. I can perfectly well make my own or drink tea, whatever's most convenient.'

As he moved towards the door, she said again, very quietly, 'You really ought to have told me before I got here, Richard.'

He nodded, but didn't turn round to look at her. There was something stiff and unhappy about his shoulders that made sympathy surge through her. She nearly rushed after him to put her arms round him and hug him in sympathy.

But she didn't dare because he'd suddenly erected a tall fence around himself, a fence that hadn't been there until they got near this damned house. It might be invisible but she could sense the fence quite clearly.

She went to stare out of the window, but all she saw was a blur of colour as tears filled her eyes. How could she make it up to Richard? And how the hell was she going to get out of owning this place?

She wanted to go home so desperately it hurt. From the first moment of arriving in Australia as a child, she'd loved life there. She'd had no such reaction here.

She'd never expected to feel homesick so quickly in England. Make that extremely homesick.

Chapter Six

Richard went down to the kitchen, where his aunt was waiting for the kettle to boil with a teapot standing next to it.

'Paula prefers coffee.'

Marian shrugged and reached up into a cupboard and pulled out a jar of instant.

'Don't we have a percolator?'

'It's in the back kitchen. We rarely use it and it needs washing out.'

He was surprised at her reluctance to accommodate a guest. 'I think she's into real coffee. If we have some ground coffee, I'll make some for her.'

'Well, there is the remains of a packet in the freezer. I don't know what it's like, though. It's been there for months.'

He went to get the old-fashioned percolator, washed it out and set it up in a corner of the kitchen.

His aunt fiddled around nearby. 'Has she recovered from the concussion now?'

'She seems all right but I'm keeping an eye on her, just in case.'

'When do we have to move out by?'

He spun round, startled. '*You* may not need to move out at all. She'll still need a someone to look after the house, after all.'

'If you have to move out, I'm coming with you. Some things are just not right and she doesn't *deserve* to inherit all this.'

Richard sighed. His aunt could be as prickly as any thornbush and he knew she was upset on his behalf as much as her own. Asking her to be nice to Paula would only make her stiffer, so all he said was, 'Let's just take it day by day, hmm? She seems a decent sort to me.'

Marian got out the biscuit tin and banged it down on the surface. 'Whatever. But however decent she is, she's still taken your inheritance so keep her away from me as much as you can, please.'

Paula stared at herself in the mirror. Nice bruise. She'd make an excellent impression on the neighbours with that. If there were any neighbours near here.

She was desperate for a shower after the long hours on the plane. She got out some clean clothes and slung her old ones in a corner, for lack of a dirty washing basket, then clambered into the bath and drew the shower curtain. She shivered as she stood there because it took her a minute or two to figure out the way the instant hot water system worked. When it did she nearly scalded herself, and when she twiddled the knob it turned icy and made her yelp.

Once the water was flowing at a comfortable temperature, she stood in the huge claw-footed bath and moved to and fro under the warm water. The curtain had a tendency to cling to her and the water trickled out of the shower head far too slowly to keep her whole body warm so she didn't spend long under it but got out of the huge bath again, towelling herself dry as quickly as she could.

She couldn't help remembering how unhappy Richard had looked as they walked into the house, even though he'd been trying to hide it. Well, no wonder he'd been upset. He loved this house and now she'd taken it away from him.

When she was ready, she looked in the mirror again. It definitely didn't approve of her. Oh, hell, her hair was still damp and tendrils were spiralling out of control. She couldn't use her hairdryer because she didn't have the right adaptor for her plug so hunted through her suitcase for a scarf. She found a bright green one and used it to tie the heavy mass of damp hair back. What did it matter if the scarf didn't match her top? She wasn't a stupid fashion plate and she liked to wear cheerful colours.

Just get on with it! she told herself. *Sort out this mistake and get back home to Oz again.*

Stovell Abbey might be Richard's home, but it'd never feel like hers. That had been confirmed the minute she saw it. It was strange how you sometimes reacted to a building before you'd even gone inside it. She'd instantly loved the wooden colonial house where she'd lived with her stepmother when they first arrived in Australia and she'd loved her canal home at first sight, too.

She'd felt the same way about the bar, though it'd been a coffee shop in those days, and a shabby one too. Well, their little business would still be there for her when she returned, though she was getting a bit worried about Nick and his friend Jonno. What if they wanted to buy her out and run the place together? No, Nick would never do that to her.

On that thought, she sent a quick text to him, saying they'd now arrived in the UK. She'd told him about their unexpected stopover in Singapore but had made light of it being caused by her accident.

As she left her room, she hesitated. Where had the others gone? Had Richard gone to the kitchen with his aunt or was he too having a shower? She didn't want to face that woman on her own.

She felt a bit nervous of poking into rooms, even though technically she owned them. As she walked along the balcony that ran round three sides of the huge, two-storey hall, she stopped to admire the stained-glass window, but scowled at the walls covered by dark paintings with heavy gold frames. There were also stiffly placed chairs every now and then that didn't invite you to sit on them, but seemed to be standing guard on the paintings.

She stopped at the top of the stairs but could hear nothing, so ran lightly down and listened again. Still nothing.

In the end she decided the central hallway would be the best place to yell for guidance, so let rip a 'Coo-ee', grinning as it echoed beautifully.

Richard thought he heard something. 'Shh!' He listened hard. Yes, there it was again. He went out of the servants' quarters into the main hall.

A voice called, 'Coo-ee! Anyone there?'

He looked into the hall and there she was, looking alien and out of place in another startling display of colourful clothing. 'This way to the kitchen, Paula, which is where we usually meet because it's warmer there. I'm afraid we only have an old-fashioned percolator, though.'

'Any sort of coffee will be welcome, as long as it's warm.'

He took her hand for a moment. 'My goodness, you are cold. And your hair's damp.'

'I don't have an adaptor for my hairdryer.'

'I've got a couple. I'll get one out for you when I next go upstairs.'

He watched his aunt blink at the sight of Paula's top, which was in shades of orange, teamed with a yellow patterned with orange cardigan and a green scarf to tie back her hair. He must be getting used to the bright colours. He even thought they suited her bouncy nature, though her facial expression was rather subdued today.

Unfortunately, the bruise really stood out. He'd explained about it to his aunt and she'd shrugged.

After refreshments and some stilted conversation, to which his aunt contributed very little, Richard took Paula for a tour of the house, taking an old shawl off the hooks near the back door first to wrap round her.

'The clothes hanging here don't belong to anyone. They're old ones we use sometimes when we go outside for temporary protection against the weather. Help yourself if needed.'

He showed off the formal drawing room, then the dining room, switching off a small panel first. 'We don't often use these rooms, except on special occasions. The furniture is the most valuable in the house and that switch was for an extra security system covering these rooms.'

She turned round on the spot, then walked across to study the massive portrait of a long-gone group of Stovells with solemn expressions, then moved to two formal landscapes in matching gold frames with no people in the scenes at all.

He couldn't help chuckling at her expression. 'Not your taste in paintings?'

'Definitely not.'

'That one' – he pointed – 'is worth about £50,000.'

'Get away with you! They're such a miserable bunch of folk, why immortalise them in the first place?'

'I agree with you.'

She looked at him in surprise. 'You do?'

'Yes. It's a boring painting, but it's by a moderately famous fellow. I'd intended to sell it and use the proceeds to do some more work on the roof before next winter.'

She snorted. 'Good idea. I'd not like to sit and look at it for even five minutes.'

'Let's leave it in peace, then.' He led the way out, switching on the security system again, then going down the hall towards the rear. 'The family mostly use the smaller rooms along this side of the passage leading off the rear of the hall.'

Even these contained valuable items, more genuine oil paintings and display cases full of delicate china. He hadn't realised how much he'd taken them for granted, but now he seemed to be seeing everything afresh through Paula's eyes. It was cluttered. Far too many objects jostled for position and the walls were nearly covered in heavy old paintings, most of only a mediocre standard.

No one needs that many possessions. The thought surprised him.

She didn't say much at all. He'd grown used to her chatting happily and missed it. 'Is your head aching again?'

'No. What made you ask that?'

'I'm not used to you being so quiet.'

'There's a lot to take in.' She sighed. 'And I feel guilty

for taking the house away from you. Why didn't you say it had been thought you were the heir before I turned up?'

Why hadn't he told her? 'I didn't want to spoil our time together. I was enjoying your company.'

'I was enjoying yours, too.'

He opened his mouth, then shut it again. He was *not* going to take his aunt's advice and try to marry her for the sake of a house. Paula deserved better than that.

What a pity they'd had to meet like this, though!

And what a pity she was so very Australian. He couldn't imagine her settling down in England, just could not picture it. Especially as he'd seen her looking happy and relaxed in her own country and Singapore.

Once he'd got used to the idea that he was the heir, he hadn't been able to imagine himself living anywhere else except the Abbey. Now, he had to get used to being Richard Crawford of no fixed abode again. He still hadn't the faintest idea where he'd go, what he'd do with himself. He was a bit like Paula in that: he hadn't had a settled home during his youth, what with boarding school, university then life in London. He wondered whether that had been one of the most appealing things about inheriting Stovell Abbey.

Fate had made a mess of her life, a really bad mess, and his aunt was wrong to blame Paula. But it hadn't dealt very well with him, either.

Strange how he seemed to be seeing the big picture more clearly now.

Only when Richard took her outside did Paula feel she could breathe properly again without the weight of the house clamping down around her. They stopped in the area off the kitchen to 'borrow' some outdoor clothes. Most of the stables had been converted into garages and outhouses, but there was a horse peering over a half door at the end of the row of low buildings.

He went across and the brown mare nuzzled his hand affectionately.

'Is that one yours?' she asked, keeping a safe distance away . She hadn't realised horses were so big.

'She belongs to you now.'

'No, thank you. I know nothing whatsoever about horses. I'd probably damage it.'

'Come and say hello to her, at least. Callie's a very friendly girl.'

She went towards the mare and held out her hand in the way he had, then stroked the animal tentatively. Callie stared at her and tossed her head, moving slightly away. She seemed to know that this human was nervous of her.

Suddenly Paula sneezed, then sneezed again. 'Damn!' She backed away, her eyes feeling itchy. 'I think I'm allergic to her, so you may as well keep her for yourself.'

He looked at her in surprise. 'Allergic to horses? Isn't it a bit soon to tell?'

'I'm not so good with cats, either. They make me sneeze pretty quickly, too. This reaction feels similar.'

The horse nudged him and he turned to caress her again.

'Keep her, Richard. Call her a thank you present from me for all your care on the journey.'

'That was my pleasure.' He stared at her, then at a nudge from the mare, nodded. 'All right. I will accept her. She's always been rather a pet of mine and she's not an expensive animal. You'll need to sign over her papers.'

His acceptance of her gift made Paula feel a bit better. Sort of. She watched the way he stroked the mare's neck. They looked like two old friends. Then she sneezed again so moved even further away.

He came across to join her. 'How about I show you the lake next? We can't go boating at this time of year, though, not unless you want to freeze to death.'

'You've got a lake here, too?'

'No, *you* have a lake. You really will need to get used to being the owner and accept its implications. It's not a very large lake, but it's quite pretty and there are a couple of rowboats. I'd intended to have it cleaned out and restocked with fish and also the correct water plants next year.'

They stood side by side near the edge of the water, staring out over the grey ruffled surface. 'I can see that it'll look pretty when the leaves are out and the sun's shining,' she admitted. 'But I think we should go back to the house now. Even with the borrowed clothing, I'm slowly freezing to death.'

'I don't think it's likely that we'll have snow, but it's going to rain tomorrow and we'll definitely have to find you something warmer of your own to wear both indoors and out.' He frowned for a moment, then said slowly, 'There are all sorts of old clothes stored in the attic. There must be something which will fit you. You don't seem to mind wearing second-hand clothes.'

'I love retro clothes.'

This time his smile was warm and genuine. 'I've noticed.'

She was trying to hide her shivers from him so he didn't

say anything, but put his arm round her shoulders and clasped one of her hands in his. Then he took her to the nearest entrance, this one at the side of the house, unlocking the door then stepping back to let her pass. But she slipped on the mossy stone step and of course he caught her.

She clung to him for a minute, then sighed with regret as he stepped away. She'd have welcomed a kiss or two but he hadn't offered any. 'Thanks for catching me.'

'You're welcome.'

She looked at the small corridor to one side. 'Where does this lead?'

'The estate office. I work there – used to work there.'

'Has someone fired you?'

'No. But I feel it might be wise for me to leave the house once you've settled in.'

'How many times do I have to tell you I'm *not* staying, Richard. I am not a cold-climate person. Oh, it's so unfair! If I can't sell the house, surely there's some way I could give the place to you? After all, you're a member of the family, too.'

His voice was tight and controlled as he stepped even further away from her, 'There's no way you can do that and besides, I'd not take anything I wasn't entitled to. It's different when something is yours to when you're just looking after it.' He held up one hand to stop her. 'Please don't labour the point.'

She could hear the pain behind the calm, measured words and shut her mouth, stuffing her chilled hands into the pockets of her borrowed coat. 'What would you do with yourself if you left?'

He answered her obliquely. 'Not if, *when*.'

'They'll still need an estate manager.'

'But will I want to go on working here with someone else calling the shots from the other side of the world, not knowing what's worth doing and what isn't – not even caring? I don't think so.'

'Oh, Richard.' Her protest came out too softly.

'I haven't always lived at Stovell itself, you know, Paula, even though I used to run tame here in the holidays. My aunt owns a house in the village. It was only when old Roy got weaker that she came to live in the big house full time. Before that she came in daily. He was rather a recluse, you see, and preferred being on his own.'

'I bet it feels like home to her now. And she's angry with me on your behalf, isn't she?'

He shrugged. 'She'll grow used to the situation.'

'Will she? Will you? It's obviously upsetting you both.'

'My aunt thought I was crazy to keep the investigations going, but there were a couple of siblings not properly accounted for and I had to *know*.'

'So my mother told you.'

'She must have kept tabs on you.'

'I wonder why. Couldn't this Roy person have overturned the trust and left it to you?'

'No. It's entailed. Legally it can only go to the correct heir. If they aren't Stovells by birth, they usually change their name to it.'

'I shan't do that. I didn't change it when I married ratface, either.'

He gave her a wry smile. 'Why does that not surprise me?'

As he fell silent, she asked again, 'You must have some idea what you will do with yourself . . . afterwards?' Then she snapped her fingers. 'That's what you were talking about, running a hotel.'

'Probably. I could find myself a job running somewhere similar to the abbey, I suppose, but I rather fancy setting up my own business. But don't worry. I'm not rushing off next week and leaving you to flounder. You'll need my help for a few more weeks to sort things out, whatever you decide to do long-term.'

Relief surged through her. 'Thank goodness. I can't imagine how I'd manage without you. And what about your aunt? Will she stay on as housekeeper for the time being? Or will the sight of me and my crazy clothes send her fleeing?'

'She is rather conservative about clothes.'

Paula chuckled. 'So I noticed. Twinsets and tweeds. Don't worry. I'm used to people thinking me weird. I dress to please myself, not others.' And she would need the bright colours even more while she was here in this big, gloomy house.

'I think your clothes suit your personality. As for my aunt, if you ask her, she'll stay on for the time being. She loves this place. When I thought I was the heir, I still felt it was more her home than mine.'

He showed her the estate office and the records room, then led her out into the huge entrance hall again. It had several doors and seemed to be the centre of the whole house. Black and white tiles that covered the floor, and the walls were white. Even the marble busts looked like dead people, white and stiff with blind eyes.

'The stained-glass window saves it from mediocrity, doesn't it?' she commented. 'I won't pretend. I couldn't live here permanently, Richard, not under any circumstances.'

'Can't you even give this place a chance?'

She shook her head. 'I love Australia. It was the first place where I ever experienced a real home. I'm not saying it to be awkward; it's just how things are.'

Silence throbbed between them, then she sighed and rubbed her forehead.

His expression changed and he reached out to move her hair gently away and study the bruise. 'You look tired. Is your head aching again?'

'A bit.'

He put his arm round her shoulders and steered her towards the stairs. 'Go and lie down for an hour or two. We'll look at the clothes in the attic later. You're probably suffering from jet lag on top of everything else.'

'I suppose.' She leant against him for a minute, wanting comfort and finding it. The warm expression was back on his face. His arms were closed protectively round her.

He spoke against her hair. 'Can you find your way back to your bedroom? I need to catch up with the business mail.'

Regretfully, she pulled away. 'Yes, of course.'

But it felt as if there were heavy weights tied to her feet as she climbed the stairs to the old-fashioned bedroom with the high ceiling and Adam-style plasterwork, where she felt so out of place in her bright, fun clothes.

She sniffed, smearing away a tear, then snuggled down under the covers and closed her eyes.

Chapter Seven

When Paula woke after an hour or so, she felt ravenous and went downstairs looking for something to eat. She followed the sound of voices and found Richard and his aunt in the small sitting room next to the kitchen, entertaining a guest.

'Oh, sorry. I didn't mean to intrude.'

Richard stood up. 'You're not intruding. Come in and meet one of your neighbours. Laurie, this is Paula Grey, the new owner. Paula, this is Laurie Blythe-Jones, whose family live just down the road if you turn right outside the front gates.'

The other woman was about her own age and stared at her with open animosity, then tried to cover her feelings with an unconvincing smile as she held out one hand. 'Welcome to Wiltshire.'

Paula shook the hand for as short a time as she could. Another person who resented her. Why? This woman wasn't a member of the family and they'd never met before.

Well, the feeling was reciprocated. She didn't like the looks of this tiny woman, immaculately dressed in shades of beige, with the drawling upper-class voice and chill expression. Laurie Thingy-Whatever had managed to make her feel like a gauche Aussie with one glance, and was so muted in colour that for a moment Paula felt like a gaudy maypole beside her.

Then her instinct reasserted itself. Who'd want to wear clothes like that day after day? Not her.

'You'll still be tired from the trip, I suppose?' Laurie smoothed back a strand of soft blonde hair with one perfectly manicured hand. 'Richard said you had an accident on the plane. Rotten luck.' Her eyes went to the bruise.

'Yes, well, I'm fine now.'

'I know some excellent make-up for camouflaging bruises.'

'I don't wear make-up. My skin doesn't like it.'

After a couple of trite comments about their journey, Laurie expressed a patently false wish to see Australia one day, then turned back to Richard. 'I came to ask if you're going to the big hop and can give me a lift.'

'Big hop?' Paula asked, intrigued by the picture painted in her mind of this woman hopping around like a kangaroo.

Laurie frowned at her interruption and said quickly, 'Oh, they put on a ball every year for the locals. We all go together usually.' She turned her back firmly. 'Well, Rich?'

She fancies him, Paula suddenly realised. *Are they an item?* He hadn't been acting as if he had a relationship with anyone.

'Better not rely on me, Laurie. I'm going to be very busy for a while. Unless . . .' He turned to Paula. 'Would you like to come, then we can take Laurie?'

'Me? I don't think so. I won't be here for all that long.'

'The ball is next week.'

'Oh.' She looked doubtfully from him to their visitor and noticed Marian frowning at the woman. She put on a drawling American accent to answer him. 'Well, shucks! I forgot bring my ballgown with me.'

He turned back to Laurie. 'Look, we're not sure of our plans yet, so you'd better arrange to go with one of the others. I'll bring Paula if she feels up to it, so we may or may not see you all there.'

Marian looked relieved and Paula wondered why, then realised Laurie was staring at her as if she'd crawled out from a hole smelling of something rotten. 'I suppose you have to play the gracious host, Rich.'

The rudeness behind this remark took Paula's breath away and made Richard and his aunt look at Laurie in disapproval.

It was a relief when the visitor said she had to go and looked expectantly at Richard as she stood up. But he turned to say something to Paula and left his aunt to show her out.

Paula took the bull by the horns as soon as they were alone. 'Look, I seem to be treading on someone's toes here.'

'Not mine.' He hesitated, then said, 'I don't want to sound conceited, but I've been fending Laurie off for years and have never ever taken her out as a girlfriend, only gone with the same group. You'd actually be doing me a huge favour if you'd come to the ball as my partner. Maybe if she sees me with you, she'll leave me alone. She's . . . rather strange in some ways and not at all my type.'

Paula put her head on one side as if considering his words. 'I think that's probably the most insulting invitation

I've ever received – though I may be wrong, of course.'

He flushed. 'Oh, hell, I didn't mean it like that.' He reached out to grasp her hand. 'Paula, I'd really enjoy taking you to the big hop. You, not anyone else. And I'd enjoy dancing with you. Will you come with me?'

She grinned and rolled her eyes. 'I'd say yes but as I already told you, I forgot to bring my ball dress. What a pity!' As if she'd ever owned one!

'I mentioned earlier that we have an attic full of old clothes from decades if not centuries ago. Something up there must have come back into fashion again.'

She perked up at that thought, then told herself firmly not to give in to temptation. 'I really don't think it'd be wise for me to be seen in public with you. People might start getting ideas about us being a couple.'

'Who cares what's wise or not? I'm beginning to think people can be too sensible for their own good.'

What had brought this on? She forced a smile. Hoped it was more convincing than Laurie's rictus had been. 'I'd rather keep on being wise.'

'We'll talk about that later. Come on. Let's get you a coffee and a snack.'

As he set a mug down in front of her, he stared at her pleadingly. 'Come to the ball with me, Cinderella.'

'Have you got a pumpkin handy?'

'No. But there is a fine old Rolls-Royce in the stables. We'll get Kevin from the village to drive us there and back in it, then I can have a drink or two.' He reached out to brush a wayward curl from her forehead. 'Please come.'

Paula felt a tingle of pleasure. It wasn't his good looks that attracted her, though they were a nice bonus; it was his kindness and the crooked smile and . . . Oh dear, it was the whole Richard that she liked. This visit would be easier if she didn't.

'We'd better leave the kitchen to my aunt now.' He gestured towards the other end, where there were signs of preparations for cooking.

Paula picked up her mug and followed him back to the sitting room.

Marian peered in shortly afterwards, not looking happy. 'Dinner won't be ready for at least an hour, I'm afraid. She wouldn't take a hint about leaving. She's . . . in one of her moods.'

'Oh, dear.'

Neither of them explained this.

'I'll bring you in some cheese and biscuits if you're hungry, Paula.'

'I am a bit. I'd appreciate a snack if you don't mind.'

'It's no trouble. Laurie arrived at the wrong moment.' She frowned at her nephew. 'You could have shown her out, Richard.'

'I didn't want to encourage her.'

Paula looked from one to the other, sensing some kind of message behind those words.

'I'll bring the snack in.' He followed his aunt out and came back five minutes later with a tray laden with cheese, biscuits, olives, sun-dried tomatoes and grapes, not prettily arranged, just dumped on it.

'That's my kind of snack!' Paula took a plate and filled it.

'You'll never be able to eat tea after that.'

She laughed. 'Just watch me.'

'You obviously don't need to diet, then.'

'I work too hard. This is great cheese. Have some.'

But he only picked at the food. And kept staring into space.

'Laurie isn't a friend of yours, then?'

'Hell no. Different generation, really. And we don't have much in common.' He changed the subject firmly.

After they'd finished eating, he said abruptly, 'I forgot to find you some warmer clothes to wear. Let's nip up to the attic and have an initial poke round, shall we? My aunt will be at least half an hour yet.'

'That'd be great.'

'I think the clothes are in the front attic.'

When they got there, she stopped for a moment in the doorway, staring. You could have fitted the whole of her house into this space and still had some room left.

'Wow. Where do we start?'

'I think the old clothes are in the trunks over there.'

He opened a few of them and stared down as if puzzled. 'I think my aunt must have been reorganising things. I don't actually know what is where now.'

'Let's rummage about and see what we can find.' She was much better than him at guessing what would be underneath the top layer in each trunk. All the people who had stored the things here seemed to have been amazingly methodical about it.

In the third trunk she found a collection of jumpers, cardigans and a couple of warm winter skirts, and immediately put on a chunky Fair Isle cardigan.

The fourth trunk gave them a rainbow display of what

looked like old-fashioned evening clothes. She pounced on them in glee. 'I wish I'd found these in a charity shop in Australia. I'd have bought the whole trunkful.'

'You don't need to buy these. They already belong to you.'

'I suppose they do, but they also belong to the house.'

She began lifting the corner of each garment, checking the colours. 'No use pulling one out unless I like the looks of it.'

Suddenly she exclaimed, 'What a lovely shade of red!' and lifted the pile to one side reverently enough to draw out the whole garment without messing it around. The vivid scarlet dress must have been from the 1930s judging by the dropped waist, scalloped hem and cape-like bolero over long tight sleeves. She held the dress against herself, squinting down at it. 'Does the colour suit me?'

'Very much.'

'Is there a mirror up here?'

'Over in that corner. It has one broken corner, so be careful you don't cut yourself if you're adjusting it.'

'Don't people in this family ever throw things away?'

'Not often.'

She went to stand in front of the mirror and held the dress against herself again. 'Oh, yes!' Then she gave him a push. 'Turn round. I need to try it on.'

'I'd rather watch.'

'Turn round this minute, Richard Crawford.'

Grinning, he did as she asked.

When she was ready, she looked at herself in the mirror and nodded. Exactly her sort of clothes. 'You can look now.'

He turned round and stared at her. 'You're beautiful, Paula Grey.'

For a moment she thought he was going to kiss her, wished he would, then he took a determined step backwards. 'You're going to need some sort of matching jacket at this time of year. You can't go out with such thin material.'

He edged round her and hunted in the next trunk, letting out a cry of triumph and waving her across to look at a dark red garment. 'Will this do, do you think?'

She beamed at him. 'Clever Richard. It definitely will. It tones in beautifully.'

She took it from him, turned towards the mirror and tried it round her shoulders. It was a knee-length coat-like garment, cut to fit more tightly round the bottom edge. 'There. What do you think?'

'I think you're going to be the belle of the ball.'

He looked at her, took a deep breath and once again stepped back. 'If you've got everything you need, I'll shut up all the trunks and you can change back into your own clothes.'

When they went downstairs, they met Marian in the hall. 'Didn't you hear the phone, Richard?'

'No. We were in the attic. Paula was trying on clothes.' He gestured to the bundle she was holding. 'We've found a few things suitable for the ball.'

She looked at it in mild surprise. 'Not many women can wear such a bright shade of red.'

'It's my favourite colour,' Paula said firmly.

'Mmm. Well, you've got the right colour of hair for it, I suppose. Anyway, our new neighbour just phoned. Well, he's an old neighbour too. Dan Peverill. Remember him, Richard?'

'No, I don't think I ever met him, though I've heard the name.'

'Well, I knew him quite well. He's just bought Beechley Hall. I invited him to join us for dinner tonight. I hope you don't mind, Paula.'

'Why should I mind?' She saw Marian start to open her mouth and held up one hand. 'Don't answer that. Just invite who you want when you want. I like meeting people.'

'Right. Thank you. So tea will be a little later than planned. It'll only take him a quarter of an hour to lock up and get here. Did you find some warmer clothes as well as those?'

'Yes. But I left them in my bedroom. I'd like to hang these out to air tomorrow, if that's all right, Marian?'

'Yes, of course. You can hang them in the laundry tonight. There are pull-down racks in there, because of the nice high ceilings. It's through that door.' She pointed.

Paula wished Marian would relax with her as she had earlier. If she didn't these two weeks were going to be very uncomfortable for them all.

Chapter Eight

It was a relief when Dan Peverill arrived and turned out to be a pleasant guy who treated her normally. Paula could not only feel herself relaxing, she could see Richard relaxing too.

Unfortunately, Marian had gone back to behaving stiffly towards her and only her during the meal, and Paula saw their visitor stare at her a couple of times as if surprised.

Was the older woman still angry about her nephew not being the heir? And even if she was, why blame Paula, who had made it clear that she didn't want the damned house at all?

She couldn't see herself putting up with this from Richard's aunt for her whole visit. Even if she vowed to try, something would touch a very hot button and she'd fire up. She was mostly in charge of her temper these days, but some things were just *too much*.

After the meal was over, Richard took Paula along to the library for a nightcap and left his aunt entertaining their guest. Not that Paula wanted a drink but she did want to get away from Marian.

'What am I doing here?' she murmured as she accepted the glass of brandy from him but quickly poured most of hers into his glass. 'I'd never fit in here, never in a month of Sundays, not even if I tried. And your aunt knows it. Is that why she's so resentful, do you think?'

He raised his glass in a salute to her and took a mouthful. 'It's a bit soon to say that you'd *never* fit in, don't you think?'

She raised her glass back at him and took the tiniest of sips, because look what had happened when she'd indulged in two glasses of champagne on the plane.

He fixed his beautiful brown eyes on her and said quietly, 'Give Stovell a chance, Paula. It doesn't deserve an absentee owner.'

She didn't argue but couldn't help shivering. It wasn't just the cold of its long, chilly corridors that upset her; she felt an awareness of all that history pressing down on her, not to mention having to keep walking past all those ancestors staring disapprovingly at her from across the abyss.

Maybe it was haunted. Or maybe she was just imagining things. All she knew was that she didn't feel welcome here.

After a couple of pretend sips, she set the brandy glass down with some amber liquid still left in it and made an excuse to go to bed.

'Shall I show you the way back to your bedroom?'

'No, thank you. I only have to go somewhere once to know my way there from then onwards. Thanks anyway.'

But the master bedroom felt no more welcoming than the rest of the place and it was a long time before she fell asleep.

Perhaps it was jet lag and she was mistaking the reason. Or it was jet lag plus her attraction to Richard.

No, it was the whole damned situation.

Tears came into her eyes and she felt a desperate longing for her own home.

Who would have thought she'd be so very homesick? Even she hadn't expected it to be this bad, hadn't realised you could feel like this. She *ached* to stroll out into the sunshine, joke with a customer at the bar or tease Nick, or simply spend a quiet hour in her home sitting outside near the water.

She had to pull herself together, didn't like feeling so helpless.

When the other two had left them, Dan said bluntly, 'Why are you being so stiff with her, Marian? She seems pleasant enough to me.'

'Because she's making no attempt to fit in here.'

'Perhaps she can't. Didn't her father tell her anything about his family?'

'No.' She hesitated then added, 'And he doesn't seem to have been a very good father in any sense. And – well, I'm annoyed that Richard's attracted to her.'

'I'd say he's very attracted, the way he looks at her.'

'Yes.'

'You can't choose who he fancies, Marian.'

'I know that in theory but in practice it annoys the hell out of me, not only that she's inherited but that she's insisting she's not going to stay.'

'Well, let's discuss something more pleasant now. When are you coming to look round Beechley Hall?'

'Whenever you like. I'll be glad to get out of this house for a while.'

'I'll get the place cleaned up first, I think. Talk about dusty and neglected.'

'There's a cleaning service in the village if you want to win brownie points with the locals.'

'Good idea. Can you give me their name?'

She scribbled it down on a scrap of paper, then said, 'I need to get to bed now, Dan.'

After Paula had gone to bed, Richard sat on alone in the library, sipping the cognac slowly. When a car drove away, he assumed Dan had gone home. His aunt joined him shortly afterwards and he went automatically to pour her a gin and tonic, after which they sat together and chatted in their usual end of day ritual.

'That young woman not only doesn't deserve Stovell,' she said abruptly, 'she's genuine about not wanting it. I thought at first that was just talk, but it isn't, is it?'

'No. But she's the heir, not me. Don't you think it's unfair for you to blame her for that?'

'I suppose so.' She sipped her drink. 'I meant it as a joke but actually, if you had any sense, you would marry her.'

He choked on the mouthful of brandy. 'Stop saying that!'

'I would have stopped but anyone can see the two of you are attracted to one another, so why not think about it?'

'If I ever get married, it'll be because I love the woman, not because I want her house. And because she loves me just as much.'

His aunt ignored his protest. 'She's pretty. And pleasant

enough. If she wasn't in the wrong place at the wrong time, I could probably like her – in spite of those ridiculous clothes. I don't think I could ever like the way she dresses.'

'I do like her. Very much. And I love her vivid clothes. They match her personality.'

Marian snorted. 'Then let yourself fall in love with her, for heaven's sake!'

He jerked to his feet. 'I think I'll go to bed now.'

But his feet took him automatically to his old bedroom before he remembered that he wasn't sleeping here now. He paused with his hand outstretched towards the door handle as he heard Paula humming inside. He'd already noticed she had a habit of humming when she was busy with something. She must be unpacking. Wacky clothes, sexy underclothes, filmy nightgowns.

Bloody hell! He strode along the corridor and slammed the door of his new bedroom behind him. After a quick cold shower, he climbed into bed, yawning. Long flights left you exhausted for days. But tired as he was, he didn't get to sleep for a long time because his aunt's words kept echoing in his mind.

'If you had any sense, you'd marry her.'

He suddenly remembered Paula in Singapore, laughing, her head thrown back, a satay stick in one hand and sauce dripping down her chin.

He turned over, punching his pillow in a vain effort to get comfortable. He was definitely not marrying anyone for the sake of a house.

He tried to turn off his brain, but it wouldn't stop churning, so in the end he lay there for what seemed like hours, thinking of her.

'Then fall in love with her, for heaven's sake!' his aunt had said.

How stupid could you get? He was in love with Paula already.

Even if he did follow his aunt's advice, he knew Paula wouldn't want to stay here. She was like an exotic bird and this was a cage.

So how could he do more to imprison her? He couldn't. Best if he thought of a way to run the place with her as an absentee owner.

Only he didn't want to stay here now.

Chapter Nine

Paula woke the following morning to grey skies and a bedroom which felt like the inside of the cooler room at the bar. She shivered as she took another sparse, unsatisfactory shower in the chilly, unheated bathroom. It shouldn't surprise her that it was consistently cold here. This was the coolest part of the year here, after all, and it would get cooler still, worse than any West Australian winter.

Even when she'd dressed in her warmest clothes, topped by a heavy cardigan borrowed from the attic, she couldn't seem to get warm and wasn't in the best of moods as she went down in search of breakfast.

She discovered Marian in the kitchen, which had a large table at one end and two cookers at the other, plus a few acres of work surfaces. Underneath the window were two huge, antiquated sinks and two dishwashers, one of near medieval vintage, she decided after staring at it.

After a curt 'Good morning', Marian showed Paula to a room at the rear of the house. 'This is the breakfast room.'

'We ate in it last night as well. Why is it called the breakfast room?'

'It just is.'

There was an array of cereals and toasting facilities on a rather battered sideboard, so Paula assumed this was where the family always ate.

Marian stood beside her, face expressionless. 'Do you want anything cooking? Bacon, eggs, porridge?'

'No, thanks. I just feel like fruit, toast and marmalade.' Paula decided to try to bridge the gap that yawned between them. 'Aren't you going to join me?'

'I had my breakfast earlier, thank you.' She left the room without another word.

'And good morning to you, too!' Paula exclaimed, feeling angry at this treatment. She made some toast, crunched her way through an apple, topped that off with a banana, and ate it all in solitary splendour. Even in this short time, she'd grown used to sharing meals with Richard and missed chatting to him. She fidgeted about, wondering where he was. Did he get up later in England?

When she'd finished, she carried her dirty dishes through to the kitchen and found him sitting at a table in the corner with a half-eaten bowl of cereal in front of him.

He smiled. 'Up at last, are you? You must have slept well.'

His aunt turned away to fiddle with something on the cooker.

Paula could barely contain her anger and went across to stand next to her. 'Why did you send me to eat alone in that other room, Marian?'

She kept an eye on Richard, wondering if he was in on this conspiracy, but unless he was the best actor in the world, he couldn't have feigned that look of utter surprise. He put down his spoon and stared across at his aunt, who stared back, replying more to him than to Paula.

'Roy always ate in there. You're the owner now, so I thought you'd expect the same standards of service.'

'If you expect me to believe that, you'll be ringing up Santa Claus for a chat come Christmas,' Paula snapped.

'You must eat in here with us from now on,' Richard said, putting a finger to his lips to warn her not to push the matter. 'Come and join me here for a coffee, at least.'

She bit off another caustic comment and sat down in the chair next to his with an angry huff of breath.

He leant closer to whisper, 'Sorry. I'll make sure it doesn't happen again. She's desperately upset about the whole situation.'

'She isn't the only one.' Paula poured herself half a cup of coffee for something to do but took only a sip. As the silence continued, she glanced at Richard, to see him chewing slowly, frowning into space. She'd had enough silence. 'So, what's on the agenda for today?'

'We might start with a walk round the nearest part of the estate. There's quite a bit you haven't seen.'

'Don't we have some paperwork we can work on indoors till it warms up?'

He looked out of the window then back at her in surprise. 'I don't think it'll get much warmer today and they've forecast rain this afternoon. Anyway, don't you want to see what you've inherited?'

Her shiver wasn't feigned and she cradled the cup of coffee in her hands for warmth, before realising he'd said something else and was waiting for a reply. 'Sorry. My mind's wandering a bit. Come again?'

'Maybe we'll drive round the estate then.'

'Fine by me as long as the car has a heater.'

Marian muttered something and walked out, leaving them together.

'Why did you tell me to shut up?' Paula demanded at once.

'Because I'm hoping you'll be generous. She's extremely upset. This has been her home for a long time.'

'You have more reason to be upset than she does after believing yourself the heir, yet you've been nothing but kind to me.'

'You didn't take the place from me on purpose and anyway, we're friends now, don't you think?'

He gave her a smile so warm she couldn't help smiling in return and nodding in agreement.

'Besides, I've only been back here for a couple of years. I'm not embedded in the place like my aunt. So . . . do you want to go for a drive round the estate?'

A gust of wind rattled one of the windows and she said, 'I'd prefer to get started on the paperwork first, if you don't mind. It's far too cold for me to frolic out of doors.'

As he hesitated, she said firmly, 'I don't intend to stay in England for longer than necessary, Richard, and there's no way you or anyone else can force me to, so shouldn't the paperwork be our first priority?'

'I suppose so.' He took her into the estate office, settling her next to him at the largest desk she'd ever seen and positioning an electric heater beside her.

The things he showed her weren't hard to understand, but when the first pile of papers was finished, he pulled another one across and her heart sank.

'I hadn't realised how complex running an estate like this is,' she admitted as she waited for him to start on the new pile.

'I have a part-time secretary, but this isn't one of her days in the office.'

She tapped the paper with the staff summary. 'Plus two gardeners, one of whom doubles as a groom, a woman who comes in on weekdays to clean the house and casual staff as needed for social events. Makes my little bar seem a very small-scale operation.'

'I liked your bar.' He smiled reminiscently. 'The second time, anyway.'

She blinked furiously, wishing she were back there.

He laid one hand on hers, gave her a quick squeeze, then turned away to fiddle with some papers while she wiped her eyes.

By late morning she was fed up of paperwork, and they'd only got through three piles of it. 'I think that's enough for today. My brain can't take in any more information. I'd have been content with a summary, you know.'

'I feel you ought to understand exactly what goes on here.' He leant back to stretch and ease his shoulders to and fro, then glanced at his watch. 'Lunch won't be ready for about forty minutes. I don't think it'll rain yet, so how about we go up to the attics again and have a quick look for a heavy winter coat. I can't show you round outside in your flimsy jacket.'

'You're on! Only I might wear the coat indoors and put another on top of it when I go outside. Race you there.'

She was on her feet and out of the door before he was and he overtook her, laughing, as they ran up three flights of stairs to the west end of the attic.

'This is my favourite part of the house,' she said.

'What made you develop such a passion for old-fashioned clothes?'

'I don't know. I just did. We've looked in those trunks. Let's try these next.' She flipped up one lid to see a trunk crammed with men's clothing. A second was just as full. 'You Stovells are real hoarders.'

'I'm not a Stovell technically. I'm a Crawford.' He smiled and led her across to a trunk which was less dusty than the others. 'I used to play up here when I was a kid. These are my favourite things. They're eighteenth century, a great era for men's clothing.'

Inside were knee breeches, a shirt with full sleeves and a knee-length, skirted jacket with big turn-back cuffs. In a wooden box next to it were some hats. He pulled out a tricorne and put it on his head, swishing an imaginary rapier.

'Is this genuine eighteenth-century stuff?' she asked in a hushed voice.

'Why should you doubt that it's genuine?'

'Well, it could be theatrical props or – or someone might have had it made for a fancy dress party.'

'It's genuine clothing, worn by my – no, by *our* ancestors.' He smiled reminiscently. 'I've actually worn some of these for parties in the past few years.'

'I thought people were smaller on average in the old days.'

'Most Stovells are quite tall and some of the clothes fitted me perfectly – not all of them of course. And don't say boys don't enjoy dressing up, because they do.' He'd been a pirate, a king, a soldier – so many figures conjured up by his imagination because Roy had allowed him to run tame in the attic and gardens.

'I'd love to see you wearing them, Richard. Where are

the women's things? Could I try some on?'

'I shouldn't need to keep reminding you that they all belong to you now.'

That was it. She'd had enough. She jabbed her elbow sharply in his ribs.

'Ow!'

'If you don't stop hanging a guilt trip on me, Richard Crawford, I'll deck you.' She bunched up a fist and waved it at him threateningly. And she was only half joking.

He laughed and caught hold of her hand, adjusting her fingers and thumb alignment. 'Not like that, like this, or you'll damage your thumb when you hit me.'

Suddenly the air seemed to be sizzling around them. He groaned and pulled her towards him.

She went willingly.

'This is not a good idea,' he said thickly. 'We're too different.'

'No, it isn't a good idea, but let's give it a whirl anyway.' She reached up to pull his head towards hers.

Suddenly they were kissing and although it started gently, it didn't stay gentle. His mouth felt so right on hers.

'Why is this happening?' he muttered as he moved his head back a few inches, breathing deeply.

She laced her arms behind his neck to stop him getting away. 'I don't know. But I'm fed up of acting as if it isn't.'

'It's not a good idea. Only adds to the complications.'

He tried to take a step backwards but she refused to let go. 'It seems like an excellent idea to me.' And since he didn't try to kiss her again, she kissed him.

She put all the frustration of the past few days into that kiss. Then she thought she heard something and he must have too, because he paused, his lips a breath away from hers.

'Someone's coming up the stairs.'

'Damn!'

They stepped away from one another. She could feel that her face was flushed and hoped that wouldn't show in the dull light up here.

Marian came across to join them, her footsteps echoing across the large shadowy space. 'I thought one of the stable cats had got into the house when I heard sounds up here. What on earth are you two doing? You got what you needed yesterday, surely?'

Richard answered. 'I'm trying to find some warmer outdoor clothes for Paula.'

'In the eighteenth century section? And you'll get things dusty if you leave the lids open.' Marian banged the lids of the various trunks shut, sending a cloud of dust flying around each time, then walked briskly across to another part of the attic.

'You might find something here, Paula.' She studied a label on a trunk, shook her head and moved on to the next one. 'Ah! This one has women's winter clothes in it from the 1930s to '90s.' She stood up again. 'I'll leave you two to sort through them.'

'Maybe you'd be of more help to Paula than me?' he suggested.

'I'm in the middle of preparing lunch and anyway she knows what she likes better than I do. You stay and help her carry her loot down.'

Paula breathed deeply and glanced sideways at Richard, seeing him scowl at his aunt's use of the word 'loot'. What unspoken messages had been passing between them this time? Marian scowled back at him, ignored her and walked downstairs again.

She gave up trying to understand tight-mouthed Poms and concentrated on finding some warm outdoor clothes. 'I'm sure I'll find what I need here. Maybe you've got something else to do while I try them on?'

'I've nothing better to do. And I enjoyed the way our last search ended. Are you still happy with the red outfit for the ball or do you want to find something more modern to wear?'

'I haven't said I'll go.'

'Aw, come on, Cinderella. You more or less agreed yesterday and your prince needs you.'

'I won't know how to behave with your posh friends.'

'Only some of them are friends. And I won't leave you alone with the local dragons.'

A bell rang just then in some far part of the house.

'Lunch. Let's go and eat.'

The meal was ready in the kitchen, a thick, home-made broth with toasted sandwiches, followed by home-made cake and fruit.

'That was delicious,' Paula said with perfect sincerity.

Marian almost smiled. 'Thank you.'

Afterwards, Richard said, 'Paula's agreed to come to the ball with me. And I'm *not* giving Laurie a lift there. I'm going to get Kevin to drive us two there in the Bentley.'

Paula tried desperately to think of a reason for not going. 'I'm a bit frightened of damaging that period outfit.'

'It won't matter if you do. There are plenty of other clothes up in the attic. They were made to be used, after all.' He turned to his aunt. 'Are you going to the ball this year?'

She flushed slightly. 'Well . . . Dan Peverill has asked me so I probably will, though I'm a bit old for balls.'

'Of course you aren't. And I liked Dan.'

'I'm still thinking about it.'

'I'm going to have to buy a pair of suitable shoes. Where would be the best place to go?' Paula looked from one person to the other.

'We have a room full of them. I'll show you.' This time Marian led them to one of the bedrooms at one side of the attic. It contained nothing but fitted cupboards and drawers all the way round the walls, with a full-length mirror fixed behind the door. 'Roy's mother was obsessed by shoes, so she had these cupboards built and all the shoes sorted out and put here. She said they were historical treasures. What size are you?'

'Nine.'

'You'll need to look for two sizes smaller in English shoe sizing. Try these.' She walked over to pull out the appropriate drawer.

Paula walked across to join her. 'Goodness. They look nearly new.'

'They probably are.' She looked at her watch. 'I have to go. I've got a hair appointment this afternoon. Make sure you shut the doors and drawers tightly after you've made your choice.'

After she'd left, Richard came to join Paula. She began fiddling with the shoe she'd picked up. 'How long is she going to stay angry at me for existing, do you think?'

'She's starting to come round.'

'At this rate she'll take about six months to relax into normal behaviour and I'll be gone long before then.' She pulled a couple of pairs of shoes out of one of the special drawers, trying them on then walking up and down the corridor briskly. 'These!'

'May I ask why?'

'They're more comfy. I'm not into torturing myself in high heels the thickness of knitting needles, whether they're in fashion or not.'

'Very sensible. Most women walk very jerkily in shoes like that. So you and I are all set up to go to the ball together now?'

It might be foolish, Paula thought, but it'd be something to remember, dancing with Richard, wearing that beautiful dress. 'I wouldn't have chosen a dress if I weren't coming with you, you fool.'

'I admit that did give me hope.'

They looked at one another, but he stepped back and said, 'Let me drive you round the estate now, the part nearest the house anyway. You'll need that warm coat we found.'

The size of the estate, even on what he called a short tour, took her breath away. How could one person own all this? The more she saw, the more she didn't want to be that person. How could she get rid of the burden of it permanently?

He seemed to have noticed her dislike of Stovell Abbey. Was that what was making him keep his distance?

She'd keep her distance too from now on, deal with what business she could, then she might not even bother with visits to any famous historical places before heading home.

Oh dear! She shouldn't have agreed to go to the ball with him but she didn't like to renege on a promise.

And he did still have the problem with Laurie. Why had that woman set her sights on him? You could see it from the way she looked at him. She was rather strange, made you feel uneasy.

The following day was to be spent on more business and a drive round the further parts of the estate and on to a couple of neighbouring villages, which were apparently very picturesque with churches built mainly in the medieval era.

'I'll leave you something to eat tonight,' Marian said as she cleared the table. Her face grew a little pinker. 'I'm going out to dinner with Dan.'

'Why don't Paula and I go and eat at the village pub? She ought to experience a traditional pub meal.'

Marian made a scornful noise. 'What's traditional about a gastro-pub? Pubs used to be there for drinking and chatting, with the occasional bag of crisps.'

She seemed determined to be negative about something at regular intervals, Paula thought. If Richard thought his aunt was starting to come round, then heaven help anyone Marian really disliked.

Richard turned to smile at Paula. 'The King's Head does a very reasonable meal and a particularly good apple pie and custard, which is my favourite dessert of all. Is it all right with you to go there?'

'Of course.'

'I'll phone and book a table. Six o'clock suit you? I know you like to eat early.'

'Fine by me.'

Marian banged a pot down on the draining board. 'Right then. I'll just clear up the kitchen if you two will leave me in peace.'

Paula wondered what had caused this sudden change back to barely polite.

'She's embarrassed about going out with Dan,' Richard whispered, eyes dancing. 'She fancied him when she was younger, but refused to go and live in America with him and he married someone else there. I gather he lost his wife a couple of years ago, so I hope things go well for them this time. She's been very lonely since Roy died, you know. They used to play chess together in the evenings.'

Paula made a non-committal murmur. 'I think I'll go and have a short nap. I'll switch my phone alarm on to wake me in a couple of hours. I was awake for three hours during the night. I don't usually nap in the daytime. Jet lag is still with me, I suppose. I wish it'd go away.'

'I'll go out for a ride, then. Poor old Callie's desperate to have a good gallop.'

She went to stand by the window and watch him set off. He looked great on horseback. Hell, he looked great all the time.

Her inexplicable attraction to him was another reason to get this visit over and done with and return to Australia ASAP.

For two pins she'd run away and simply go home again. She pulled her Australian passport out of her shoulder bag and stroked it. Silly to carry it around with her but it was comforting to have something from home.

In the car on the way to the pub that evening, Richard said abruptly, 'I'd better warn you – the locals will stare at you.'

'Don't they like bright colours, either?' Tonight she was wearing a brilliant purple leather jacket, with a shaggy mock fur collar and cuffs, that she'd found in the attic. It was warmly lined with a brightly flowered material and was so warm she was almost comfortable in it.

'Since you've inherited Stovell, you're the lady of the manor now. That's why they'll stare.'

'Oh, no. I'm not the lady of the manor and I never

will be. I don't think I want to go out now. Couldn't we find a pub where you're not known?'

'You'll have to face the locals sometime, Paula.'

If it'd been left to her, she'd have stayed right out of the public eye. She sighed. She couldn't keep complaining and protesting when he was being so kind, so she'd just have to put up with people staring tonight.

But they did more than stare. Some of them came up to the table and asked to be introduced.

The worst was a young man who was a journalist on the local newspaper. 'Mind if I take a photo?'

As Paula opened her mouth to refuse, Richard squeezed her hand. 'Sure. Jack, meet Paula. Make it quick, would you? We're hungry.'

Jack went to get his camera and Richard whispered, 'Better play nice. That chap can be a spiteful devil if you upset him. He and Laurie have had a feud going for years. He only publishes unflattering photos of her now. She's not bad looking—'

'In a long-faced, horsy, *beige* way.'

He ignored that and continued, 'But he can make her look raw-boned and ugly.'

'I like him already.'

Paula did as he'd suggested, answering a few questions without betraying her irritation, posing for a photo with Richard, then also pleading hunger.

The food was good but she'd lost much of her appetite. She'd planned to whiz into the Abbey, sort out the paperwork as quickly as possible, then whiz out again. Now that she was getting cosy with locals at the pub, her photo would appear in the community newspaper and she wouldn't be able to go anywhere without attracting attention. She was even preparing to go to a damned ball. She never normally went to formal functions like that.

It worried her that she'd let herself be sidetracked into socialising formally.

It worried her even more that Richard hadn't touched her in a romantic way since that time in the attic.

She tried to tell herself that it was probably a good thing. Richard was a complication she didn't need.

Only, it was hard enough to stay calm when he was close to her and how was she to keep her cool while dancing with him? That closeness would be difficult not to respond to.

She could only hope others wouldn't notice their attraction to one another.

In London, Amanda de Vanne flipped open the newspaper, fed up of waiting for her husband to get ready. *Never marry a Frenchman*, she thought. *They spend nearly as much time getting dressed as women do.* Her first two husbands had been much easier to live with, but she'd look such a fool if she broke up a third marriage, and besides, this one enjoyed the same sort of lavish lifestyle as she did, though unfortunately he wasn't nearly as rich as she'd thought.

She yawned and turned to the society pages, stiffening suddenly at what she found. 'I don't believe it!'

'Don't believe what?' Jean-Pierre said from behind her.

She tapped the newspaper article. 'My daughter has just inherited Stovell Abbey, a stately home in Wiltshire. It must be her, can't be anyone else, not with that name and coming from Australia. Besides, she looks like her father.'

She smoothed out the newspaper and read aloud, 'Missing

heir found after over a year of searching. It was believed that Richard Crawford was next in line, but at the last minute an Australian woman has become the chatelaine of the stately home Stovell Abbey in Wiltshire. Paula Jocelyn Grey was running a bar in Perth when she was told of her good fortune.'

He was suddenly very interested. 'Is it a big place, this Stovell Abbey?'

'I don't know. I'll have to look it up online. Tony only mentioned his family home by name once or twice.' Amanda stared at the paper. 'That's definitely my daughter, though. There can't be two women with that name. Tony said it was a family tradition to use the name Jocelyn, but I wasn't having it for her first name, so I called her after my own father.'

'Must be a rather juicy inheritance.'

'Yes. And a good entrance card into Society with a capital S. You know, I never believed Tony when he said he might inherit a stately home one day. Just goes to show.'

'You don't sound pleased about it, *chérie*.'

'I'm not. If I'd stuck with him, I could have been living in a stately home by now, instead of scrimping and scraping while your family home is leased out.'

'You thought you were marrying into money while you have only me, a flat in Paris and a stately home in the Dordogne. Poor you.'

'And you thought you were bringing money into your impoverished family.'

He shrugged. 'Well, at least you're good in bed.'

She couldn't help smiling. 'We are good in bed.'

'And you'd miss that.'

'Yes, but it's a pity you can't stay faithful for two minutes.'

'I always come back to you, *n'est-ce pas*? Just as you come back to me after your little encounters.'

She ignored that. 'Sorry. Don't mind me. I'm just jealous of Paula.'

'We're going down to Dorset next week. We could pop in on the way, see whether there's any way we can profit from her good fortune.'

She stared at him thoughtfully. 'So we could.'

'Shall I find out her phone number, then you can make contact first?'

'No. She might say she's busy or doesn't want to see me. After all, I did give her away to Jenny quite happily when her father died and I haven't bothered to keep in touch with her very often. No, you just find out where exactly this Stovell Abbey is and let's surprise her. I doubt she'll turn her birth mother away.'

Chapter Ten

Paula and Richard went through all the main paperwork and she signed a few apparently important documents, which were couriered off to the lawyers in London. Now she had to wait for the lawyers to draw up some other documents she'd insisted on, giving authority to manage Stovell Abbey to their firm.

She'd tried to give responsibility for this to Richard, but he'd refused, saying he'd probably not stay on there, after which he changed the subject every time she tried to ask about his plans. Why would he not let her do this for him, at least? It'd mean he could live in the house he loved. Surely that would be some compensation?

Oh, what did she know about anything?

Marian had booked to have her hair done on the afternoon of the ball, but Paula had no need for that. If she washed her hair and put in a couple of vintage hair slides, it'd be perfect for the outfit she was wearing tonight. She had learnt to avoid hairdressers, who always made her hair seem stiff or, worse, they tried to straighten it. When they did that, it bounced back into curls bit by bit, making her look like a badly shorn sheep, she always felt.

She wasn't planning to make a grand entrance, but by the time she walked down the main staircase of the Abbey to join the others, she was a little late and they were standing in the hall waiting for her.

Marian turned round to watch her, head on one side, thoughtful.

As Richard turned, his mouth fell open and he walked forward to meet her at the foot of the stairs, one hand held out. 'You look wonderful.'

'Do I? You look pretty hot yourself.' The dark formal evening dress suited him perfectly. No wonder Laurie Whatsit had been chasing after him for years. If circumstances were different, if only their lives weren't firmly fixed at the opposite ends of the earth, Paula would be chasing after him too. As it was, she treasured the memory of their encounter in Singapore and had given herself permission to enjoy his company to the full tonight. She was sick and tired of being sensible.

And she wanted some more good memories to take back with her. Why she had to fall in love with someone out of reach, she didn't know. She stiffened as that thought settled firmly in her mind. *Fall in love?* No such thing. She wasn't that stupid – or was she? A horn sounded outside and thank goodness for that.

Marian went to peer out of the window to one side of the front door. 'It's Dan. See you there. Um . . . we've booked to stay overnight at the hotel, in separate rooms, mind, so can you get your own breakfasts? See you tomorrow.' Face a little pink, she hurried out.

Richard let out a low whistle of surprise. 'I never

thought she'd sleep with him openly. And so soon. She must be getting more deeply involved with him than I'd expected.'

'She said separate rooms.'

'But did she mean it?' He shrugged. 'Her choice either way.'

Paula began pacing up and down the hall, her borrowed shoes making neat little clicking sounds on the marble tiles.

Richard leant against one pillar and watched her. 'Kevin will be here with the car in a minute. And I can't believe how gorgeous you look in those clothes.'

She stopped for a moment, feeling embarrassed, as she always did when someone complimented her about her appearance. 'Me? I'm not the gorgeous type.'

'You are, you know. You're not classically beautiful. I think the best word to describe you is vivid, in looks and personality. That shines through, whether you're dressed up or have thrown on some casual clothes. Oh! I nearly forgot.' He walked across to the hall table and came back with a corsage, a dark red rose with a halo of baby's breath and some tiny leaves.

She took it, sniffing, disappointed that it had no scent. Still, it was beautiful to look at. 'Where should I put it?'

'Shall I pin it on for you?'

She held it out and waited, motionless, as he unfastened the pin and secured it on her dress between her left shoulder and the neckline of her bodice.

He didn't move back and her breath caught in her throat as he bent to kiss her gently on her lips.

Before she could respond, he stepped quickly away to pick up the purple outer jacket and help her put it on. 'I'm glad I'm the one taking you to the ball, Paula.'

She didn't pretend. 'So am I.'

As they sat in the back of the grand old car, letting Kevin drive them there, he said, 'I haven't forgotten Singapore. I doubt I ever shall. But things are different here.'

'Are they? Well, you should know. Anyway, I'd appreciate it if you didn't leave me on my own for long tonight. I shan't know anyone there except you and your aunt. Oh, and Laurie Thingy.'

'I'll have to dance with one or two other women but I'll make sure you're safely disposed of to another partner before I leave your side.'

'Does that include you dancing with Laurie?'

He sighed. 'Yes. But only once. She'll want more and . . . Look, I've been wondering . . . No, it's too much to ask, not fair to you.'

'What?'

'Would you mind pretending we're together? In love, even? I'd like to put an end to her pursuit of me once and for all.'

Paula considered this, wondering if it'd lead to a dangerous level of . . . togetherness. Then a memory of Laurie's rudeness and scornful attitude made her agree. That woman had really got up her nose. 'It's only make-believe,' she warned.

She thought she heard him mutter, 'Pity,' but didn't comment. She agreed with him, though. It was a pity.

But he seemed so firmly rooted in the UK, it'd be foolish to let herself follow up on the attraction. She'd had enough experience of that with Simon, who'd lied about wanting to stay in Australia and gone back home to America when his visa expired, leaving her a brief note. He'd known she wouldn't even try to follow him. And he hadn't written again after that, not one word of regret, though they'd been living together for months.

She didn't think Richard would use her in quite the same way. They'd had a holiday fling, that was all. There was no point in continuing with something that couldn't end happily.

She wouldn't let herself be stupid enough to expect more from him.

'Here you are!' Kevin called as he pulled to a halt. 'One of the best hotels in the county, this is, Miss Grey. I hope you two enjoy yourselves. I'll be at my sister's, Mr Crawford. Just give me a ring and I'll be there to pick you up in ten minutes max.'

'Thanks, Kevin. Will do.'

Richard handed Paula out of the car as if she couldn't have managed without him and for once, she didn't protest at being treated like a fragile flower. It seemed to go with the outfit.

As she tucked her arm in his, she put on a breathless, girly voice. 'Do I have to give you melting looks to keep up our charade?'

'Only if I can look at you as if I'm about to eat you.' He mimed a snarl and they both laughed.

It was warm enough inside the hotel even for her and when their outer coats had been taken away, he led her into the ballroom.

'I've just seen someone I know,' he whispered and kissed her. 'Let's start the show.'

He turned as a woman's voice called sharply from their right, 'There you are, Richard. We've saved you a place.' She indicated an empty chair next to herself.

He pulled Paula closer and dropped a quick kiss on her cheek. 'We need two places together.'

Laurie scowled at Paula. 'There is another empty place over there.'

Richard ignored her, greeting his friends without removing his arm from Paula's shoulders as he introduced her, then called out, 'Could you three move along to the next chair, please? Paula and I want to sit together.'

She saw the speculative glances exchanged at this and wished suddenly that she hadn't agreed to tonight's mockery of a relationship. Then she changed her mind as somehow, in the shuffle of chairs, Laurie managed to end up sitting on Richard's other side, scowling across him at her.

That did it! Paula took hold of his hand, fondling it against her cheek as she leaned forward to whisper in his ear, 'Come on. Let's give her a run for her money.'

'Why not?'

'Would you like a drink, madam?'

She turned to see a waiter holding out a bottle of champagne. 'I'm no good at alcohol. Could you get me a long drink, please? Lemon, lime and bitters would be nice.' She had to explain how to make her favourite non-alcoholic drink, as they only seemed to do lemonade and lime in the UK.

'I'll only be a minute, madam.'

He moved on to fill Richard's glass, then vanished into the crowd.

When Richard reached out to pick it up, Laurie stretched out her arm at the same time and knocked it out of his hand, showering Paula's skirt with droplets.

'Oops, sorry!' she said, not even looking directly at Paula. 'Here, take mine, Richard. I'll get another.' She'd shoved it into his hand before he could stop her.

The waiter returned a couple of minutes later with a glass of lemonade with a good dash of lime cordial, all turned a delicate orange colour by a few shakes of bitters added to it. Another waiter had handed Laurie a fresh glass by then.

Richard waited until they all had drinks to raise his glass and clink it against Paula's. 'Here's to us.'

'To us.' She held his gaze with a soulful look for as long as she could manage it then nearly burst out laughing at Laurie's shocked expression. She took another sip then set her glass down, deliberately knocking his glass off so that the liquid went in Laurie's direction.

'Oops, sorry!' she said.

His chuckle was faint but definite and he began to fiddle with her fingers, kissing them one by one. Which was a bit unnerving, to say the least, because her body responded as if it were a real caress.

The evening passed quickly and she couldn't help noticing that Laurie was drinking champagne steadily and was soon slurring her words.

'If she goes on at this rate, someone's going to have to take Laurie home,' one man muttered to Richard as they were all walking off the dance floor just before midnight.

'Well, it won't be me, my friend. I'm otherwise occupied tonight, and very happily so.' He pulled Paula to one side.

'Let's go for a stroll round the atrium.'

Once out of the overheated ballroom, she let out her breath in a whoosh. 'Is your friend Laurie always so obvious? She's expecting you to rescue her now that she's well oiled, isn't she?'

'I'm afraid so. I've had to do it before when no one else would because I go past their house on the way home.'

'Why does she live at home?'

'She's not been well, doesn't have a job.'

'And are you going to play Sir Galahad tonight?'

'Not if I can help it.' He looked up at the clock. 'How about we go home now? You're looking tired and I've had enough of crowds and loud music.'

As if to emphasise his words, there was a sudden burst of loud laughter from some group inside the ballroom. He winced.

Paula fought with her conscience and it won. 'How will she get home if you don't take her?'

'Someone will probably pour her into a taxi.'

'That's not safe when you're as drunk as she is. I'm amazed at the lengths she'll go to, in order to spoil our evening.' She stopped walking.

'Nothing seems to discourage her, either. What the hell do I have to do to escape her?' He stopped walking and looked longingly towards the exit.

'You could marry someone else,' Paula said lightly. 'Even she will get the message then.'

'It's not very likely. I'm about to lose my home and job. I'll be too busy sorting my life out to go a-courting.'

'You don't have to lose either home or job, as I've told you. And anyway, no woman worth falling in love with will care whether you can provide for her in luxury.'

'You wouldn't care at all, would you?'

'Of course not. I'm used to earning my own living and—'

Before he could finish, one of his friends came hurrying across the atrium to join them. 'Thank goodness you've not left yet.'

Richard stared at him in dismay. 'What's wrong?'

'Laurie's collapsed. Out cold. I daren't put her in a taxi, well, I doubt any of them would take her, and you're going in her direction.'

Feeling furious at Laurie's strategy succeeding, Paula rolled her eyes. 'What rotten timing! We just get engaged then we have to ferry a drunk home.'

He gaped at them. 'You two are engaged?'

She smiled brightly at him. 'Yes. Richard just proposed and I naturally said yes. You can be the first to congratulate us.'

He beamed back at her. 'I do congratulate you, Paula. You not only look as if you're together, you're helping him escape a fate worse than death.'

Richard sighed and pulled out his mobile phone. 'All right. We'll see her home. It'll take Kevin ten minutes to bring the car for us.' He turned away to speak on the phone.

'Where is she now?' Paula asked.

'On a sofa in that far corner of the foyer. My wife's keeping an eye on her.' He bent forward to kiss Paula's cheek. 'Great news about the engagement. He's the best of fellows. My Louise will be delighted to hear your news. She's not a fan of Laurie.'

When Richard turned back to them, his friend clapped

him on the back. 'I'm delighted about your engagement.'

Richard managed a smile and when he turned to follow his friend across to join his wife, Paula grabbed his hand and fluttered her eyelashes at him, whispering, 'We need to stay together, *darling*.'

'You're a devil!'

'I sure am.'

'You don't mind doing this?'

'It'll be fun.'

'Pay attention, everyone! These two have just got engaged,' someone announced in a loud voice before they got to the corner where Laurie was lying. Everyone nearby immediately turned round to stare.

Paula was wondering if she'd gone too far with her impulsive announcement because Richard hadn't touched her as he spoke. Then he put one arm round her shoulders and dropped a kiss on her cheek. That felt nice, more than nice.

People were calling out congratulations, so she smiled and nodded, leaning against him and keeping a tight hold of his hand as well.

If only this were real and happening in Australia.

A porter turned up with a wheelchair and when Richard made no move to help get Laurie into it, another man stepped forward to assist the porter.

Laurie wasn't fully conscious, her clothes were disarranged and she looked slack-faced. If she saw this as a way to catch a man, she had rocks in her head, Paula thought as the porter started to wheel Laurie towards the door.

'I'll ring her mother to say you're bringing her home,'

one of Richard's friends called. 'And again, congratulations on your engagement, you two.'

Kevin was waiting by the door and clearly heard this because he stared at them open-mouthed before taking charge of Laurie. 'Is she drunk again? Just a minute.' Before he helped lift her in the back he spread newspaper around her in case she threw up.

Richard insisted on Paula riding in the front for the same reason. She tilted the sun visor and watched them in the rear-view mirror. He didn't look happy and was sitting as far away from the drunken woman as he could.

'I couldn't help overhearing your news,' Kevin said. 'Congratulations, Richard, Miss Grey. Everyone in the village will be really happy for you.'

Paula glanced in the mirror. Richard nodded and forced a smile, but he didn't look genuinely happy.

At the Blythe-Jones residence, he was greeted with relief by Laurie's mother. 'Thank you. I always know she's safe with you.'

'She wasn't with me. I was with—'

Paula wasn't having him paired with Laurie, so moved forward to join them, slipping her arm into his. 'He was with me, his fiancée.'

Liz Blythe-Jones looked at them in shock. 'You're – engaged!' She looked down at Paula's left hand. 'Where's the ring?'

Like mother, like daughter, Paula thought. 'We haven't chosen one yet. He only proposed tonight. It isn't obligatory to have a ring before getting engaged, you know. It's the promise that counts.'

Richard, who'd been standing as if frozen, stepped

back and beckoned to Kevin, who had been standing in the doorway after helping carry Laurie inside and depositing her on a sofa in the hall. 'We'd better carry Laurie up to her bedroom for you, then we'll leave you to deal with her, Mrs B.'

Laurie's mother didn't say a word to Paula while she waited for the two men to return, but she stared at her, or rather scowled.

When he came down again, Richard went over to Paula. 'Come on . . . *darling*.'

He said nothing as Kevin drove them back home but Paula was beginning to worry that she'd gone too far this time. Well, serve them all right. Talking about nothing wasn't her way of chatting or getting to know people.

'I think I'll go straight to bed,' she said airily as Kevin drove away.

Richard paused in his struggle with the ancient key to the front door to say grimly, 'If you do, I'll come after you.'

She stuck her tongue out at him. 'I'd like that.'

The lock clicked and he swung the door open, moving quickly to switch off the alarm system in the lower part of the house. 'We'll go into the library. I need a brandy. It's not every day a man gets engaged, after all.'

She'd seen him in several moods but not angry, so she sat down and kept her mouth closed, watching him with interest.

'Want anything to drink, *darling*?'

'Tonic water, please. And darling yourself.'

He poured himself a large brandy and her a glass of tonic water, then threw himself into the chair opposite, letting the silence continue for a few minutes before tossing words at her. 'What the *hell* made you say we were engaged?'

'You. You asked earlier what you had to do to escape her. I suddenly saw a way of providing you with it. I'm not expecting you to actually marry me, you know.'

'No, but half the county will be by morning. I guarantee you Mrs Blythe-Jones will be phoning all her friends before breakfast to ask if it's true.'

She shrugged. 'Well, we can pretend we're engaged till I go back to Australia, then we can break it off, so you'll only have to put up with a fiancée for about a week longer. And after all, it was you who suggested we pretend to be in love. This was merely the logical next step.'

'It's also a step that makes me look like a fortune hunter.'

'Oh, pooh! No one who knows you would ever consider you that. Especially if we keep up the pretence of being in love.'

He scowled at her. 'And the ring? The engagement party? All the usual trimmings will be expected, you know. What do we do about those?'

'Haven't you got any collections of old family jewels here that I can borrow a ring from?'

'You don't borrow your own possessions.'

'Well, *use*, then. And we don't have to throw an engagement party.'

'Even if we don't, people will still give us presents.'

That shocked her. 'Presents? Without a party? Oh, no. Are you sure?'

'Very.'

'Oh, hell!' She shrugged. 'Well, you'll just have to send them back when we break up.'

'You're mad. Did you know that? As in crazy.' He gulped down some brandy.

'It's no biggie to pretend for a week,' she coaxed. It might be unkind, but she rather liked the idea of publicly spiking Laurie's guns.

'It may not be a biggie to you, but it's going to cause me considerable embarrassment when we break it off. And what do you think Laurie will do then? She'll begin stalking me all over again, that's what.'

'Hmm.' Paula couldn't resist teasing, he looked so frazzled. 'Perhaps you should pretend we broke it off because you're gay?'

He sat bolt upright and glared at her. 'Don't even think of it!'

She chuckled.

He couldn't hold back a smile. 'Why someone hasn't strangled you before now, Paula Grey, I can't think.'

'Oh, stop complaining and give me a sip of your brandy. It looks like a rather good one. Such a beautiful deep colour.'

'I thought you didn't drink.'

'Only a sip here and there, just enough to get the taste into my mouth. I've seen too many drunks make fools of themselves to go down that path myself.'

He brought his glass across and held it out to her.

Smiling, she drank a little, rolling it round her mouth. 'Mmm. Very good.' She held the glass out to him.

He grabbed hold of both glass and hand, yanking her to her feet and keeping hold of her as he dumped the glass on the nearest surface. Before she'd realised it, he was kissing her and then she lost track of everything else until he moved his head back to take a breath.

'You are the most infuriating woman I've ever met.' He kissed her again.

'Well, you can be pretty annoying yourself.' She kissed him back.

When he let her go, she clung to him, struggling to breathe, then wondering why she was even trying to pretend, so said it out loud. 'It's not going to go away, is it, this thing between us? We didn't succeed in leaving it behind in Singapore.'

'No. I seem to be attracted to crazy Australians.' He opened his mouth to say something, then shut it again.

She said it for him. 'In that case, why don't we simply make the most of our engagement till I leave?'

After a very pregnant silence, he asked, 'Are you sure?'

'That's what you asked in Singapore. I was sure then and I'm sure now.'

She laced her arms round his neck and nibbled his earlobe, enjoying the involuntary gasp that elicited from him. 'As long as you remember this isn't a long-term affair because I'm not staying here in England, whatever anyone says or does.'

'You said earlier that it was only make-believe, but what if it turns into more? We're playing with fire.'

'We won't let it turn into more, Richard. It can't, anyway. I'm going back to Australia as soon as I can. I really miss it.' Her voice wobbled on the last word and to her horror she felt her eyes well with tears.

'Poor Paula. I hadn't expected a feisty woman like you to be so homesick but you're not pretending about that, are you?' He cradled her close, rocking her slightly and dropping a kiss on her forehead.

'I hadn't expected it to hit me so hard. And of course I'm not pretending. I don't often pretend about anything. Only, I feel such a fool.' Tears spilt over, so she pulled away, took out a tissue and blew her nose on it good and hard. 'You can say that's why we broke up.'

'I find that weakness endearing. It makes me want to hold you very close and comfort you, not push you away.' He picked up his glass and took another sip, watching her.

She guessed he was leaving it to her to make any further moves. His care for her feelings, his desire not to take advantage of her were as attractive as his tall, elegant body and his gorgeous smile.

She tossed the damp tissue into a wastepaper basket and pretended to study him. 'Now . . . where were we? Ah, I remember. We were about to celebrate our engagement.'

She took the glass from his hand and put it down again, then tugged him to his feet. 'Your room or mine?'

His smile was as warm as a caress and made her breath catch in her throat yet again. 'Yours.'

Holding hands, they walked out into the hall and up the stairs.

'Just a minute. I need to secure the ground floor.' He went across to the keypad on the landing and typed in the code number. A tiny red light began flashing down near the front door.

She led the way into her bedroom and, after he'd closed the door of her room on the world and its problems, she walked gladly into his arms.

She wanted a few more golden memories from this trip.

Chapter Eleven

In the morning, Laurie woke with a thumping headache. Groaning, she made her way to the kitchen looking for the painkillers.

'Serves you right.' Her mother thumped the packet down in front of her, following it with a glass of water. 'If you will drink yourself silly, what do you expect?'

'I had a very good reason for getting legless. Did Richard bring me home?'

'Yes.'

She smiled triumphantly at her mother. 'Then it was worth the headache to stop him getting too cosy with that Australian bitch.' She swallowed two tablets and turned towards the coffee percolator.

'That Australian woman is not as stupid as you are. *She* is engaged to him. You missed the big news last night because you were out of your mind drunk. You know you shouldn't drink more than one glass, if that, with the pills you take.'

Laurie swung round. 'She's isn't engaged to him. She can't be.'

'Well, that's what they both told me last night after he

and his driver had carried you up to bed, and apparently they'd made an announcement about it at the ball.'

Laurie set the coffee cup down empty. 'They didn't say a word about it at the start of the ball. Surely they would have done if it was true?'

'Not if he'd only just proposed. I must say it's the most sensible thing for him to do. It means he'll still be able to hang on to the Abbey. You know how he loves it.'

'Well, she's not having him!'

'Laurie, if he was going to marry you, he'd have done it years ago. Face facts, my girl. You lost him years ago when you pretended to commit suicide because of him. Why you ever thought that would make him care for you, I've never understood. Anyway, you've lost him completely now so you might as well get on with your life. How many times do I have to tell you that?'

'I won't believe it till I see them actually get married. I just – won't! They're only pretending to be engaged.'

'Why would they do that?'

'How do I know? Perhaps you're right and he's doing it to get hold of the Abbey. I just know he doesn't love her.'

'You can't know that. But may I remind you that everyone knows he definitely doesn't love you.'

Laurie poured herself another cup of coffee, putting sugar in and stirring it round and round. 'I'll make him love me once we're together. I'll be so good in bed that he won't want or need to look elsewhere.'

'Love doesn't work like that.'

She ignored that and continued to stir until the coffee slopped over into the saucer. 'Have you discussed this so-called engagement with anyone? Who knows about it?'

'The phone has rung hot this morning with people itching to tell me and ask how you'd taken the news.'

'I wish you'd denied it. If people like your friends accept it that means it'll be harder for him to split up from her.'

Mrs Blythe-Jones shook her head. 'You're still fooling yourself. It was already public by the time you were carried in here last night.'

When she'd gone, Laurie said quietly. 'Well, she's *not* having him. I'll do whatever it takes to split them up. He's mine. He's always been mine. I'd rather he were dead than married to someone else. Far rather.'

Paula woke to see Richard still sleeping beside her. She studied his face and smiled as he opened his eyes.

'It wasn't a dream,' he muttered and reached for her.

At the sound of a car outside, she glanced at the clock. 'Richard, it's nearly eleven o'clock!' She jumped out of bed and went to peep down at the circular drive in front of the house. 'Someone's just turned up. Do you know them?'

He joined her at the window. 'No. The fellow's a stranger to me.'

'I can't get a good view of him. I've not got good distance vision.'

A woman got out of the car, taking her time, straightening her skirt, then tossing back her hair with a gesture Paula knew only too well.

'Oh, no!'

'Does that mean you know the woman?'

'Unfortunately, yes. She's my birth mother, who doesn't usually bother to visit me. How the hell did she know I was here?'

'The national newspapers must have picked up on that story about you inheriting. Better get dressed quickly.'

'I feel more like hiding under the bed.'

He turned in surprise. 'You mean that, don't you?'

'Oh, yes. I don't get on with her and never did. I've only seen her a few times since she dumped me on my father when I was five years old. She was never a presence in my life, you know. Never. She hasn't a motherly bone in her body. Jenny was my real mother.'

He was pulling on his dress trousers as he spoke. 'Shall I go and tell her you're not at home?'

'No.' She yanked on her jeans and dragged a huge, multicoloured sweater over her head, tying her hair back with a scarf which echoed its colours. 'You need to put something else on before you appear in public. Wearing last night's dress trousers is a dead giveaway that you haven't been back to your own room.'

She took it for granted he'd do what she asked and went racing down the front stairs, only to be stopped dead by the sound of a siren.

Still only half-dressed, Richard grinned at her over the balcony. 'You must learn to switch off the alarm system in the mornings.' He went across to the upstairs keypad and the shrill wailing stopped.

She turned back to the front door and unlocked it. Her mother was standing looking out over the home park, so Paula took a deep breath and turned to the man waiting patiently. 'Hello, Jean-Pierre. Long time no see.'

He reached out to kiss her on both cheeks, and she pushed him away, stepping back quickly. She'd only met him a few times but she had never felt comfortable with the way he touched her.

'You look as if we've only just got you out of bed,' he said with a knowing smile.

'I have. We went to a ball last night and got in rather late.'

'Darling!' Her mother moved towards her, arms outstretched.

Paula forced herself to stand still for an air kiss that came nowhere near to actually touching her skin, then pulled away as quickly as she could from the grasping arms.

Her mother grimaced and said in that sharp voice, which carried all too well, 'Still don't like embracing anyone? How are you ever to find a husband if you keep people at a distance?'

Paula heard footsteps behind her and turned with relief to Richard. 'Richard, this is my mother, Amanda de Vanne, and her husband, Jean-Pierre.' She'd nearly said 'her third husband' but stopped herself in time. No use making bad worse. 'And this is Richard Crawford, a very distant relative of mine on my father's side.'

He put his arm round her shoulders. 'Let's bring our guests inside, darling. It's supposed to be a bit warmer today, but it doesn't feel like it.'

Her mother raised her eyebrows. 'You called her darling as if you meant it.'

Richard glanced sideways at Paula, a question in his eyes, and at her reluctant nod, he turned back to their visitors and announced, 'Paula and I got engaged yesterday evening.'

Her mother's expression suddenly turned sour and it

was left to Jean-Pierre to offer congratulations. 'If we'd known, we'd have brought you a present. As it is, I'll send you some rather special champagne from my own vineyard.' He gestured round them. 'It seems to me you have all the physical possessions you're ever going to need now.'

Richard said, 'Thank you. We'll look forward to that.'

Paula watched her mother walk confidently forward then stop to turn slowly on the spot and study the entrance hall, and she was sure that Amanda would be mentally valuing the place. That was probably what had brought the sour expression back to her face.

She wished, as she had many times before, that she had half that poise and confidence, but not that greed for money.

Amanda turned and began giving all her attention to Richard. Of course. When did she ever talk to a woman, even her own daughter, if there was a man available, especially a good-looking one?

The voice echoed back to them. 'You know, Richard, I didn't believe Tony when he told me there was a stately home in the family. But he always added that there were probably several cousins between it and him. How did it come to my daughter?'

She threaded her arm through his and Paula could only admire the way Richard kept his smile steady as he began moving towards the kitchen, saying, 'Let's find you some coffee, Amanda.'

Maybe he'd been taken in by her mother's charm, as many men were, and his smile was expressing genuine pleasure at meeting her? That thought did *not* please Paula.

'Shall I close the front door now?'

'Oh, sorry, Jean-Pierre. Yes, of course. Let's follow them to the kitchen,' said Paula.

Jean-Pierre gestured ahead. 'I like your young man.'

'So do I.' And she meant it. That must have shown because he pursed his lips and nodded slowly.

They followed the sound of voices to the kitchen, where her mother was perched on a stool, with her shapely legs showing to best advantage while Richard dealt with the ancient coffee percolator and kept his gaze on the preparations.

'Were you passing by or did you make a special journey?' Paula asked, wondering if their visitors were going to expect a bed for the night.

Jean-Pierre smiled. 'We made a small detour on our way to Salisbury. Your mother was anxious to see you again, and of course, she was intrigued by your inheritance of this place.'

'I bet she was.'

He smiled and lowered his voice. 'I'll take her away soon, but you must allow her some curiosity and I too am rather surprised. From what you said when you first settled in Australia, you were never going to live elsewhere but there.'

'I haven't changed my mind about that. I'm not staying here any longer than I have to. I never wanted this inheritance in the first place.'

Her mother proved yet again that she was perfectly capable of listening to two conversations at the same time. 'You can't mean that, Paula!'

'Oh, can't I?'

Amanda looked at Richard. 'Surely she's not dragging

you off to Australia and away from this lovely house?'

'Why not, if it's where she wants to live?'

'Instead of here? Even she isn't that crazy, surely?'

Paula ignored that and went across to get out the cake tin and bang it on the kitchen surface. 'Would you like a piece of cake with your coffee?'

'Of course not.' Amanda gestured to herself. 'One doesn't stay slender if one eats cake.'

'Paula seems able to eat anything and stay beautifully slender.' Richard took some plates out and joined her. 'Jean-Pierre? My aunt's home-made fruit cake is delicious.'

'I'd love a piece.'

'So would I.'

He dropped a kiss on Paula's head as he passed as if offering her comfort, and for some reason that made her want to cry. She couldn't remember her mother ever giving her a genuine kiss.

To her relief, Marian came home just as they were finishing their snack, and Paula let Richard whisk them away from the kitchen so that her mother could look round the ground-floor rooms before they left.

Amanda paid far more attention to the two rooms full of magnificent artworks than her daughter had and Paula could imagine her going online that night to check the value of some of them.

Half an hour later, Jean-Pierre insisted they move on. 'We mustn't be late, *chérie*. Our friends will be expecting us.'

'We'll come back another time,' her mother said. 'You really should invite some people down for the weekend. It's a perfect place for house parties. In fact, you could earn good money hosting card parties here.'

'I don't do house parties. It's not my sort of thing at all. And I'm not into gambling.'

Amanda shook her head sadly and frowned at her daughter. 'You might have to learn to bring in money with a house like this to support, as Jean-Pierre has to do with his family home.'

Paula didn't attempt to answer that, just led the way to the front door and stood on the steps outside it, waving goodbye. She let her forced half-smile fade the minute their car pulled away.

'If she comes back to stay, I really will hide under the bed.'

'She's an unexpected mother for someone like you.'

She looked at Richard warily.

'It's all right. I wasn't taken in by her oozing charm all over me. I prefer honest faces and tactless comments any day.'

'I always feel guilty that I don't even like her.'

'Why? She might be beautiful, but I didn't like her either. Or her husband, for all his affability. They looked as if they were valuing everything they saw.'

'They probably were.' She had to give him a big hug for that remark, doing it as Marian came in to see if they wanted something to eat and earning a speculative glance from his aunt.

'We'll come and pick up a scratch brunch in a minute,' Richard said. 'We'd only just got up when Paula's mother arrived.'

Marian lingered by the door. 'Is it true?'

'Is what true?'

'That you two are officially engaged. I left the party quite early and Dan stayed on. I didn't wait to see him before I left this morning so it wasn't till Liz phoned me that I found out.'

Richard put his arm round Paula's shoulders. 'Yes, it is true.'

He waited, then prompted, 'Aren't you going to congratulate us, Aunt Marian?'

She gave them a distinctly puzzled look. 'Of course. I hope you'll be very happy. Does that mean you'll be settling here in England after all, Paula?'

'No.'

'We'll let you know what we've decided when we figure it out ourselves.' He guided Paula out of the kitchen, one hand firmly round her waist.

'I'll bring you some brunch,' Marian called after them.

In the breakfast room, he sighed and flopped down in an armchair opposite Paula. 'That's only one of the anomalies we'll have to reconcile with the facts later on. It might help if you didn't say quite so firmly that you are not going to live here in England.'

She shrugged. 'I don't really know what to say and, as you keep pointing out, I'm not noted for my tact.'

'An old lady I knew always used to tell me, "If in doubt, say nowt." Do you think you could manage that for a while?'

'I'll do my best. I'm sorry.'

'What for?'

'I shouldn't have said we were engaged, should I? It's made things more difficult, not less.'

'Who knows? I don't mind, actually. I'm hoping that at

the very least it'll get rid of the Laurie problem. And it does have a few benefits.' He blew her a kiss and winked.

'Don't hold your breath. Laurie has to be crazy to hang on to you as she has done.'

'She's had mental health problems in the past.'

'Well, I reckon if she can't break us up, she'll try to murder me.'

He shot her a worried look. 'She might not murder you but she might try to get at you in some way. She can be a spiteful bitch. And a bit chancy in what she does.'

Paula shrugged. Laurie was a minor problem compared to what to do about this damned inheritance – and even more important, about her attraction to Richard.

Chapter Twelve

Aubrey Lloyd stared at the oncologist in near disbelief, unable to form a single word for a minute or two. Then he asked in a near whisper, 'How sure are you that I'm clear of it?'

'We're pretty sure we've nailed it. This type of leukaemia is mostly treatable if caught early. You have a good chance of living a normal lifespan now, Mr Lloyd.'

And heaven help him, for all he was fifty-seven years old, he put his face in his hands and wept. He hadn't dared let himself expect this whatever they said about how effective the treatments could be. He simply hadn't dared hope, had only been able to cope with one day at a time and keeping control of his fears in public.

His daughter, who had been sitting beside him, got up and hugged him, then looked across at the specialist and said it for him, as if she knew he couldn't force two coherent words out. 'Thank you so much for your help, Dr Wiler.'

As Rhona drove him home, Aubrey said, 'You must think me a fool, bursting into tears like that.'

'Not at all. You're a human being just like the rest of us,

Dad, and these days men don't have to keep a stiff upper lip whatever happens. You're looking a bit more relaxed now.'

'And feeling a lot better.'

When they reached his country retreat in the small village just across the Welsh border from Hereford, she made them both a cup of tea and sat down beside him on the sofa.

'Are you in a fit state to discuss your future and that of the business now, Dad? I'd have preferred to give you a few days to settle back into normal life, but there are a few things that desperately need sorting out, I'm afraid.'

She was right and he'd rather have spent some time alone but he'd trespassed enough on his daughter's life, so he tried to pull himself together. 'Yes, of course. I'm so grateful to you for bearing with me this past year as I fled from the world. To tell you the truth, I'm sure the peace and quiet of the village and walking in the hills did contribute to my recovery.'

He looked at her. 'Go on. Fire away. Which problems are you referring to?'

'It's about time you came out of hiding where the Stovell side of the family is concerned, don't you think? Are you able to face doing that now? There are problems to sort out about the inheritance.'

He leant back and summoned up all his self-control. 'I thought we'd settled it and got rid of their investigators.'

'I'm afraid not. There's something I need to tell you about.'

'Go on, then. I'm not fond of some branches of the Stovell family, though, and would rather stay away from them. What's so urgent?'

'I didn't mention it two months ago when I was contacted again, because you'd asked to be left in peace until you saw how the treatment went. And I could understand that. The trouble is, the man the first investigators said was the heir didn't feel certain their findings were correct and he appointed another set of private investigators to make another search.'

She gave him a sympathetic glance. 'They thought they'd nailed it when they found the descendant of Percival in Australia, only it was the wrong person for a second time due to your vanishing act. And sadly, the woman in question doesn't want such an inheritance, or to move to England. Do you really want to leave it at that? It could lead to big trouble for everyone concerned in the future, including me as your heir. And anyway, it isn't fair to her.'

He stared at her, feeling as if the whole room was sending back echoes of the bombshell she'd just thrown at him. 'Oh, no.'

She waited, letting him take his time, wishing her mother were still alive to help him through this. Sometimes it could be as hard getting used to good news as to bad. Only, which type of news was he facing now?

She watched him stare out at the view: gently swelling hills, with villages and farms nestling in their folds. It was beautiful here.

'Can't we just let sleeping dogs snore for ever, Rhona?'

She stared down at her hands. 'I can't lie to you, Dad. I think it's your moral duty to accept it. And if she were still alive, I'm sure Mum would say the same thing.'

'Yes. Sylvia was big on doing your duty. But it'll not only be me who'll be affected if I step out of the shadows.

It'll affect you just as much in future. Do you really want a major burden like that thrust upon you and your children?'

'If it's the right thing to do, yes.' She hesitated then said, 'I wasn't sure so I went to look at the house without telling you. You never said how beautiful it is, and the countryside round there is even prettier than it is here. I could easily fall in love with it.'

'I remember the house and its surroundings but I also remember the arguments and problems caused by my great-uncle Roy's behaviour, the ongoing financial worries that kept his land agent fretting and burning the midnight oil, and how my mother couldn't wait to get away from the people there after my father died. She was so glad she wasn't the one called upon to inherit.'

'Well, it's your choice, I suppose, so I'll leave you to think about it. Let's turn to our own business next.'

'You and Ken have been doing well running our investigation agency. I'll happily sign it over to you both: lock, stock and barrel. I don't want to go back to work in that area and I don't need to earn any more money, thanks to my investments and other inheritances. In fact, apart from what I need to do to wind things up, I don't think I'll ever try to work in that field again. How would you feel about you and your husband taking over completely?'

'Ah. Well, actually, I wouldn't mind a change from running a detective agency too, Dad. Especially as I need to get right away from Ken.'

He looked at her in dismay as this slowly sank in. 'Are things still not going well between you two? I thought you were finding the counselling helpful.'

'We're not getting together again if that's what you're

asking. We did consider staying together but we've grown too far apart. He's offered to buy you and me out and take over the agency. I'd be happy to agree to that.'

'I'm sorry about your marriage.'

'That's water under the bridge now. The counselling did make us both less antagonistic about our break-up, which is a good outcome as far as I'm concerned. And Ken has no desire for the children to live with him, which would have been a sticking point with me, because I do want them.'

'I see.'

She waited.

After a few moments, Aubrey took a deep breath. 'Look, can you give me a day or two to think it all over and retake possession of my own mind and body, so to speak. Some of those treatments I've gone through seem to play havoc with your brain, and clarity of thought is only just coming back to me. How about I talk to you in two days' time about what I want to do about Stovell Abbey? I think a big change of lifestyle will do me good and it sounds as if you're wanting something similar, so I'll probably make myself known to the lawyers.'

'I am.'

He stared into the distance, relieved that she was being so patient with him. 'I wish your mother were still with us. I'm still missing her even after three years. Or perhaps it's having someone around to discuss things with that I miss. Yes, that's it. I don't think I was programmed to live on my own, love.'

Rhona gave him a big hug. 'Two days it is, then, Dad. The legal wallahs can wait a few more days for the big revelation. Give me a call and I'll arrange a meeting when you're ready and if you need more time than that, take it.'

He watched her drive away, thinking what a wonderful daughter she was.

Then he walked back into the quiet house and sighed in utter relief, beaming at his engagements list on the fridge door. No more visits to hospitals and treatment venues were listed. No more prodding and poking by the various medical specialists and technicians would be coming his way, followed by anxious waits on his part for results to the latest round of tests and treatments.

And perhaps no more involvement in helping provide information for acrimonious divorce cases, or for catching villains trying to get away with stealing other people's money. Being a private investigator had been fascinating once, and the knowledge he'd gained in his work had come in very useful when he wanted to disappear from the world.

Now, who knew what lay ahead? He was definitely ready for something different to build his new life around. But was he glad or sad that it was his duty to take on such a big project as Stovell Abbey?

Did he even have any choice in that, though? You had to live with your conscience and his had already started twitching uneasily.

Chapter Thirteen

Two days after the ball, Richard and Paula got up late and sat enjoying a long lazy breakfast in the kitchen.

'Let's go away for a few days,' he said suddenly. 'In fact, let's go today.'

'That's rather sudden, isn't it?'

'Yes. But don't you think it'd be good for us to spend more time together given how close we've become in certain rather delightful ways? There always seems to be something or someone interrupting us here when we try to have a serious discussion about our future.'

Paula considered this, head on one side. 'Hmm. Good idea.'

'And you did say there were places in England that you wanted to see. We could perhaps visit one or two of them together.'

She beamed at him. 'You've persuaded me. How about we start with Hadrian's Wall?'

'You're on. I like Northumberland. It's a beautiful county. You'll be fascinated by the wall itself and I'll take you to a partially excavated fort I've visited before.'

'Even better! It'll only take me ten minutes to pack.'

'It might take me a little longer, because I have to check my car before I bring it round. I've only been using it for pootling around the neighbourhood.'

The doorbell rang just then. Richard grimaced and stood up. 'Marian's doing something in her own quarters, so I suppose I'd better answer that.'

To his dismay, he found Laurie standing outside.

She pushed past him without being invited in.

'Hold on a minute.' He grabbed hold of her jacket and tugged her back to stand beside him.

She shook him off. 'I won't put up with being ignored by such an old friend as you, let alone being denied entry to a house I've been in and out of freely for years.'

He stared at her in surprise. '*Won't put up with*? What the hell do you mean by that?'

'What I said.' She dodged past him again and started running towards the kitchen.

He reacted quickly, ran after her and grabbed her sleeve, pulling her to a stop. 'We're just going out so it isn't convenient for you to come visiting at the moment.'

'Who's *we*?'

'Don't play stupid. Who do you think? Paula and I.'

'Well, what I'm here for won't take long, so you two alleged lovebirds can still go out, but I need to see you first, and *her* as well, I suppose.'

He kept hold of her jacket. 'Why?'

'I'm bringing an invitation from my mother to you two and your aunt to attend a party at our house tomorrow night. Mother's already invited several other people. It's to celebrate your engagement, us being such old friends of the family. We were going to make it a surprise but Mother changed her mind and decided we'd better check that you'll be free.'

'Sorry, but we won't be here tomorrow.'

'Surely you can change your plans when Mother's gone to so much trouble?'

'She can't have gone to that much trouble because we only got engaged a couple of days ago.'

'Richard, don't you think you should wait and—'

Laurie had begun to play with his sweater sleeve, walking her fingers up and down. He let go of her and stepped away hastily, wondering what the hell she was up to now. 'Another time perhaps,' he said soothingly, not liking the look in her eyes.

She grew angry again, as she sometimes did, shouting now. 'The party is already arranged! It's tomorrow. You *have* to come or my mother will look a fool!'

He'd seen her like this a couple of times before and knew her mother was starting to worry about her mental health again but he still didn't want to go to a party at their home, where he never felt comfortable these days. Nor did he want to subject Paula to it.

To his relief, his aunt came into the hall just then. He looked at her and flickered his eyes towards Laurie, hoping for her support, but she shook her head slightly as if warning him about something.

'Paula has just told me you're planning to go away for a day or two. Surely you can postpone your departure to attend this party, Richard? It's so kind of Liz to hold it for you.'

By now Paula had come to lean against the kitchen door frame, arms folded, scowling back at Laurie.

He looked helplessly at his aunt, wondering why she'd got involved in this, why she wanted him to accept.

'We'll be there, Laurie,' she said soothingly. 'You can go back and tell your mother.'

'Good. Don't let anything or anyone put you off. I'd hate Mother to have arranged all this for nothing. See you tomorrow, Rich.'

She stared at him as if expecting an answer and when he said nothing, only looked meaningfully at Paula, hinting that she should be included in the farewells, Laurie simply turned and left without attempting to speak to his fiancée.

His aunt said, 'Shut the door and come into the kitchen. I need to tell you both something.'

When they were all sitting down, she said in a tight voice, 'I've just had Laurie's mother on the phone. Liz is afraid her daughter might be on the verge of another major nervous breakdown.'

'*Another* major breakdown?' he exclaimed.

'We didn't tell you about the first one, because you weren't living here at the time, Richard, but she had a rather serious one a few years ago. She had to be committed to hospital for a few weeks and has been on medication ever since. We managed to keep it quiet by pretending she'd gone away on holiday.'

'Hmm.'

'Liz would really appreciate it if you'd play along with this arrangement for tomorrow night. She's hoping that if her daughter sees you two looking lovingly at one another and Paula sporting an engagement ring, Laurie will accept once and for all that she has no chance whatsoever of getting together with you.'

'She definitely has no chance of that whatever she does!' he snapped.

Paula joined in. 'I think that's a stupid way to deal with

it. Even if Laurie does have another breakdown over this, it's not Richard's responsibility and he shouldn't be expected to get involved. He's merely collateral damage. What you'll be proving to her is that she can blackmail you into doing what she wants. I reckon this is some sort of a trick on her part.'

'I'd really appreciate it if you two would go along with it just this once, for Liz's sake. She's helped me out a time or two and she sounded desperate just now on the phone.'

Richard let out a little growling sound, ran his hand through his hair and turned to Paula. 'I'm truly sorry about this. I don't want to go to this party and if we do, I promise you that I'll only be doing it because my aunt wants to help Liz, *not* because I want to spend any time with Laurie. Because I damned well don't.'

She hesitated.

'And I promise you, Paula, I'll not let anything Laurie does stop me taking you away for our planned trip the day after that.'

He turned back to his aunt. 'Will you tell Liz that I shan't co-operate in this sort of ridiculous charade again? If Laurie needs help in future, it should be from her doctor.'

She nodded, then they both looked at Paula, who sighed and gave in. 'Oh, very well. A couple of days won't make much difference to our sightseeing, I suppose. After all, that wall has been there for nearly two thousand years, give or take. It's not going to fall down before we get there.'

Marian nodded at her. 'Thank you, Paula. I really appreciate you doing this.'

At least her tone was more friendly than ever before, Paula thought. It might be worth doing this to get on better terms with Richard's aunt.

Marian hesitated then added, 'If you don't mind my saying so, it'd look better if you were wearing an engagement ring tomorrow, Paula. I know you haven't had time to buy one, but there are various rings in the safe that you could use for the time being. Perhaps Richard could help you choose one. And – thank you again for doing this. Liz has had a hard time with her daughter. I feel really sorry for her.'

Paula could only nod and go with Richard to find a ring.

'At least this has made your aunt speak to me in a more friendly manner,' she muttered.

'Yes. She and Liz go back a long way. And I too appreciate you helping us out.' He heaved a heavy sigh. 'I'm *not* looking forward to the dinner party, though. And I meant what I said: this will definitely be the last time I let myself be persuaded to gallop to the rescue with Laurie.'

He'd said something similar the night of the ball when he agreed to drive the stupid woman home, Paula thought. The ties of families and friendships could be very difficult for outsiders to negotiate.

'I'm sure we'll manage to find you a ring that fits.'

She stopped dead. 'I'll mark this down as another highly romantic incident.'

'What?'

She clasped her hands together. 'Say after me: darling Paula, I want to give you an engagement ring as a sign of my affection.'

He flushed. 'This is only a temporary engagement ring. If we do manage to sort out something more permanent between us, which I'd really like to do, you'll have your own choice of ring, believe me.'

She felt a lump come into her throat at what he'd said. She was taking all this one day at a time. Unfortunately, she couldn't see their relationship coming to a happy resolution when they went back to living ten thousand miles apart. She tried not to say anything else but her feelings escaped her control. 'Damn Laurie Blythe-Jones! I was looking forward to seeing Hadrian's Wall.'

'I've cursed her a good few times over the years.'

'Have you any idea what she might be plotting?'

'No. But we won't let her come between us. And even if you weren't in the picture, I can assure you that I'd never in a million years get engaged to her.'

'She's been playing you all for fools for years and as far as I can see, you've let her.'

He rolled his eyes. 'You may be right, but she's playing her mother most of all. I've managed not to do any socialising with her except in groups. I'd as soon go on a solo date with a rattlesnake.'

'Even those group outings must have given her hope, Richard.' She frowned. 'How does she earn a living?'

'She doesn't. She has a small inheritance and lives with her mother so has no living expenses.'

'Lazy devil. But I warn you: I won't let her start playing tricks on me. I'm not afraid to take drastic action.'

'It's a bit different when you've known someone since childhood, I suppose. She was younger than the rest of the group but managed to tag along with us because she had no friends of her own age living nearby. I suppose we all felt sorry for her.'

Paula didn't say that she would be surprised if Laurie had ever had any real friends, whether during her childhood or in recent years. There was something . . . different about her. In one sense it was very sad; in another it was infuriating. But it would do no good to labour the point.

Aloud she said, 'Well, you're neither of you children now. Let's see how firm your resolve holds this time. Now, where are these damned rings?'

He took her into the estate office and got the tray of family rings out of the safe, letting her choose one. He wasn't surprised when it was fairly plain yet colourful, a rather nice amethyst surrounded by a circle of tiny diamonds.

He put it on her finger and it fitted perfectly. He would have kissed her to seal the bargain in the traditional way – and because he really enjoyed kissing her – but this time she backed away quickly, waving her finger around.

'There you are. We're officially engaged now. I hope it's fully insured in case I mislay it.'

She started to leave the office, then stopped just outside the door to say abruptly, 'I need some fresh air and peace now, Richard. I'm going out for a walk. On my own.'

'You don't want company?'

'Not this time.'

'There are some old jackets on a hook in the corridor.' He pointed them out. 'You could take one of those and use the side door nearby to get outside.'

'Thanks.'

He went to the office window and watched her walk out of the house. She strode off round the corner, hands thrust into her pockets, shoulders sagging, not looking back.

He nearly went after her, worried that she looked upset,

but he hadn't locked the safe and by the time he'd done that and hurried to the back door, there was no sign of her.

He felt a presence behind him and swung round.

His aunt was standing there. 'I made a mistake about Paula, didn't I?'

'In what way?'

'She's not after the money or status, and she really is homesick for Australia.'

'Desperately homesick. She had an unsettled early childhood and Australia gave her a proper home for the first time ever. She owns a lovely house on the waterfront there, which she's struggled to buy. I really admire her.'

'I'm not trying to rain on your parade, but even though I'm starting to appreciate her good points, I can't see how you two will be able to make things work long-term.'

'I'm hoping to find a way.'

'You care about her that much?'

'Yes. And I can be rather stubborn when I want something. The more I get to know her, the more I like her.'

'Yes. I've watched how you look at her. If it's any consolation, she looks at you the same way sometimes when she thinks no one's watching her. I wish now that I hadn't pushed you into going to dinner at Liz's tomorrow.'

'Well, it's done now. Did you want something?'

She nodded. 'Just to tell you that I'm going over to Dan Peverill's this afternoon. There are some steaks in the fridge, rolls and a bowl of salad. And there's always cake in the tin or ice cream in the freezer for afters.'

'Thanks. I have been known to cook a meal or two before now. Um, can I ask something a bit personal? Only, I don't want to put my foot in it tomorrow evening. Are you getting together with Peverill again? I know you were quite close to him at one stage.'

'No, I'm not getting together with him. Definitely not. But he's good company and I like being asked out occasionally on dates. Eligible men of my age aren't exactly plentiful round here, or anywhere that I go actually. He says he wants my advice about renovating the Hall in a tasteful way that acknowledges its history. It's been neglected for far too long and I've felt sad to see it deteriorate, so I was happy to agree to do that. Houses are like people. If they're to become real homes, they need loving. That one hasn't been loved for a long time.'

Another hesitation, then, 'I don't think you love the Abbey nearly as much as I do, Richard. Especially after what's happened.'

'I don't know what I feel about it now.'

'Hmm.'

He watched his aunt leave, then gave in to temptation and strolled down to the lake, stopping when he heard a sound he couldn't identify. Then he saw Paula in the distance sitting on one of the wooden benches, sobbing so hard her shoulders were shaking. She kept wiping her eyes then bursting into tears and sobbing all over again.

He nearly went running to her but knowing her fierce independence, he didn't think she'd want him to see her in such a state, so he moved quickly back towards the house.

Oh hell! What a mess this all was. There were so many conflicting needs and duties, he didn't know which way to turn sometimes.

Only, he didn't want to lose her. The more time he spent with her, the more sure he became of that.

He suspected she felt the same about him but was what they felt enough to keep them together against such odds?

When Marian arrived at the Hall, Dan came out to greet her. He tried to kiss her on the lips but she pulled back and splayed one hand on his chest to keep him at a distance.

'I enjoy your company and I'm happy to help you with renovation ideas, which I'm good at if I do say so myself, but I don't want to re-start our relationship, Dan.'

He pulled back, looking rather surprised, but after staring at her for a minute or two, as if to read the truth in her face, he gave a little shrug and started chatting about how run-down the place was.

'Are you really going to live here?' she asked after a while. 'You don't sound as if you're doing this renovation for yourself.'

He hesitated, then admitted it. 'I'd rather you kept this to yourself but no, I'm not going to turn this into my permanent home. I doubt I'll ever want one. I like change. However, it was a relatively cheap buy and I'll make a good profit from it – and what I'm doing will save it from deteriorating further, which will be a win for the district as well.'

She was puzzled. 'How?'

'I'll be subdividing the land and will be partnering with a friend who has a building company specialising in housing suitable for the more affluent type of retiree. We'll be using the big house as a social focus to attract them. I'll put in a club-cum-bar with simple dining facilities, a gym, a beauty parlour, that sort of thing.'

'I thought the council was against subdivisions.'

'They'll come round if it's that or demolishing the Hall.'

She didn't comment but that confident remark left her

wondering if he'd already been bribing the council with an offer to provide some local amenity to sweeten the deal. She felt sure the council wouldn't fall into line with his wishes without some benefit to their area.

Then she shook off her concerns. Whatever became of the place, he was right about one thing: it would do no good to let it fall into ruins when it could still be made beautiful again. And after all, there were no members of the original family left to live there.

By the end of her visit, they'd discussed various options and he'd pounced on a couple of her suggestions. 'You're good at this, Marian, better than I'd expected if you don't mind my saying. You should set up a consultancy to advise people on renovating smaller stately homes and country houses. You've got the experience as well as the ideas. You could make some good money. I would certainly put business your way and recommend you to business friends.'

It took a minute or two for that to sink in, then she said slowly, 'Maybe I will do something like that if Richard leaves here permanently.'

'Are those two really engaged? Go on. You can tell me. After all, I told you about my development.'

'It's looking that way. You can tell by the way they look at one another. I gather you've been invited to the party at Liz's tomorrow night to celebrate their engagement, so why are you doubting it?'

'I don't know. I ran into Liz when I went for a walk this morning. From what she was saying, her daughter not only suggested but insisted on the party. I don't know about you, but I think Laurie is more than a little strange. I'm wondering if she's plotting something.'

She looked at him in exasperation. 'Everyone says that but Liz has assured me that she's keeping an eye on Laurie and that nothing underhand will happen.'

'Who's keeping an eye on Paula, though? I doubt she'll put up with someone going after her man. Or trying to interfere in her life. She's a lively one, isn't she?'

'Yes, she is. I'm starting to like her now I know her better.' Marian stood up. 'I'd better go home now, Dan. Thanks for the meal and chat. Chez Lucette do good food, don't they?'

He let out a crack of laughter. 'You recognised that café's takeaway cuisine?'

'Of course I did. I've lived in this district all my life.'

'Waste of a good woman and good brain, if you ask me, you burying yourself deep in the countryside.'

'I don't think so. I love it here. I could never live in a town now.'

She got herself out of the house and into the car before he could try to kiss her again.

As she drove home, she thought how strange it was that she'd been so in love with him in her younger days. She'd not even consider him as a steady partner now let alone a husband. In fact, she didn't even want him to touch her in that way, though he was an interesting companion socially.

Everything he said and did screamed that his attitude to life was business-dominated and he was focused mainly on money and his own needs. A woman would always come second to him.

Had he always been like that?

Should she warn Richard about what Dan was planning?

She'd have to think about it. After all, the Abbey wasn't his responsibility now. Or hers.

Chapter Fourteen

The following morning, Richard took Paula to see Stonehenge, not saying anything about what they were looking at but waiting to see whether she reacted as he'd guessed she would.

She studied the queue of people straggling a long way back from the entrance and turned to grimace at him. 'I bet it'll be a long wait.'

'Yes. Couple of hours at least, I should think. I know a place where we can look at it from a distance if that'll do instead. And I brought some binoculars with me.'

'Good idea. I hate queuing.'

'Now why doesn't that surprise me?'

She pretended to punch him in the arm, then took hold of his hand instead and walked along with him.

'Afterwards I'll take you to look round Avebury, a village I enjoy much more. It's not a circle like Stonehenge but there are some enormous standing stones scattered through the village and at least there you can touch them.'

'Actually touch them? Oh, I'd love to do that.'

'There's also a small manor house in the village that the

National Trust have done up, with various rooms furnished in the styles of different eras. I think you'd enjoy that as well. I certainly did and it merits a second visit.'

'Lay on, Macduff!'

'You quoted that accurately. Most people mistakenly say "Lead on", which makes me wince.'

She sketched a mock curtsey at him. 'We aim to please.'

And they did please one another, enjoying a pleasant few hours of sightseeing and chatting about all sorts of topics, without any serious disagreements.

Eventually he looked at his watch and said with a sigh, 'We'd better start back now.'

'Can't we elope together instead?'

'I wish.'

Marian said she'd drive herself to the party at Liz's house in case she wanted to come home early.

Paula gave her a sharp look at that but didn't comment. She enjoyed keeping Richard to herself and doubted she'd be allowed to do that once they got there. She still felt uneasy about this party.

Liz's house was a pretty, three-storey detached residence, probably built in the eighteenth century, Paula guessed. It was symmetrical in the classical way with just the right amount of creeper gracing part of its walls to soften the golden stone.

So why didn't she want to go inside?

Since there were already three cars parked in the drive, Richard backed out onto the road again. 'I'll leave our car here so that we don't get boxed in. And we won't stay late whatever anyone says.'

'Agreed.'

'Stovell Abbey is only about half a mile away if you go down that minor road. I often walk here, but showery weather and the muddiness of the footpaths make that impractical tonight.'

'Pity.'

Richard made no attempt to get out of the car. 'I don't want to go in,' he said abruptly.

'Neither do I. Come on. Let's get our big entrance over and done with.'

He took hold of her hand. 'Stay close to me.'

'She'll find a way to get you to sit next to her at some point in the evening.'

'Heaven help me.'

Inside, they had to run the gauntlet of congratulations and a couple of queries about when the happy day would be.

Paula felt annoyed when Laurie ignored her and congratulated Richard, adding loudly, 'If it's really what you want.'

He put one arm round Paula's shoulders. 'Of course it's what I want, Laurie. The two of us fell in love almost as soon as we met.'

That brought a dark scowl to her face, but someone else arrived just then and she had to turn and greet them. As they moved on, Paula whispered, 'The look on her face would have soured milk.'

She accepted a glass of wine from her hostess but treated it like the glass she 'drank' in the bar and only wet her lips with it. The thought of the friendly atmosphere in the bar, and Nick's smiling face made her feel homesick all over again.

When Richard got cornered by an older woman, Paula stepped to one side, jumping in shock when someone said right next to her, 'For a newly engaged person, you're not looking happy.'

She turned to face Laurie. 'I was thinking of my family at home. I miss them a lot.'

'The Abbey will be your home from now on, surely?'

'We'll see.'

She managed to move away from the dratted woman and chat to a pleasant older man instead until they were called to the buffet to fill their plates with finger food.

Laurie said, 'I've put place names to show where you're all sitting.'

'You've made a mistake, then,' Richard said. 'On an occasion like this, I should be sitting next to my future wife.'

'She'll have you for years so you can jolly well share yourself around.'

Laurie took his arm and literally pulled him to the place next to hers on a two-seater sofa and, to Paula's annoyance, he gave in.

The evening seemed to be progressing slowly and she didn't feel hungry, especially as she watched Laurie chat up Richard and refill his glass once with wine and once with what she called a special 'after-dinner cocktail'. She kept hold of his sleeve and he couldn't get away without making a scene.

He seemed to Paula to have given in to the situation and was moving rather slowly, leaving most of the chatting to Laurie and not even looking across at his fiancée.

Paula had had more than enough of this so-called engagement party. Everyone here knew one another well, and although they made sure she wasn't physically left sitting alone, they kept exchanging reminiscences she couldn't join in, so she still felt as if she were on her own.

She was growing increasingly angry that Richard hadn't yet come across to rescue her, but simply continued to sit there on the small sofa with Laurie. It was placed sideways to the room, so that when she moved out of someone's way, she couldn't even see his face properly.

'I need to use the cloakroom,' she told her hostess.

Liz immediately showed her where to go. 'I'll get Laurie away from Richard soon,' she offered.

'If he can't get away from her himself, let him stay there. Please excuse me. My need is urgent.'

She didn't close the door of the cloakroom fully and took a quick look through the narrow gap to make sure Liz wasn't waiting for her nearby. After using the amenities, she went across the hall to peep into the living room at the other guests. Richard was still sitting on the small sofa but was now leaning towards Laurie, his head touching hers and – was he? – yes, he was holding her hand.

That did it! Anger seared through Paula and she snatched her coat down from the stand in the hall and left the house by the front door, shutting it quietly behind her.

As the cold air hit her, she hesitated for a moment, then there was a burst of laughter and she recognised Laurie's shrill whinny of sound. A peep through the window of the room full of guests showed Richard with his head on Laurie's shoulder. That was the final straw and sent her striding down the drive, breathing in the chill night air with relish after the over-heated rooms, and setting off along the road towards Stovell Abbey. Thank goodness it wasn't far away and she'd worn sensible shoes.

As she walked, she thought how much she'd hated the evening. She couldn't bear the thought of living here and facing social events with 'the crowd' regularly. She simply couldn't do it. And she wouldn't let any damned inheritance force her to put up with a life like that, just would not.

She shouldn't have initiated the pretend engagement to Richard, but how was she to get out of it now without looking a fool? It'd be difficult to pretend to fall out with him if she stayed here because he was so attractive.

Suddenly, she felt a surge of homesickness. She needed to go home quite desperately. She stopped walking as that thought sank in.

By hell, she was going to do it. What's more, she was going to leave straight away before anyone could prevent her or persuade her to give it 'just a little longer'.

Only, by the time she'd walked back to the Abbey, someone would probably have noticed that she was missing and Richard would feel impelled to come after her.

Could she run away now? Did she dare?

She checked in her shoulder bag and yes, her passport was still there in the zipped compartment at one side. She hadn't liked to leave it in her bedroom because it felt like an ongoing contact with home. And now her sentimentality was going to pay off big time. Well, it was if she could get a last-minute seat on a plane.

She stopped under a street light and got out her phone. It was the work of seconds to find the number of a taxi service and call for a vehicle 'urgently' to pick her up at the crossroads and get her to Heathrow for a family emergency flight to Australia.

If Richard's car appeared, she'd hide behind a tree.

But to her relief, the taxi arrived within two minutes.

'Bit of luck for you, that was,' the driver said cheerfully. 'I was driving home when I heard your journey called.'

'I need to get to Heathrow quickly,' she said.

'No worries.'

'I'll sit in the back and try to book a flight. I'm urgently needed in Australia, you see. A family member is ill.'

'Good luck with that. I hope everything goes well for you.'

'Thank you. So do I.'

She called the airline and fell lucky. They'd just had a cancellation and if she could get to the airport within two hours, she could take that seat. It was in what Richard called 'cattle class', but that suited her just fine. She didn't want to waste her hard-earned money on a mere twenty-four hours of improved comfort.

She gave them her credit card details and it was done, then she asked the driver to step on it.

'They were lucky to find someone available to take the empty seat,' he said.

'I was lucky to get it.'

'We'll be there in just over an hour, unless we encounter any traffic jams,' he assured her. 'And I don't usually have much trouble at this time of day.'

'Oh, good.' She sank back and closed her eyes, not allowing herself to cry. It might be cowardly to flee but Richard was falling for Laurie's blandishments and wasn't backing her up. Fine fiancé he made!

And in fact, he'd been sitting staring round rather blankly, closing his eyes from time to time as he listened to Laurie. He'd not even once glanced across towards his so-called fiancée.

Surely he hadn't just been chatting her up because she'd inherited Stovell Abbey? She couldn't have been that mistaken in his character.

What the hell was going on, then? Whatever it was, she didn't intend to play stupid games.

Marian frowned as she watched Richard. Something was wrong. Her nephew was sitting there looking as if he was on the verge of falling asleep and he hadn't been near his fiancée since the food had been served, or maybe even before that.

Laurie was cuddled up close to him, looking smug, and he'd made no attempt to push her away. He never normally allowed her that sort of closeness. What was he thinking of?

She turned to see whether Paula was looking upset and could see no sign of her.

'If you're looking for your future daughter-in-law, she went to the cloakroom a while ago,' Liz said. Then she glanced at her watch. 'In fact it was nearly fifteen minutes ago. Perhaps she's got an upset stomach.'

Or perhaps she was upset by Richard's behaviour, Marian thought. *And rightly so*. 'I'd better go and check that she's all right.'

There was no sign of Paula in the cloakroom. Marian stared at the coats hanging near the front door, wondering what had changed. It took her a minute to realise that the brightly coloured anorak was missing. Had Paula gone outside for a breath of fresh air?

She'd better find out. There was no sign of Paula in the

front garden and Marian began to get worried. Where had she gone?

She went back inside and across to Richard. But when she spoke to him, he didn't respond, just gave her a glassy-eyed stare. He looked . . . stoned out of his mind. Surely not?

She glanced sideways at Laurie and was disturbed by the expression on her face, not just smug but triumphant.

'He prefers me to that stupid Australian bitch,' Laurie said suddenly.

Marian shook her nephew's arm and he still didn't respond. Indeed, if she hadn't kept him propped up, he might have fallen sideways. She saw Dan staring at her and beckoned him across. 'Something's wrong with Richard.'

He repeated her own thoughts. 'He looks stoned out of his mind.'

'I know. But Richard doesn't do drugs,' she said firmly. 'He never has.'

Dan bent over and shook him, but he hardly reacted. 'There's definitely something wrong with him.'

Laurie gave a high-pitched giggle. 'No, there isn't. We just had a little puff or two. Go away and leave us to enjoy the nice floaty feeling.'

Marian turned to study Laurie on a sudden suspicion. 'What have you given him?'

'Never you mind. He was happy to try it.'

She turned back to her companion. 'Dan, he never takes drugs, says he likes to keep his brain in good working order. There's something very wrong.'

'He doesn't look right. And he's very pale too.'

'I'm worried about how out of it he looks.' She shook

Richard's arm and this time he fell slowly sideways and his eyes closed.

She and Dan looked at one another in horror.

'Something's badly wrong,' he said.

'Will you help me get him to A&E?'

'Let's get him outside first and see if the fresh air revives him. If it doesn't, I definitely ought to seek medical help. If he doesn't do drugs and she's given him too much of whatever it was, he could be in serious trouble. Where's Paula?'

'That's the other strange thing. She's vanished and so has her anorak.'

Dan was tugging Richard's arm and she broke off to help pull him up. They had to hold him upright and tug him into stumbling along with them.

'I definitely don't like the look of this,' Dan said.

'He doesn't look at all well,' the woman in a nearby chair said.

They helped Richard out, both guiding and pulling him along. Liz followed them but before they got him to Marian's car, he grunted and crumpled to the ground, totally unconscious now. So they didn't attempt to take him home or even search for Paula; they lifted him into Dan's car and took him straight to the nearest A&E.

There he had to be taken inside on a stretcher trolley and the first responder felt so worried she called for a doctor immediately.

The man who examined him was also worried and when Marian explained that she thought someone had slipped him a drug and he'd never have taken anything voluntarily, he insisted on Richard being admitted so that they could keep a proper eye on him.

He summoned a nurse and they began hooking him up to some machinery to monitor his vital signs.

When Marian was handed her nephew's possessions, including his phone, Dan said, 'You could try calling Paula. They may have had a quarrel because of Laurie but she'll come back when she finds out he's in hospital.'

Marian tried to phone, but there was no answer, so she left a message on voicemail.

The medical staff said he'd be there until he recovered consciousness, so she left Dan keeping an eye on him and went home to change her flimsy party clothes for something more practical. Then she went back to wait with her nephew.

'I'll stay with you,' Dan said.

'Thank you. I'd appreciate that.'

Richard was semi-conscious now, which was a sort of improvement but she was worried sick about him because he still wasn't making sense.

And she was worried about Paula too. Where the hell was she?

Paula sat on the plane, finding the middle seat of the central trio so uncomfortable and her own space impinged on by the large people on each side that she was unable to sleep.

She was already regretting her impulsive behaviour in running away. She didn't usually run away from anything, prided herself on that. But remembering the way Richard had snuggled up to Laurie and ignored her completely still made her fizz with anger.

Anyway, she'd been growing increasingly homesick,

feeling totally out of place whenever she spent time with Richard's friends and neighbours. And though she was still extremely attracted to him as a man, reason said their backgrounds were too different and they were never likely to make a relationship work long-term.

Reason could make a harsh guide to life choices.

She had never liked cold weather and the non-stop wintry days had made it feel chilly inside the Abbey as well as outside, because the huge old house had been built well before central heating was thought of and was too big to have central heating put in now. You'd have to be a billionaire to do that.

The huge, echoing rooms had made her feel uncomfortable and although Marian had thawed a little, the two of them were never likely to become good friends.

Nick would tell her she'd been an idiot to run away. But he'd give her a big hug when he saw how upset she was. She could always rely on his support, whatever mistake she made. After all, no one got through life with a perfect track record.

Anyway, that mess was done with now and she wasn't going back to England, whatever those lawyers said or did.

If Richard wanted to see her in person, he'd have to come to Australia. She doubted he'd do that.

At least from tomorrow onwards she'd be in her own home in her own country again. She needed that so much.

And if it was weak of her, she couldn't help it.

Chapter Fifteen

Aubrey spent a couple of days re-orienting himself to his wonderful new life expectations, then phoned his daughter. 'Want to have that chat now? I'm ready to make a few plans.'

'Yes. Do you want to come into the office in case we need to access any business records in preparation for our sale of it to Ken?'

'Not really. It's mainly the inheritance side I'm concerned about dealing with first. From what you've told me, I feel that's far more urgent. Besides, I don't think Ken will try to cheat us.'

'No, I don't think he will either. He has faults as a husband, but has been a good business partner. I'll drive out to your place, shall I? I can be with you in just over an hour. I've been feeling like getting out of the office.'

'I'll look forward to seeing you.'

He had the coffee machine percolating when she arrived and they sat down together in the small conservatory, which had lovely views over what he called 'small, bumplety hills'.

He gestured to the scene outside. 'I'm going to miss this.'

'Which means?' She cocked her head to one side and waited.

'You were right to give me a nudge. I've been neglecting my duty to my family. I was brought up in comfort and inherited money. That enabled me to start up a business for the sheer fascination of solving puzzles but it was enough that I didn't need to work if I didn't want to. And now that I've been given a second chance at life, I can't simply take, take, take. I need to do some giving back to the world.'

As usual, she got straight to the point. 'What's your first step going to be, then, Dad?'

'I shall get in touch with the lawyers for the Stovell estate and let them know of my existence. After we've proved that I'm the heir, I'll discuss with them how best to proceed.'

'Shall we phone them straight away? They were really anxious about the situation and it's been a couple of months now since they thought they'd found another heir. That's a long time to let them keep the wrong Stovell descendant in place, only I felt that your health needs were rather more pressing than the question of inheritance.'

'Yes. It took time to recover and I'm not fully there yet, still get tired easily. But I have enough energy to make a start so I shall contact the lawyers straight away.'

'Do you want me to do that for you?'

He gave her one of his charming smiles but she could see that he was well on his way to being his old independent self again, so she listened without interrupting.

'No, darling. You're the best daughter on the planet and you've done far too much for me over the past year as well as running your own life and working through your troubles with Ken. You've been truly wonderful but it's more than time I shouldered my own responsibilities again.' He reached out to squeeze her hand. 'I don't think there are words to express how grateful I am to you.'

'You don't need to put it into words,' she said softly and they smiled at one another.

'I would prefer that you do the negotiating with Ken for what he should pay to buy us out, though, Rhona, because you're far more in touch with the business than I am after my year away from work.'

'OK. It's a bargain, Dad.' She fumbled inside her shoulder bag and held something out. 'I have the Stovell main lawyer's business card here if you want to phone him now, but how about I stay with you while you do it in case I can help in any way?'

'Good idea.'

As he took the business card from her and sat staring at it, she flapped her hand at him. 'Go on. Get it over with.'

He picked up his phone. 'I'll put the call on loudspeaker once I'm through to this Perett fellow. It'll save me going over it again with you.'

He got through to the lawyer's office quickly and spoke first to a woman who sounded like a junior secretary. Unfortunately, she seemed inclined to dismiss the importance of his call when he refused to tell her exactly what it was about.

'Kindly put me through to someone at a higher level immediately.' He heard his voice go chill and businesslike for the first time in ages. 'This matter is extremely important.'

'But I can't—'

'It's crucial information and that's all I'm going to tell you.'

'Very well. Your name is?'

'Lloyd.'

Silence, then, 'Just a moment, sir.'

She put him through to the chief clerk, who must

have known more about this case than she did because he listened for a moment, then said quietly, 'I'll connect you to Mr Perett, sir. He's in charge of the Stovell case.'

When the lawyer came on the phone, he told him bluntly, 'I'm Aubrey Lloyd. I gather you've been looking for the heir to Stovell Abbey for a while and I believe I'm that person. I'm sorry to have been avoiding you, but I've been recovering from cancer for the past year and that took precedence over everything else.'

'And indeed it would! I hope you're all right now, sir?'

'Yes. I got the all-clear a few days ago.'

'How exactly do you fit into the family, Mr Lloyd?'

He guessed that the lawyer knew that already but explained patiently that he was Jonathon Stovell's grandson, his mother had been Jonathon's only child and she had married Ernest Lloyd. 'And I'm her only child.'

Silence, then, 'You can prove all that?'

'Yes, of course. Easily.'

'One of our investigators spoke to an employee of yours, a Ms Feltham according to his notes, and she gave him the impression that you'd died.'

'She's my daughter and Feltham is her married name. She was acting on my instructions the first time she spoke to your investigators, because I wasn't sure at that stage whether I'd recover from the cancer or not. And the second time, I was at a delicate stage, so we continued to deceive you, for which I apologise.'

'Hmm. Right. Can you come into the office with your various proofs?'

'It'd be better if you came to my family home in Cheltenham, Mr Perett, because I have all the necessary documents there, as well as some family diaries from way back if you need further proof. There's too much to carry around and we can't be sure exactly what you'll need to see. I have a photocopier there that you can use.'

'Yes. Right. Good thinking. Oh dear, this is going to cause a big upset if you're correct. It's been only a few weeks since we told a woman from Australia that she was the heir and brought her to England to Stovell Abbey.'

'I can't apologise too much for the inconvenience I've caused to all of you. I'll make sure this woman is recompensed for any expenditure she's had to make, and your firm too.'

'Er, you're definitely fully recovered now?'

'So the oncologist told me. She said that I could look forward to a normal lifespan because this type of cancer is treatable if caught early, as mine was. From now on I'll be facing the same life challenges as everyone else.'

'I'm glad for you, of course I am, really glad. But goodness, this does put us in an awkward position.'

There was a pause, then the lawyer asked, 'Would it be all right if I came to see you this afternoon? I don't think we should leave things wrongly attributed for an hour longer than necessary.'

'Yes, of course. I retreated to a cottage in the country for a while and haven't been living in the family home so I'll meet you there. My daughter has been living in the house and I'm sure she'll be happy for us all to gather there.' He looked questioningly at Rhona, who'd been listening, and she nodded vigorously.

'Give me the address and I'll set off straight away.'

Once Aubrey had finished speaking to the lawyer, he decided he would pack a few things and spend the night with

Rhona and his grandchildren in Cheltenham after the meeting.

'I'm sorry for the way we've messed people about,' she said. 'As I told you earlier, at first Richard Crawford was informed that he was the heir, then this Paula Grey was discovered in a final check by a second private investigation service. What a can of worms it now is for all concerned. I'm sure our company would have done better than that first group of investigators. I found their representative who came to see me incredibly easy to fool.'

She patted her father's hand. 'I'm not sorry, though, that we bought you some peaceful time and gave you the best chance possible of regaining your health.'

'No. Me neither. But we must try to make amends for that now if we can.'

'I'd better start for home immediately, Dad, so that I can make sure of being there when the lawyer arrives.'

'I'll sling some things into a suitcase and follow you shortly.'

As he drove to Cheltenham, Aubrey steeled himself to face his former home again. He and his late wife had lived there for most of their years together but he didn't plan to move back permanently whatever happened because it still reminded him of Sylvia. He continued to miss her greatly, even though it had been three years since she died so suddenly. He needed a new start in a home where he wouldn't encounter memories of her in every room.

Then it occurred to him that he'd be living at Stovell Abbey soon and he couldn't get a much better start than that because there would be all sorts of problems to sort out if it was like other large old homes, and he'd enjoy solving them.

He'd only visited the place a couple of times when he

was a lad because its long-time owner, Roy Stovell, had always been something of a recluse and hadn't encouraged visits from any of his siblings or their families.

However, Aubrey had a photo of what it looked like from the outside and it had a certain elegance, he felt. He was looking forward to getting to know and care for it and would relish having a real purpose in life again.

Richard continued to be in a coma-like state, due to whatever drugs Laurie had slipped into his drink or food and the doctor in charge at the hospital asked Marian to try once again to find out exactly what she had given to the poor chap.

However, when she phoned her friend, Liz had no success with Laurie, who still refused point-blank to say what drugs she had used and what liquid the concoction had been administered in.

Marian had had enough of treading softly with her friend's wayward and devious daughter. If Laurie acted in a similar way again, she might kill someone.

She didn't hesitate to phone the police from the hospital car park to report the incident and was asked to go to the police station at once to make a statement and answer further questions.

She rang Liz again before she set off and told her in no uncertain terms to meet her at the police station straight away if she didn't want to be charged with aiding and abetting. Marian didn't know whether this was true, but was determined to get Liz to co-operate.

Her friend hesitated, clearly reluctant to dob her daughter in.

'You have to report this, Liz. She could have killed him.

And she's still refusing to tell you what she gave him, which has prevented him receiving the best treatment as quickly as he could have done. Are you really going to let her stay free to do something like that again?'

Marian heard a sob, then Liz gave in and agreed between more sobs to come to the police station.

'And bring Laurie with you.'

'She won't leave her bedroom and she's locked the door.'

After she'd made her own statement, Marian left it to the police to deal with Liz and get Laurie out of her bedroom. She was furiously angry with her friend's daughter and wasn't sure she now considered Liz a friend.

When she went back to the hospital, she was told that Richard had regained consciousness enough to answer a couple of personal questions, so she closed her eyes for a moment as relief surged through her.

'I'm afraid your nephew is still a bit hazy about what's happened to him,' the sister in charge told her. 'We've had his blood checked and fortunately no unknown substance has been found. This female seems to have given him a cocktail of prescription drugs and a common recreational drug and he's reacted badly. We shall have to report it to the police.'

'I've already made an initial report to them and they'll find your medical information very useful, I'm sure. Laurie's mother has gone to make a statement and told me she would go with the police afterwards to pick up her daughter from home. Laurie will probably have to be sectioned.'

'I'm glad you did that, Mrs Saunders. Your nephew is lucky she didn't kill him because she gave him a hefty amount. Now, I'm sure you'd like to speak to him.'

'I would. Can he come home now?'

'I'm afraid not. Perhaps tomorrow if he continues to make good progress.'

Richard's first question when he saw his aunt was, 'Where's Paula?'

Marian was worried at how slurred and jerky his voice was. 'We don't know. She isn't answering her phone.'

'Oh, hell! What did I say or do to upset her when I was under the influence of whatever Laurie slipped me?'

'Who knows? Speaking of Laurie . . .' She explained that the police should have picked her up by now.

'She's completely lost touch with reality,' Richard said quietly. 'Never been this bad before.'

'There's something very wrong with her, that's for sure. Is it my imagination or has she been getting worse lately?'

'She's been more of a nuisance to me, that's for sure. I'd guess that she's stopped taking her medication. Poor Liz must have been having a hard time keeping that quiet.'

'Yes. But she shouldn't have kept protecting her. At times like this I'm glad I never had children.'

'I really want children one day.' He looked at her anxiously. 'I wonder where Paula went last night.'

'Two nights ago.'

'Oh hell, yes. So it is. I've not only lost track of time, I still don't feel as if my brain is firing on all cylinders.'

'I went back to the Abbey for a nap and change of clothes, but Paula hadn't gone back there or picked up any of her belongings. They were all in the drawers still. She simply vanished into the night.'

'I can't think where can she have gone. As far as I know, she doesn't know anyone else in England. Do you think she's simply found a hotel and is staying away from the family for a while? I wouldn't blame her for doing that.'

'Who can tell? I don't know her well enough to guess and I'm sorry I misjudged her.'

'What worries me is that she was desperately homesick, worse than any of us had realised. I saw her the other day sobbing her heart out down by the lake when she thought she was alone.' He looked at his aunt and frowned. 'She couldn't have—'

'Couldn't have what? Thrown herself into the lake? Surely not?'

He gave a wry smile in spite of the seriousness of the situation. 'No, not Paula. She'd be more likely to shove someone else in if they got in her way. No, I'm wondering if she's gone back to Australia.'

'She can't have done. She'd need to have booked a seat on a plane, not to mention having her passport with her.'

'She used to keep her passport in her handbag, said she found it comforting.'

'Oh. Richard, surely she wouldn't have just taken off so suddenly, and in her party clothes too?'

'I wouldn't put anything past Paula once she set her mind to it. And if there had been a spare seat on a plane she'd have had to claim it immediately. It wasn't just Laurie messing us all about that was upsetting her, you know; it was the homesickness. Once I'd seen her weeping, I realised I wasn't allowing for how unhappy her childhood must have been, how badly the constant moving around must have affected her.'

'She'd probably benefit from some long-term counselling.'

'And from some feeling of security – which she found in Australia but not here.' Richard stared into space, then yawned and closed his eyes. 'Sorry. I'm in desperate need of another nap.'

Marian gave him a little shake. 'Stay with me a minute. Paula would have got to Australia by now if she'd gone straight back, wouldn't she? Do you have the name of that bar of hers? I'll contact them if she's still not answering her phone and find out whether they've seen her.'

'Yes. It's called Nick's Bar. I have the phone number of it but I don't know it by heart, obviously. It's in the folder with her name on it in the top drawer of my filing cabinet at the Abbey. I think it's at the front of the drawer.'

'If you don't mind me poking around in your office, I'll look for it as soon as I get back.'

'Go for your life.' Another yawn overtook him. 'If you manage to speak to her, tell her I love her, will you? I don't think I ever quite said the words, though I'm pretty sure we both knew we were heading in that direction.'

'Good heavens, I can't do that, Richard! You should be the one to tell her.'

'Mmm.' His eyes closed and his breathing slowed down.

A nurse came up to the bed. 'I was about to tell you that Mr Crawford needs to rest now, but I see his body has sent its own message.'

'When he wakes, can you please tell him I'll come back to see him this evening?' Marian asked.

'Yes. I'll put a note on his treatment sheet because we'll be changing shifts before then.' She indicated the clipboard hanging on the end of his bed.

As she was walking across the hospital car park, Marian switched her phone on again and saw that she'd received a phone call from the Stovell lawyer. She didn't attempt to answer it. She felt it was much more urgent to trace Paula and make sure the poor woman was all right than to fiddle around with what were probably only trifling legal niceties.

Aubrey got to the Cheltenham house before Mr Perett. His daughter came to the front door to greet him, linking her arm in his. 'Have you had anything to eat since breakfast?'

He shook his head. 'I wasn't hungry. Food doesn't seem as important these days.'

'Well, come and have a quick snack before Perett gets here. I've made some sandwiches.'

He only had time to eat one small chicken sandwich before a big Mercedes drew up outside and Mr Perett came to the front door, accompanied by a young woman.

'I hope you don't mind but I brought my assistant to take notes and act as witness if necessary. This is Elaine.'

'We don't mind at all. Nice to meet you, Elaine.'

Aubrey spent the next half hour going through the details and papers, and letting them photocopy the various birth and death certificates from his branch of the family. It was easy enough to validate his own identity by showing them his passport and driving licence, which had unflattering but recognisable photos of him.

In fact, proving he was who he claimed was as easy as he'd expected.

After a while, Mr Perett leant back and scowled at Rhona. 'I don't know how you managed to persuade our investigator that the heir wasn't in this branch of the family, Ms Feltham—'

'It's Lloyd again now,' Rhona interrupted.

'Right. Lloyd. It must have been perfectly clear to you that your father was the rightful heir to Stovell Abbey.'

She shrugged and continued to stare blandly back at him.

Aubrey had to clear his throat loudly to get their full attention again. 'Let's not waste time on recriminations. I feel the most important thing to do now is to find Paula Grey and let her know that the situation has changed.'

'She'll be glad of that, actually,' Mr Perett said. 'She told us several times that she has no desire to live anywhere else but Australia.'

'I can get our company on to it immediately, if you like,' Rhona offered. 'I can guarantee we'll be more efficient than the people you've employed up to now.'

The lawyer hesitated. 'And the charge for that will be what?'

'There won't be any charge at all. And my father and I will both work on finding her. We're fairly experienced investigators.'

Aubrey managed not to smile at that understatement, then it suddenly occurred to him that this would probably be his last job before he moved permanently to Stovell Abbey. He realised Mr Perett had spoken and was waiting for an answer. 'Sorry. Could you repeat that, please?'

'You'll be asked to change your surname to Stovell, Mr Grey.'

'If you wish.'

'It's specifically requested in Roy Stovell's will that the heir do that.'

'Then I'll be happy to oblige.'

The lawyer nodded towards the woman who had accompanied him. 'I'll get my assistant to ask the second investigation company we were using to share their information with you.'

Elaine handed Aubrey her business card, then gathered together their newly photocopied information and the two visitors left.

Rhona closed the front door behind them and re-joined her father. 'I'd like to get on to the sale of our business straight away as well.'

'You go for it, love.'

She studied him. 'You don't look upset or tired.'

'I'm fine. You can stop worrying about me from now on and get on with your own life.'

'Yes. Big changes for me too. Shall you mind taking a new surname?'

He'd temporarily adopted a variety of surnames when working as a private investigator, didn't care about doing that permanently. 'No, not at all. Do you want to change yours to Stovell while we're at it? After all, you're the heir-in-waiting now.'

She stared at him in surprise. 'So I am! That part hadn't sunk in. Yes, I might as well do that. I hope I'll have to wait a long time to inherit, though.'

She leant forward to squeeze his hand. 'Wow. Big changes for us both, eh, Dad? And I don't just mean the names.'

'Absolutely huge ones, but most of them good, don't you think? I can't wait to see Stovell Abbey.'

Chapter Sixteen

By the time she got off the plane in Western Australia, Paula was so exhausted it was all she could do to put one foot in front of the other until she could find a taxi willing to take her from Perth to Mandurah.

She negotiated a set price for the journey because traffic could be so variable on the freeway heading south. She was never too tired to be careful with her money.

After giving the driver her home address, she told him she'd prefer to ride in the back, almost falling into the vehicle in her desperation to sit down and rest. *Nearly there*, she kept telling herself. *Nearly home. Just hold on for a little longer.*

The man was in a chatty mood and Paula had to say, 'I'm sorry but I'm too tired to chat. If I fall asleep, will you please wake me when we get there?'

'Long journey, eh?'

'Yes, I've been awake for nearly two days.' The plane journey was tiring enough but for her it had come at the painful end of a long day.

She managed to stay more or less awake but it seemed a

long time until they got there. When at last the taxi pulled up in her drive, tears came into her eyes. She couldn't see the water from the street side of the house but she would go outside to look at it as soon as she got in. She'd kept her front door key in her shoulder bag as well as her passport, simply because she'd forgotten to take it out of the small inner pocket. She couldn't wait to get inside her beloved home.

She used her credit card to pay the taxi driver and since she had no luggage, the man wished her a good night's sleep and drove straight off, leaving her standing alone in a dark street lined with garages since this was the rear side of the canal dwellings.

It took no time to open the front door and bring the house to life by switching on the hall and stairs lights. It must have been a hot day because the interior felt uncomfortably warm and stuffy, so she switched on the air conditioning for the living area and master bedroom. As she opened the door from the hall into the great room, she remembered the water heater and half turned to fumble for the switch to that as well. Tiredness made you so clumsy.

She calmed down considerably as it slowly sank in that she really was home. 'I'm back!' she called as loudly as she could.

After standing for a moment or two gazing happily round the huge living area, she walked across to unlock the door that led to the patio at the canal side of the house and slipped outside. She stood there for a few moments, enjoying the sight of the water sparkling with the reflections of the lights from houses along both edges of the canal and also the lights of passing boats bobbing past now and then.

Usually she would have stood there for longer, but she was in desperate need of a shower and the fancy clothes she'd worn for the dinner party looked crumpled and dirty now. She was also ravenously hungry.

She caught sight of herself in a mirror and grimaced. She must have looked ridiculous travelling in these clothes but she didn't care. She was home!

She locked the water-side door carefully behind her because you had to be careful in a house with access from two sides, then walked slowly across to the kitchen area. Thank heavens for freezers and fridges! She made herself some cheese on toast and ate it with cold baked beans, spooned out of the tin into her mouth. To hell with setting a place properly at the table, or even sitting down to eat.

When she'd eaten as much as she wanted, she got out a tub of her favourite vanilla ice cream and put a couple of scoops into a bowl, topping it with tinned fruit and sprinkling chopped nuts and dried cranberries over the top. She made happy murmuring sounds as she ate the impromptu dessert.

Sleep was rapidly gaining control of her and making her feel dopey so, once she'd eaten her fill, she shoved the leftovers in the fridge, picked up her shoulder bag and went into the front hall. Her bag got in the way as she fumbled for the light switches for the big room downstairs and she set it down on the hall table.

'Done!' she muttered and walked slowly up to her bedroom. She wanted to lie down on the bed and sleep for ever, but she needed a shower to get the stale smell of the aeroplane off her skin.

She'd phone Nick tomorrow morning and let him

know she was back, then go and chat to him at the bar later in the day. She wanted to explain to him in person how unhappy she'd been in England, far worse than she'd expected, and to confess what a mess she'd made of dealing with the unwanted inheritance and the people there.

She wouldn't tell him she'd fallen in love with Richard, though. What was the point? There wasn't likely to be a happy ever after. But she bet he'd figure out that something had gone on between them. He seemed almost able to read her mind at times.

Standing under the shower, she wondered yet again why Richard had behaved like that at the dinner party after earlier claiming not even to enjoy Laurie's company. He hadn't stirred from the couch and had been cuddled up to her. That had made her furious.

She'd phone him tomorrow and ask him straight out. She should have confronted him there and then, except that she hadn't been able to face doing it in front of all those well-dressed people with their upper-class accents.

She grew angry all over again at the memory and summoned up enough energy to phone Richard immediately. She needed to let him know where she was and apologise for running away, because that was no way to solve a problem. Even before the journey was half over she had begun to feel ashamed of herself for doing it.

She dried herself more or less and slipped on a light summer kaftan, then realised she'd left her phone downstairs in her bag. She was so tired she couldn't be bothered to go down and fetch it, let alone explain her sudden flight from England.

'I'm sorry this has happened, Richard,' she whispered

aloud. 'You're probably better off without me. I'm an impulsive fool, the sort who rushes in without thinking things through clearly, or in this case rushes out of a situation.'

She didn't usually run away, though, wasn't normally such a coward. Didn't normally care so much, either.

One problem had been that Stovell Abbey gave her the shivers, with its big rooms where your footsteps echoed and arrogant faces of dead ancestors gazed down disapprovingly at you from the paintings on the walls. Marian had stared at her in a similar way at times.

She was better off away from it, she was quite sure of that. But was she better off without Richard? She wasn't nearly as sure of that. It wasn't just that she was attracted to him; she had felt utterly comfortable with him whenever they managed to spend time together on their own. She'd thought he felt the same about her – until the incident with Laurie after dinner.

His behaviour still puzzled her. Ah, who knew anything? Not her, that was sure. She was definitely not an expert on men or romance.

She closed her eyes and let the world fade gently away.

Some time later, Paula was woken abruptly by someone grabbing her and dragging her upright in the bed. She screamed and began to struggle until a voice she knew exclaimed, 'What the hell are you doing here, Paula Grey? Why didn't you let me know you were coming home?'

'Nick!' She flung her arms round her friend. 'I might ask you the same question. What are you doing in my house?'

'You didn't switch off the security system properly or

else you knocked it and switched it partly on again. The firm monitoring it thought there could be an intruder so when they could see nothing wrong, they called me in as per your rather vague instructions to them before you left. I met them here and couldn't see any signs of your luggage, so didn't think it could be you returning from the UK. Nor could I see who was under the covers so I grabbed the intruder and voilà! It's you.'

He turned towards the landing, waved and stuck one thumb up to show that everything was all right and she saw a man standing there, arms folded, looking wearily patient.

Nick gave her one of his shrewd, assessing looks. 'Just a minute. Let me tell them who you are, then I'll show them out and we'll be able to talk in private. You might want to get properly dressed while I'm doing that.'

She looked down at herself and squeaked in dismay at how transparent the kaftan was. Once he'd left the room, she put on the first garments that came to hand, a pair of shorts and a tee shirt, and joined him downstairs. Oh, how lovely it was not to need to put on layers and layers of winter clothes!

When he'd locked the front door behind the security guys, he came and sat down next to her on the sofa. 'You've lost weight and you look deep down unhappy, my girl. You need a big hug before we talk about it.'

She knew she was home when he folded her in his arms. 'I wish you really were my uncle,' she murmured against his chest. But after a few moments, she pushed away from him. 'I made a horrible mess of it all, Nick, and then I ran away. How stupid can you get?'

'I'm sure you didn't muck things up on purpose or on

your own, love. Don't be so hard on yourself.'

She gave him a summary of what had happened in the UK, ending with the mock engagement party and Richard not only ignoring her but cuddling up to Laurie.

Nick listened in silence, letting her unburden herself till she ran out of words and was able to dry the last of her second set of tears.

At that moment, her phone rang and when she only stared at it, he nudged her. 'Find out who it is.'

'It's an international call and I don't recognise the number.'

'Where is it from?'

'The UK. And it's not Richard's number. Who can it be?'

'You'll need to answer it to find out.'

'I'm not awake enough to talk sense. They'll have to ring again later.' She set aside her phone. 'Thank you for listening to me so patiently, Nick.'

'It's what friends and adopted uncles do. But I think you need sleep now more than you need to continue talking. Come and see me at the bar tomorrow morning and we'll resume the inquest on your trip.' He glanced at his watch. 'No, it's officially morning already, so I should have said come and see me later today, before things get busy if you can, and we'll discuss everything and solve all your problems in one swell foop. Jonno will be there to deal with customers so that we can talk.'

She chuckled. 'I know I'm home when I hear you mangle "fell swoop" in that tone of voice.'

After seeing him out, she concentrated hard to be sure of setting the security system properly before climbing wearily up the stairs and lying down on the bed. She switched off her phone completely and pulled a sheet over herself, letting sleep start to overtake her.

She'd work out what to do after she and her brain joined forces again and both woke up properly. And she'd listen carefully to any advice Nick offered her. He was such a savvy guy.

Marian went back to Stovell Abbey and found the file giving Paula's details and background information where Richard had said it would be in his immaculately tidy filing cabinet. She did a quick calculation about time and decided it'd be early morning now in Western Australia, so she tried Paula's phone again.

The phone rang on and on but no one answered it. She tried again a little later with the same result so phoned the bar. To her relief, someone there picked up the call.

'Nick's Bar. How may I help you?'

'I'm calling from England, from Stovell Abbey. My name's Marian Saunders and I'm Richard Crawford's aunt.'

'Ah. Pleased to meet you. Nick here.'

'Paula's uncle?'

'That's the one.'

'Is she there?'

'She's not at the bar.'

'She is back in Australia, though? We've been worried sick about her and she isn't answering her phone.'

He sighed audibly. 'I suppose it's time someone here started communicating about what's going on. If I tell you what I know, I hope you'll be open in return about what Richard did at the party and why? He really upset her.'

'That's a bargain. I'd say the party was a comedy of errors except that there was nothing remotely funny about what happened.'

'Well, Paula arrived in Mandurah last night looking dreadfully upset. She'll probably not have woken up yet, which is why she isn't answering her phone.'

'But she's all right?'

Again, Nick hesitated. 'As I said, she's upset.'

'It was a misunderstanding and I need to explain what really happened. I hope you'll pass it on to her so that she doesn't think Richard was behaving like that on purpose.'

'Shouldn't he be doing the explaining?'

'He's still in hospital. He was slipped something to eat or drink by a woman who wanted to separate him from Paula. Unfortunately she gave him too much and it did more than just knock him out. He reacted badly to it, collapsed and had to be taken to hospital.'

Nick's voice grew sharper. 'Good heavens! Was his life in danger? Who did that and why?'

'He lost consciousness and needed medical help, certainly, but he's coming good now. As to who did it, there's a young woman who's been obsessed by him for years and resented him getting engaged to Paula. She's – not thinking clearly and the police are now dealing with the incident.'

'Good heavens! That must be Laurie. Paula's mentioned her.'

'Yes, it was. Look, can you get Paula to phone me on this number when she wakes up? It doesn't matter what time it is here, night or day. I'd like to explain everything to her and give her an important message from Richard.

He's recovering but he's not fully coherent yet, so they're keeping him in hospital, which is why I'm the one phoning to explain.'

'Yes, I'll get Paula to do that.'

'If I don't answer the phone straight away, I may be driving him home from hospital. She can leave a message and I promise faithfully that I'll get back to her as soon as I can.'

'All right.' Nick put the phone down with a soft 'Wow'.

'What's the matter?' Jonno asked.

He explained to his friend, then said abruptly, 'I'd better go round to Paula's and tell her about this in person and privately. We don't want her bursting into tears here. She thought Richard was deliberately avoiding her and she must care deeply for him or she'd not have got so upset. Can you keep an eye on the bar?'

'Of course. I can always call someone in from your list of casuals to help out if I need it.'

Marian's phone rang again a few minutes after she ended the call to Australia and, since she recognised the lawyer's number, she was tempted to ignore it again. But in the end she decided she'd better not do that and answered it.

'George Perett here.'

'Hello, George.'

'Marian, I've been trying to get hold of Paula and she's not answering her phone. I tried Richard too, but he's not picking up either. Is everything all right? I have something rather important to tell them both.'

So she explained for a second time that her nephew was in hospital, not going into details of why.

'Oh, dear! Oh, my goodness, how terrible for him! The trouble is, I was hoping he'd be there when I explain the situation to Paula.'

'Explain what?'

'That she isn't the heir.'

'What?' Then Marian's voice became grim as she said pointedly, 'So another mistake has been made about who inherits and another life has been disrupted.'

'I'm afraid so. We've been given some new information and I can assure you that we're one hundred per cent certain we've found the correct heir this time. I don't think Paula will be upset about that, though. Do you?'

'I doubt she'll be at all upset. She made it very plain to us all from the start that she didn't want the Abbey or to live in England. But she'd have the right to get rather angry about the disruption of her life and take legal action. I certainly would.'

'I'm afraid you're right. I need to tell her what's happened as soon as possible. It would be wrong for the news to get out before she's aware of the situation.'

Marian was sure she felt more upset about this turnaround than Paula would, possibly more than Richard would either. Her life was likely to be disrupted too if the inheritance went to a stranger. Presumably this new heir would want to change things at the Abbey, and if he had a wife who wanted to take over as housekeeper, Marian could see herself losing not only her job but her home there, both of which she loved.

'Who is this heir, George?'

'He's called Aubrey Lloyd and he's the only grandson of Jonathon Stovell.'

'I thought that branch of the family had died out.'

'No. We were misinformed about that or, rather, an inefficient operative was nudged into assuming it. But it turns out that the heir has been rather ill, which is why they did it. He's better now, thank goodness.'

'Could you tell me about him? Because with Richard unavailable, I might be the one who has to welcome him to the Abbey. Naturally, I shall be quite happy to show him round whenever he wants to visit, or help him to move in, or do whatever is needed.'

'Yes, of course. Very kind. And who knows the place better than you? I'm glad you reminded me of that. You must excuse me for not working out your likely involvement myself. We've only just found out about Mr Lloyd and, well, we've all been upset, not to say dreadfully embarrassed, about a mistake being made for a second time. Ms Grey really should be told about it as quickly as possible. And since we'd heard that she and Richard had got engaged, we were hoping he could help soften the news about the mix-up.'

'My guess is that it'll be a welcome relief to both of them. I can't go into details at the moment because it's in police hands, but the reason he's in hospital is because someone spiked his drink two nights ago and he reacted badly to the drugs. He also unknowingly behaved unkindly to Paula and she went back to Australia. I don't blame her for being upset, either.'

'She's gone back to Australia?'

'Yes. And she doesn't know that Richard's in hospital.'

'Good Lord! What next?'

Marian felt angry all over again at the mere thought of

what Laurie had done. She'd like to strangle her for causing that dangerous reaction. Only, you couldn't hold someone accountable who was clearly mentally ill. What a mess it all was! She realised George was speaking again and made an effort to concentrate.

'I'll have to try Paula's number in Australia, then. I really must contact her. In the meantime, I wonder if I can give Aubrey Lloyd your direct phone number, Marian? You will definitely be the best person to show him round the Abbey and I think he's planning to visit it straight away. I've seen how much you love the place.'

'I do. Hasn't Aubrey seen it before?'

'Not since a couple of quick visits as a child decades ago. As you will be aware, the older Roy Stovell became, the less he wanted anyone to visit him. He was a strange man, an archetypal recluse.'

'Yes. But he's left us with a superb library that's been listed as a heritage site. If I owned the Abbey, I'd charge people to visit the library and use the money to pay for the professional upkeep of it. And at least Roy had the good sense to hire Richard as well to look after the fabric of the place properly and do the main maintenance jobs. So it's remained weatherproof, even if it hasn't been prettied up as it could have been.'

Poor Roy, she thought. All he'd cared about was his beloved library. He had been another person not eager to inherit. Did the family own the house or did the house own them?

Aloud, she said, 'Anyway, you're welcome to give Aubrey my direct phone number. Tell him to leave a message if I don't answer and I'll return his call as soon as

I can, probably within the hour. Explain that I'm waiting to hear when Richard can leave hospital and may have to go and fetch him.'

'Have you any idea at all when that will be?'

'This morning sometime was all they could tell me. You know how vague hospitals can be about such things. Actually, I'd better get off the phone now in case they've been trying to contact me.'

They hadn't. Her phone would have beeped at her if someone else had been trying to get through to her. She ended the call without waiting for George to say goodbye. He was a pleasant chap but rather long-winded and fussy once he got talking.

Only after she'd signed off did she realise that George hadn't given her much detail about the heir. His marital status and age would have been helpful for a start. Oh well, she'd soon find that out one way or another.

She felt as if she were riding a roundabout with bystanders hurling information at her as she passed. She'd better take care she didn't fall off. At the moment she was the only one available to handle all this.

Her stomach growled at her and she decided to grab something to eat while she could.

Chapter Seventeen

An hour later, the hospital called to say Richard was ready to come home, so she set off.

Of course, her phone beeped at her while she was driving there. Well, if that was Aubrey Lloyd, he'd have to wait for her to get back to the abbey before she returned his call. You had to switch off your phone in most parts of the hospital and she wasn't having what could be an important conversation taking place in one of the public areas with every person nearby able to listen in.

She found Richard sitting in a waiting space near the nursing staff's counter in that ward.

He looked rather heavy-eyed but his face brightened when he saw her come through the self-closing doors.

She went across and explained that Paula had gone back to Australia and didn't even know he'd been hurt.

Then the sister beckoned her across and held up one hand to stop Richard joining them. 'Please remain seated, Mr Crawford. There's just a little more paperwork for your aunt to complete, then you can escape our clutches.'

Caged tigers sprang to Marian's mind as she looked at

him and she had difficulty hiding her amusement in spite of the seriousness of the situation. She read and signed the final document as quickly as she could.

The nurse came across to Richard with her and wagged one forefinger at him. 'Remember, Mr Crawford, the doctor said you're not to fly anywhere for at least two weeks.'

'I know what he said but I may have to go to Australia quite soon on important business.'

She looked at Marian and rolled her eyes. 'See if you can talk sense into him.'

'Tell me what exactly he can and can't do.'

'He should take it easy for a few days and not fly anywhere for at least two weeks.'

She turned back to Richard. 'You don't want to risk damaging your mental processes permanently, Mr Crawford, now do you? Your body and brain need to be totally clear of whatever was put into it and fully functioning again before you subject yourself to the physical stress of flying. If you're tempted, bear in mind how severely you reacted to what you'd been given.'

'But I need to see someone down under.'

'Are you actually booked on a flight to Australia?' the nurse asked.

'No, but there's no way the person I'm desperate to see will agree to come back here, that's for sure.' Paula was like a different person there or when they were alone.

'Please don't risk it,' the nurse repeated. As he stood up, she added, 'And don't try to leave the ward yet. You'll need to be taken out of the hospital premises in a wheelchair. Health and safety regulations.'

He turned to his aunt, spreading his arms wide. 'What

the hell can go wrong walking out of the hospital?' He breathed deeply and walked across to stand near the double doors, shoulders hunched, arms folded and back turned towards them.

'He has good reason to be upset,' Marian murmured apologetically.

'He has equally good reason to be careful.'

When Marian joined him, he muttered, 'How ridiculous can you get? A wheelchair indeed. I've a good mind to simply walk out. What could they do about it? Bring me down with a rugby tackle? Health and safety wouldn't like that either.'

'Only a few more minutes to wait,' Marian coaxed. 'That nurse doesn't make the rules and she'll be the one who'll get into trouble if you walk out.'

Not till they were finally outside and sitting in her car did he say, 'I do have to see Paula. I need to talk to her, make sure she knows I was under the influence of a mixture of sedatives and drugs and would never avoid her on purpose or cuddle up to that stupid bitch.' After a slight hesitation, he added, 'Have you spoken to her yet?'

'No.'

'Well, I need to make sure she knows I really care for her. Please! If you speak to her first, tell her that for me.'

'I've only spoken to her friend Nick, but he assured me she was all right. She was sleeping off her exhaustion after the flight so I didn't get a chance to speak to her. And before you try to phone her, I have some other news to catch you up on, and I think I'd better tell you exactly how you behaved at the dinner party when you were under the influence of those drugs, because that's what sent her rushing back to Australia.'

'Oh, hell! What did I do? I can't remember that part of the evening at all.'

'No, I realise that now, but I don't blame Paula for jumping to the conclusion that you didn't care about her, thanks to Laurie. She sat cuddling up to you and you leant against her, making no attempt to stop her or to get away. We know now that you were only semi-conscious but that wasn't obvious then.'

He groaned and buried his head in his hands.

She didn't start the car, sagging for a moment with her arms resting on the steering wheel. She wished she wasn't the one who had to take care of everything at the moment because she was feeling pretty tired, too.

'You look exhausted too,' he said quietly. 'Sorry it's fallen on your shoulders to sort this out.'

She forced herself to sit upright. 'Yes. I am rather tired, but it needed dealing with. It's been an eventful couple of days. Let's leave the serious talking till we get home, eh? I need to concentrate on my driving.'

'I could drive.'

She speared him with one scornful glance and set off.

Once they were back at the Abbey, Marian took Richard into the kitchen and pointed to the chairs at the table where they ate their meals. 'Sit. We'll have our talk here. It's a chilly day and this is always the warmest place in the house. I'm feeling shivery even if you aren't.'

She went to put the kettle on and, after plonking a cup of instant coffee down in front of him and getting one for herself, she sat down opposite him. She sipped her own with an appreciative murmur, sitting there silent for a few moments before she looked across at him.

'Right, Richard. The big news is that they've found the real heir to Stovell Abbey, guaranteed one hundred per cent certain to be the right one this time. So Paula is off the hook.'

'Really? Oh, thank goodness for that! It made her so unhappy. And me too. Who is it?'

Once she'd explained the relationships that had led to Aubrey Lloyd and why he'd been in hiding, Richard gave her a beaming smile. 'That's good. I'm glad he's recovered, but I'm even happier that it'll take the biggest stressor completely off Paula.'

'You'll be sorry not to live here, though, which you might have done if you'd married the heir.'

'I've told you before: I'd never marry anyone for the sake of a house. It upset me when I first found out I was the heir and then it upset me all over again when I found out I wasn't. But I'm used to the situation now. If fate socks you in the face, you move on, don't you? I need to make a life elsewhere. But first I need to sort out my emotional life. It's Paula avoiding me that I'm most worried about and I shan't lose those worries till I've seen her in person and talked to her properly. I do still believe and pray that there can be an "us".'

'Then I hope so too.'

'But if I can't fly out to Australia, how am I to persuade her that I care about us getting back together?'

'There are such things as phones and other devices or computer programs for communicating long-distance, you know. Presumably she's already given you reason to hope.'

'We were starting to make a – call it a connection. I'm hoping it will still be there. Only, I want to make sure our relationship has time for nurturing.'

He smiled before continuing. 'If neither of us is legally tied to Stovell Abbey, I believe we'll have a far better chance of making a happy life together. I not only find her physically attractive, you know. She's also interesting and amusing. Or she was in Australia and some of her liveliness came back whenever we were on our own together. I doubt I'd ever grow tired of her.'

She studied him, head on one side. 'I've never heard you talk like that about any other woman.'

'I've never met anyone like her. And I'm quite prepared to go and live in Australia. In fact, I rather like the idea of doing that and I'd looked into it a little of my own accord before I was told I was the heir.'

'I'd miss you horribly.'

He reached out to squeeze her hand. 'I'd miss you too. We'll have to find you a husband to keep you happily busy.'

She let out a scornful puff of air. 'As if. And the authorities might not allow you to stay there. The rules for settling permanently in Australia are pretty tight, I gather.'

'I had a quick glance at the requirements when I first considered it and you need to have enough money to set up a business. It's a no-brainer. That's what I'd want to do anyway.'

She didn't say anything else. Putting relationships right was easier said than done in her experience, and in the end it was wisest to leave it to the two individuals concerned.

She coaxed her nephew into having something to eat and, while he was enjoying a toasted sandwich, she picked up her phone and returned Aubrey Lloyd's call. The poor man must be getting extremely impatient by now.

He answered the call almost immediately. 'Mrs Saunders?'

'Yes. Sorry to keep you waiting, Mr Lloyd. I was picking up my nephew from hospital.'

'Do call me Aubrey. I'm not keen on formality.'

'And please call me Marian. I'm not the formal type either.'

'Marian it is. Is your nephew all right now?'

'He's fine, thank you.'

'I gather you're the domestic manager at Stovell Abbey.'

'Yes. Fancy title. I just call myself the housekeeper.'

'The lawyer said you know the house better than anyone and have quite a lot of expertise in caring for historical buildings.'

'Probably. I've lived here for well over a decade.'

'I've been wondering . . . Look, I know it's short notice, but can I come there this afternoon and have a look round? I can take a leisurely drive back to Wales afterwards. I'm dying to see it because I have only vague memories of it from when I was a child.'

'Yes, of course you can come. Actually, Aubrey, as the new owner, you don't need to ask anyone's permission.'

His laugh sounded slightly embarrassed. 'I haven't quite got used to it yet, though I'm delighted about it, naturally.'

'Will you be coming on your own? What about your wife and family? Mr Perett didn't give me any details about them. I think he was too upset by the news that his firm had made such a big mistake to think clearly.'

'He did seem rather flustered at my sudden appearance on the scene, to put it mildly.'

They both chuckled at the same time, then he said, 'To answer your question about family, I'm a widower with one grown-up daughter. Rhona won't be able to join me on this visit, though. She has to deal with an important business matter and she's in the middle of planning her divorce, fortunately a fairly amicable one.'

'That would keep anyone busy.'

'Yes. But she'll cope with it all. She's a brilliant organiser. So, back to my original question: if I set off now, I can be with you in just over an hour. Will that be all right?'

'Of course it will. When you get here, you'd be best coming round to the back of the house to park your car. There's plenty of space. If you continue along the drive it'll lead you there. I'll look forward to meeting you.'

She ended the call and turned to Richard. 'The heir, Aubrey Lloyd, is coming here this afternoon to look round. He has a rather nice speaking voice, not to mention a good sense of humour.'

'That's great.'

But she could see that Richard's mind wasn't on their visitor. He was definitely in love, and about time too. She just hoped Paula really felt the same way about him.

'I think I'll go and make some phone calls before he arrives, if you don't mind, Aunt Marian.'

'Of course I don't. Shall I let you know when he gets here?'

'No. I want to try to catch Paula and I'm also late contacting a couple of people about quotes for ongoing work on this house. And to tell you the truth, I'll probably need a nap by the time I've finished. I'm still not feeling all that bright. I'll join you when I can but if I don't appear during his visit, please tell him what happened and give him my apologies.'

'Do what you need to. I can cope.'

Story of her life, that, she thought, not for the first time: *Marian can cope!* She'd lost count of the number of times people had said that to or about her over the years, usually while dumping another unwanted task on her.

Her nephew would probably be trying to contact Paula at this very moment and she could only hope he wasn't letting himself in for further disappointment.

As she stood up, she glanced at the kitchen clock. Oh dear! She'd been intending to find time to ring Liz and ask how Laurie was but she didn't think she'd better try now because looking after the heir was far more important. Not that she cared particularly about Laurie, but she did care about Liz.

It must be very painful to have a daughter who was – well, so damaged. Why did these things happen? Perhaps one day medical experts would find a way to put them right. Not likely to happen in what was left of her lifetime, though. Medical progress usually seemed to move along in small, careful steps, with only occasional leaps forward.

Aubrey arrived exactly an hour and ten minutes after his phone call. When she heard him stop outside, Marian couldn't resist peeping out of the kitchen window and thought he looked as pleasant as he'd sounded, if a trifle frail still. You could sometimes tell when people were recovering from serious medical problems. By her age, you'd been trained to do that because it was a rare person who hadn't seen bad things happen to some of their friends and relatives.

But at least this man was recovering and the clear, bright half-smile he presented to the world as he studied the back of the house showed his nature, because he didn't know he was being watched and he was still smiling.

She went outside to greet him and he shook her hand warmly, clasping it in both his like a man who had what she called the touchy-feely gene and was quite at home with his own emotions.

'It's lovely to meet you,' he said.

'Nice to meet you too, Aubrey. Welcome to Stovell Abbey.'

'I'm excited to be here and it's great that I'm going to be shown round this first time by someone who really knows the place. I've always loved old buildings.'

'I enjoy showing people round who're appreciative of the historical aspects.' She waited to lead the way inside because he was still standing outside staring up at the house.

'Lovely brickwork, isn't it? They used much smaller bricks back in the times this house was built. I stopped to look at the front façade on my way round to the back, and it's even more beautiful in real life than it looks in the only photo I have of it.'

'I'm biased, I admit, but I think it's a very special house.' She studied him surreptitiously. He looked like a member of the Stovell family with that lean, elegant face. His hair was thinning a little on top but still retained plenty of that rich chestnut colour with only threads of grey. And he had beautiful eyes of a vivid blue colour with long eyelashes. Strange thing to think that way about a man, that, but there you were. His eyes were beautiful.

When they were inside, she asked, 'Would you like a cup of tea or coffee first?'

'I'd love a cup of tea, if that's all right with you. I'm not a coffee drinker.'

By the time she'd put the kettle on, he'd wandered across the big, square kitchen and disappeared into the hall as if the house was drawing him in further. She followed him, stopping to find out what was catching his attention this time. He hadn't gone far and was staring up at the huge stained-glass window next to the stairs with an expression of awe on his face. And no wonder. It was about three metres wide by five metres high, a triptych featuring St George and the Dragon, surrounded by fanciful fairies and other fabled creatures. It was one of her favourite features of the house.

'That window is abso-bloody-lutely fantastic!' He turned a beaming smile on her. 'I can't believe this is all mine. Why don't I remember the window from my childhood visits?'

'How old were you?'

'Eight and ten.'

'You were probably restricted to the nursery wing and the grounds because Roy didn't like visiting children to go anywhere near his precious library. Come and see it. I think it's magnificent but not everyone is lit up by the sight of two storeys of bookcases.'

They went in and he stood in the doorway, shoulder to shoulder with her, letting out a long, low whistle. 'Well, this definitely lights me up. Fancy having an upper gallery lined with books and stairs leading up to it. Oh, and there's a ladder on wheels giving access to the upper shelves downstairs.'

'All the trappings of a real library,' she said quietly. 'Are you a reader?'

'Oh yes! I absolutely love reading. I've done a lot of it in the past year because I was rather limited physically. I've found some superb new authors.'

'Then you'll enjoy exploring the library's contents. Roy had some rare old illustrated texts which he kept locked under glass display areas, because they're valuable and he considered them museum-class treasures. He believed ordinary books were for reading, though. There are a few rows of murder mysteries half-hidden in one corner, his secret weakness.'

'I like those too.'

'I have the key to the glass cabinet safely hidden from view here.' She showed him the secret place.

'I'd better not get started on studying titles or I'll never leave. I think it's best that I begin with an overview of the whole house then as time passes I can get to know the details of each room.'

He gave a happy-sounding sigh at that prospect and again she smiled with him.

'There's a small modern cloakroom over there under the stairs, which you might like to use. I'll finish making our cups of tea then we'll continue the tour.'

In the kitchen, she smiled and nodded approval of what she'd seen of him so far. Even on the phone she had thought him very pleasant, and in person he was physically attractive too. Somehow she felt as if the house liked him as well. It was fanciful of her, but she'd always felt Stovell

Abbey had a character and opinions of its own.

Hope crept through her on tiptoe. Perhaps, just perhaps, if he didn't have a wife, she might be kept on as housekeeper. She certainly didn't want to leave, was in the middle of a couple of small improvement projects that she'd put a lot of planning into.

After he'd gulped down the tea, he gave her a slightly embarrassed smile. 'Would you mind if we carried on with our tour now? It's all so exciting.'

'Of course I wouldn't mind. We'll finish off the ground floor but I think the cellars can wait till another day. They're dark and hide a couple of fiddly secret areas, which I'll demonstrate on your next visit.'

'I'm hoping to move in next time I come here.'

'I'll make sure the master's bedroom is ready for your arrival. I'll have a quick peep in on my nephew when we go upstairs, if you don't mind. I need to keep an eye on him.' She gave him details of what had happened to Richard.

Aubrey looked at her in shocked surprise. 'How terrible!'

'Yes. But he survived.'

They did a walk-round, not lingering to examine any of the rooms in detail and after about another hour, he smiled at her apologetically. 'You were right about how much we could fit in today. I'm sorry but I still get tired more quickly than I used to. I need to rest for a while before I leave, if you wouldn't mind.'

'How about you do that with your feet up on the sofa in the morning room and a slice of my fruit cake disappearing into you bite by bite?' She made a snapping gesture with her fingers and he clasped his hands together in mock ecstasy.

'You've caught me by the heartstrings. It's years since I've had home-made fruit cake. My daughter isn't interested in cooking but I used to enjoy it and fruit cake is one of my weaknesses.' He licked his lips involuntarily at the thought of it.

'Do you prefer it plain or Lancashire-style with sharp cheese?'

'Lancashire-style. My wife was from there so she trained me in what she considered to be the correct way of eating it.'

When she would have left him in peace, Aubrey insisted she stay and continue chatting. 'It's physical tiredness mainly so if you stay for a while I can rest as well as continuing to enjoy your company.'

That made her feel good. She was enjoying his company too and was surprised at how quickly time had passed. When she noticed that nearly an hour had gone by, she excused herself to go and check on Richard again because he hadn't come down to join them.

She eased his bedroom door open a little and saw that as she had guessed, he'd fallen fast asleep. He'd been looking drowsy when she peeped in earlier so she hadn't worried about introducing him to Aubrey yet.

On coming back downstairs, she found that Aubrey was also asleep. What should she do? Wake him and send him on his way or suggest he stay the night? She glanced at the window and frowned. It was getting dark already.

Well, it wasn't for her to dictate what he did but she didn't like to think of him driving all the way to Wales when he was so tired, so she'd offer him the option. It'd take over two hours for him to get there, maybe three, depending on traffic flows and exactly where his country cottage was located, something she wasn't sure about.

She went back into the kitchen and started getting ready to cook tea. She'd planned to do a stir-fry so could easily add a few more ingredients if he stayed.

It was a further hour before Aubrey re-joined her. She'd peeped in twice but he didn't seem to have stirred.

Footsteps sounded in the hall and he came into the kitchen, looking rueful. 'I'm so sorry to have fallen asleep on you. Not very polite of me, is it? I've not recovered my physical energy as much as I thought yet, I'm afraid.'

'I let you sleep because you looked so tired. Um, I wondered if you'd like to stay the night? We have a selection of clothing oddments and sleepwear that have been left behind over the years, so I can supply your needs and there are some items of clothing bought for Roy which he never wore, so they haven't even been out of the packets. You're about the same size as he was so you can even have clean clothes tomorrow.'

'Are you sure you wouldn't mind my staying?'

'Heavens, no. I'd enjoy your company. It can get too quiet here at times.'

'Well, then, I would like to spend the night. But fortunately I've just been staying with my daughter so I do have my own nightwear – though a warm dressing gown and maybe a clean shirt tomorrow wouldn't come amiss.'

'That's settled, then.'

Footsteps on the stairs had them both turning round and Richard came into the kitchen.

She introduced the two men and gestured to the seating area, setting an example by sitting down there.

'So sorry. I wasn't avoiding you, Aubrey; I was sound asleep.' Richard rubbed his temple and added, 'Those damned drugs that fool woman fed me have left me with an ongoing headache. Do you have any suitable painkillers, Marian?'

She stood up. 'Yes, of course. Did you get through to Paula?'

'No. She doesn't seem to have her phone switched on so I couldn't even leave a message.'

'Perhaps she's jet-lagged and not into Australian time yet.'

'Could be. It certainly hit me hard when I went there to see her the first time. I made a real fool of myself.' He took the packet of pills she was holding out to him and popped two out while she got him a glass of water.

After he'd swallowed them, she explained that their guest would be spending the night there with them. 'I'm going to put you in the owner's suite, Aubrey. After all, it's where you'll be sleeping when you move here if you follow tradition.'

'I shan't mind where I sleep tonight but I must admit the owner's suite was lovely and I shall enjoy waking up there tomorrow.'

But it was Richard who went back to bed first and left the other two chatting as they sipped a nightcap of cognac.

'Your nephew doesn't look well at all,' Aubrey commented.

'He isn't. Now, before I start enjoying this cognac, I'd just like to phone my friend, who is the mother of the young woman who drugged Richard. The police have been involved and I haven't managed to speak to Liz yet and find out what action they took. I won't be long.'

But there wasn't any answer from Liz so she could only leave a message. Was no one answering their phone today?

She re-joined Aubrey and they enjoyed sipping their nightcaps and chatting about this and that until they both yawned at the same time.

'I think I need my bed now,' he said. 'It's more or less my usual time anyway.'

'Mine too.'

'When time do you have breakfast?'

'About seven usually because I'm an early riser. Don't worry if you're not. I can easily put something together for you when you get up.'

'I'm an early riser too.'

'See you in the morning, then.'

Chapter Eighteen

Paula woke feeling lethargic and when she opened her eyes, it took her a while to realise that she really was back at home and this wasn't a dream. She reached out for a tissue from the bedside box as happy tears filled her eyes, then she suddenly remembered that Nick had told her Richard had been hospitalised and guilt shot through her.

He'd been ill enough at the dinner party to be taken to A&E! She'd known something was wrong and all she'd done about it was throw a huff and run away. She felt deeply ashamed about that now.

Only, she couldn't have stayed in England much longer, just could not. She frowned and wondered, not for the first time, why she only ever felt right here in Australia.

She really ought to phone Richard and find out how he was. She hesitated. Perhaps she should wait a day or two until she'd sorted out what she wanted from life, and also until she was in better control of her own emotions. She'd never felt so wobbly and tearful. The slightest thing kept setting her off.

Still lost in thought, she got out of bed and made her

way across the room to the en-suite bathroom, stopping for a moment to lean against the door frame as she felt slightly dizzy. Flying such long distances certainly played havoc with your body.

She smiled at the window. Sunshine from outside seemed to fill the whole house and it certainly brightened up her bathroom and made her feel instantly happier. She took another shower, then grabbed a skirt and top. For once it didn't matter what colour they were as long as they were lightweight and summery.

She danced round the bedroom, finishing up with a curtsey and a loud 'Ta-da!' in front of the full-length wall mirror.

She wondered what the temperature was going to be today, always an important consideration at this time of year, so went downstairs and switched on her desktop computer. Now that she was no longer occupying the granny flat, this was sitting in its old home in her spacious office, positioned so that she looked out at the water when she sat there. She had spent many happy hours working in here.

She must remember to go and check out the granny flat, not to mention moving the rest of her personal possessions back into the main house. She wasn't letting the flat out again, would manage somehow. And though she didn't want to take money from the Stovell inheritance, she did think they owed her the cost of coming back to Australia. She'd claim that another day.

She clicked on the weather forecast site. Aha! Today's maximum would be about 30 degrees Celsius and it wasn't going to be humid. Perfect weather, her favourite temperature of all. Not screaming hot but warm enough that there would be no need for a cardigan, let alone having to top your indoor clothes with an outer coat, scarf and gloves whenever you left the house, even if it wasn't raining.

Some of the people she'd met in England had shuddered at the mere thought of the higher temperatures, but you got used to staying out of the direct sun during the hottest part of the day because people were more careful these days about protecting their skin. And she suspected English houses were built to keep the warmth in, whereas Aussie houses tried to keep it out.

Anyway, just about all the places people used regularly in Western Australia were air conditioned: houses, cars, shopping centres, offices – and of course their bar was too.

She pulled her phone out of her shoulder bag and stared at it. She really ought to get in touch with Richard. No, it was after midnight there now, so he'd have gone to bed. Not a good time to try to explain her panic-stricken flight from England, especially when she couldn't even explain that fully to herself. She felt such a fool for fleeing like that.

And what about their ongoing relationship? Did it even exist? She didn't know for certain how she felt about the possibilities and Richard might not either. One minute she wanted desperately to make a life with him and the next the mere thought of trying to do that terrified her. He might love Stovell Abbey and Wiltshire but she'd felt as if she were in an alien land there. So in which country would they be able to make a life together?

It was even possible that he wouldn't try to get in touch

with her again; she might have put him off already. Then she shook her head. No, Richard wouldn't change his mind so easily! And neither would she.

She'd never met a man she felt so attracted to – well, she loved him when they were on their own, but not as much when he was surrounded by his friends and neighbours. *Loved?* She sighed at the idea. Trust her to fall in love with someone hedged about by difficulties in carrying things through to the usual conclusion.

The one thing she was certain of was that she wasn't going to live in England, so if that was the price of being with him, she wouldn't pay it. Couldn't.

And if those lawyers continued to pester her to take up residence at Stovell Abbey, she'd hire a lawyer of her own here to put an end to it once and for all. Surely there must be some way of getting out of accepting an inheritance you didn't want and passing it on to a family member who did want it.

Someone rang the doorbell and she ran down the stairs to peep through the 'squint' and check who was outside. Nick. Normally she would be delighted to see him but today she found it hard to face even him. Only, he had a key and if she didn't answer the door she knew he'd come in to check that she was all right.

She unlocked it and opened it wide, staring at him numbly, unable to form a single word. If you didn't see your way clearly inside your own head, how could you talk about a problem, especially a major one like this?

'Let me give you a hug first of all, Paula love. The only other time I've seen you look unhappy for this long was just after your stepmother died.'

'I still miss Jenny.' She nestled against him for a moment, then pulled away. 'At the moment I'm bewildered more than unhappy. I don't know what I want to do, Nick, haven't the faintest clue. I wish those damned lawyers had never found me. I do not want to own Stovell Abbey and I refuse point-blank to live there. Oh dear! That visit to England seems to have knocked all the stuffing out of me.'

'Well, Australia will soon put it back again. Let's make some coffee and sit down with it to have a chat. Have you had any breakfast?'

'No. I'm not hungry.'

'Oblige me by eating one piece of toast, at least. I don't want you fainting on me.' He didn't wait for an answer but rummaged in her freezer, pulled out some bread and set a slice in her toaster.

She did as he asked, feeling too lethargic to protest and she still felt a little nauseous, so perhaps the toast would settle her stomach.

After she'd forced it down, he suggested another piece but she shook her head. 'Tell me what else has happened, Nick. I can see you're bursting with news.'

'Let's sit on the sofa.' He came to sit next to her and took her hand. 'They've found another heir, one with a closer claim to it than you or Richard.'

She stared at him. 'Really?'

'I never lie to you.'

Anger welled up inside her. 'Those stupid lawyers messed my life about and it's all been for *nothing*?' Her voice had risen to a shrill pitch by the end of this.

'So it seems. Only, it did have its good side.'

'What?'

'You met a guy you liked rather a lot. That hasn't happened for a long time.' He gave her a teasing look and added, 'And he likes you in return if his attempted phone calls are anything to go by.'

'Phone calls? Richard's been phoning me here? He's out of hospital then?'

'He's been trying to. Only you've kept your phone switched off. But I'm getting ahead of myself. Let's go through things in the order they happened to me. His aunt phoned here first to find out whether you'd returned to Australia.'

'Why was she the one to phone? She doesn't even like me.'

'Richard was still in hospital at the time and in no state to phone anyone.'

'How long was he in hospital? I thought it was just a quick trip to A&E. Is he all right?'

Nick went through what Marian had told him, pausing patiently to wait for Paula to take it in and look up again once she was ready to hear more.

'Then they found out about the real heir. That's pretty important to you, eh?'

'Yes. But talk about a mix-up!'

'Isn't it just?'

'Still, I'm free of it all now, for certain.' She gave him the first unalloyed smile he'd seen.

'Do you want to be free of everything and everyone, though? What about Richard?'

Another silence, then she muttered, 'No, I don't want to be free of him. Well, I think I don't.'

He frowned at her. 'It's not like you to dither around.'

She scowled at him. 'How can I be sure? He and I have only known one another for a couple of weeks and for most of that time we've been with other people. I haven't even spoken to him for a couple of days. What exactly did he say when he phoned? Is he out of hospital now? And is he pleased about them finding a new heir?'

'He didn't say much, wants you to phone him when you wake up so that you two can talk properly. Oh, and I'm to tell you that he isn't allowed to fly anywhere for two weeks because of how that drugging incident affected him, so he can't come to see you yet or else he'd be on a plane to Western Australia already.'

Nick waited expectantly and though she didn't comment on that, he saw her smile. 'You could go back there temporarily, though, if you're eager to talk to him.'

The smile vanished and she shuddered. 'No, thank you. It'll take me a while to get over that last flight. I suppose it's the time change that's left me feeling wobbly and nauseous. Or else I may have picked up some sort of virus on the plane. I had to travel economy and you're crammed together like sardines.'

'If you're not rushing back to see Richard, perhaps you don't care enough about him to want an ongoing relationship?'

Her response was swift. 'I do care.' Then she clapped one hand to her mouth as if the words had escaped her control.

He couldn't stop himself smirking at getting her to admit that without any ifs or buts. 'If you think I can't tell that you care about him, whatever you say or do, you've got rocks in your head, my girl.'

She began fiddling with the edge of her tee shirt. 'I just don't want to rush into a relationship blindly with someone so different from me.'

'People usually talk to one another and feel their way through differences and difficult situations. Indeed, differences can make an ongoing relationship more interesting.'

'It's not easy to get past differences from ten thousand miles away, Nick.'

'No, I suppose not.'

'And people don't usually mess up the early stages as I've done. I may have put him off me for good.'

'You know you can talk to me about anything, Paula love. I'm not so far away.'

She gave his hand a squeeze. 'I know that, Nick, and I probably will talk once I'm feeling clearer-headed.'

'Give me a quick summary of what's holding you back from contacting Richard now.'

'I can't see him transplanting to Australia. He's so very much the English gentleman.' She sighed. 'You should see him in evening dress.'

He kept silent and waited for her to continue.

'It's one of the things I love about him and yet, you saw him in our bar that first time. He stood out like a sore thumb.' She smiled reminiscently, then it faded as she added, 'Just as I stood out like a sore thumb in his territory. He loves Stovell Abbey, you know. His aunt does too, even more than him, I'd guess.'

'She was very pleasant on the phone.'

'Ha! She was distinctly hostile to me at first and

she's like a mother to him. Our relationship might come between them or theirs might come between us.'

'It's not like you to look at all the negatives. You usually bowl right through obstacles to get past a bad situation.'

She shrugged. 'I don't usually feel so dopey. Jet lag sucks.'

'What about this Laurie person? Does she stand between you now that you know what she did to him?'

'No. Of course not. She's deluded, needs medical help.'

'Right, then. Here's my initial take on it. You should phone him and make a start at talking about your feelings and then you should use that app on your phone so that you can see each other's face as you talk. Then you should slowly and carefully work out together what to do about it.'

'I hate talking to faces on screens, you know I do. I prefer real life encounters.'

'In my experience, it's a life enhancer to have a significant other you care about, so get over that and sort it out. I don't want you to spend your life alone, Paula love.'

'I don't, either.'

'Did you realise your voice goes softer when you talk about Richard? I'm not sure whether you're trying to persuade yourself that it won't work because you're afraid of getting into another relationship after your marriage failed, which, as I've said before, was Phil's fault. We're told not to speak ill of the dead, so don't get me started, but I could say a lot about him. He didn't know much about pulling his weight in a partnership, how wonderful it can be.'

She could guess what was making him say this. 'Things going well with Jonno, are they, Uncle Nickykins?'

He gave her a beaming smile. 'Yes. He and I are getting along really well.'

'I'm glad for you.'

'So you'll stop rearing back like a frightened rabbit and contact Richard, give him a chance?'

'Yes. But not till I've got over this jet lag. I'm not feeling all that well today. And . . . will you tell me honestly: can you really see him transplanting permanently to Australia? I know what it's like to be in a foreign country and feel as if you're a different species to the people you meet.'

Nick was just about to speak when she added, 'And that's not only from my visit to England, but also from when I was a child. Tony moved us somewhere new every few months. I still have nightmares about those years and trying to make friends in so many new places, always being the odd one out from kindergarten onwards. And I couldn't invite other children to play with me at home because we were usually renting a caravan or somewhere seedy. If I hadn't had Jenny to love me, I don't know how I'd have survived.'

'She was a fine woman.' He waited and when she said nothing, urged, 'Phone him, love.'

'Not today.' She rubbed her forehead. 'In fact, I think I'll go back to bed, I feel so dopey.'

'Will you at least answer the phone if he rings?'

'Not today, Nick.'

He studied her. 'You're definitely looking pale. I think you've either run yourself ragged or else you have indeed picked up some sort of virus. Or both. Take as much time as you need off work. I have Jonno to help me at the bar now.' He waved one hand in the direction of the stairs. 'Go on back to bed. I'll see myself out.'

Richard's phone rang just as he was getting ready to join his aunt and Aubrey for breakfast. He pounced on it, but saw to his disappointment that it wasn't a call from Paula but from Nick.

'Richard here.'

He listened to Nick explaining how confused Paula was, not to mention jet-lagged. He could understand that. Look at how he'd messed up his first encounter with her because he'd underestimated his own disorientation after the long flight.

'She and I do need to discuss this face to face, Nick, but I daren't fly out to see her yet. I was warned so fiercely about the risks I'd be taking by the doctor and the nurse that I'd be stupid to try it. Especially as I'm still feeling ridiculously weary if I do much.'

'My advice would be that you wait anyway and give her the time she clearly needs. She has hang-ups from her childhood to face as well. As soon as she starts to come out of her shell, I'll push her into contacting you.'

'If she tries to break our relationship before we get a chance to talk, I'll do more than that, Nick. I'll come out to see her on the next plane, risks or not. I won't believe it's not possible for us to at least try being together till I see her face as she talks about it and as I put my arms round her.'

'I'm glad to hear you say that. You stick to it. She's worth it, believe me.'

A minute's silence, then Richard said, 'Thank you for

your help, Nick. Would you do one more thing: remind her that I love her?'

'Yes but only because I can tell that you do. Dear me, I should run an agony column in the newspaper, shouldn't I?'

'You'd be brilliant at it.'

Richard put the phone down, worrying about what a tangle this all was. 'I'm not giving her up,' he muttered.

When he went downstairs, he looked at the food Marian had set out and said, 'I was woken by a phone call from Australia but I'm not feeling really hungry so I'll just go back to bed. You two enjoy your breakfast. See you next time, Aubrey.'

Once they'd finished eating, Aubrey said, 'I'd normally do the clearing up since you cooked, Marian, but I don't know where anything goes here yet.'

'It's not a big chore with a dishwasher.'

'Could you leave things for a while? Because I have to leave soon and I'd like to discuss your position here before I go. Perhaps we could grab another cup of tea while we talk?'

When they were sitting down, he asked, 'Are you planning to leave when I take over or can I persuade you to stay on as house manager or whatever you'd like to call the position?'

'I'd very much like to stay on. I love Stovell Abbey, as you might have noticed.'

'I'm delighted to hear that.'

They beamed at one another across the table.

'That's settled then, but I think we ought to hire additional help around the place.'

'There hasn't been a lot of money to spare for such extravagances, as Roy called them.' She grimaced at the memory. 'I just dealt with the rooms we used and left the others to gather dust.'

'I need to find out exactly how the finances stand, but I do have some money of my own from my father's family, so I think we can safely add another cleaner to start going through the rooms I shall need to use to house Rhona and the grandchildren when they come to visit me.'

'I shall enjoy arranging that.'

'And we should surely put dust covers over the furniture in the rooms we don't plan to use. We'll discuss which they are after I move in.'

'We'd have to buy some covers first. The ones that had been used here over the years have mostly disintegrated. And some items don't do well with the cheapie plastic covers, which can make things sweat.'

He grinned. 'I can afford to buy new covers of whatever type is needed.'

'Sorry. Of course you can. I'm still not used to a saner approach to money. Roy wouldn't spend a penny on anything but the library if he could help it.'

'I'm not Roy. Do you know anyone local who'd like a job as a cleaner or shall we need to advertise for help?'

'I know an older married couple who'd love to do it by job-sharing, if you're OK with that sort of thing. They're partly retired and looking for part-time jobs.'

'I'm fine with that. Now, next question. How soon can I move in without upsetting things too much?'

'What have the lawyers said about that?'

He rolled his eyes. 'I couldn't get a straight answer out

of them, so I'd rather ask you because you're in charge of the house. I doubt the lawyers will chuck me out again once I'm in, not if you've accepted me.'

'As far as I'm concerned you can move in as soon as you like. Tomorrow if you wish. The rooms are always ready, except for last-minute dusting and airing of beds.'

'Then I'll see how soon it can be arranged. Not tomorrow but I can pack up and move everything in a few days. Would that genuinely be all right with you?'

'Absolutely. In fact, it'd be good to have company, as I already said.'

'Excellent. I'm ready for company too, after a very quiet year. It'll be great to go out and about whenever I like. I'd stay over another night and do some more poking round the house, but unfortunately I've already made arrangements to see someone later this afternoon. And also I need to put my Welsh cottage on the market. It served its purpose wonderfully but it will always remind me of, well, times I'd rather forget. I shall be happy to leave it behind.'

He glanced round the room, smiling, then said simply, 'I don't know why I felt at home so quickly here but I did.'

She waved him goodbye a little later, sorry to see him go but looking forward to spending more time with him once he moved in. She'd really enjoyed his company and thought he'd felt the same easy connection between them as well.

What a delightful person he was.

Chapter Nineteen

Richard tried several times to phone Paula and she didn't answer any of his calls. He left a brief message on her answering service saying he was looking forward to hearing from her, then he sat on his bed staring at the phone. Nick had told him she needed time to get used to the latest happenings. *How much time?* he wondered.

Talk about life's ups and downs. Well, he had a lot he could get on with here and would turn his attention to that while he waited for her. He didn't believe in wasting time. The first thing would be to clear his personal possessions out of the big house and sort out what he needed and what he wouldn't need till he had a permanent home of his own.

Whatever happened, he wasn't going back to working at Stovell Abbey. That was one thing he was sure about.

He'd made enquiries about settling permanently in Australia a while ago, before he'd been told he was the heir. He had felt then he would easily be able to meet their criteria by starting up a business there.

Now, he was going back to those plans, whether his move was to be with Paula or not. But surely she'd not changed her mind about them as a couple? They got on so well. And that easy feeling had happened so quickly.

He left notes in the estate office about any project still in progress, together with his mobile phone number and email address in case something needed further explanation. He didn't think the new owner would mind him leaving his possessions in one of the old stables. He left a note about that too, in case he didn't get a chance to ask him, after which he felt so desperately sleepy he simply had to lie down.

To his great disappointment, when he got up he found it had been a longer nap than he'd expected and Aubrey had already left to drive back to Wales. 'Damn! I wanted to give him my resignation and work out with him how best to do the handover. I'll have to send my resignation to the lawyers instead.'

'Don't you want to wait and see how things go with Paula before resigning?'

'No. I'd already been thinking of moving somewhere else, maybe to a galaxy far, far away.'

She laughed gently at that. He'd been addicted to the *Star Wars* movies as a lad. 'Have you any idea what you may do with your life?'

'I hope to set up a business that will put me in regular contact with people. Being the architect in charge of repairs here left me on my own in the estate office much of the time, and that's not how I want to spend my life.'

'You always were the gregarious type. What sort of work are you looking at, then?'

'Something in the hospitality area, I think. I might buy a country house that I can turn into a hotel, one where I can run small functions such as weddings or other family celebrations, as well as offering accommodation on a nightly basis. I don't want to take on a big place and run massive functions. I just need somewhere to enjoy life, meet people and bring in an income. I'd begun to consider that for my next step in life before I was told I was the heir but felt I had to set my other plans aside and do my duty by the family.'

'I shall miss having you around, Richard.'

'Ditto. I'm lucky that I've been left enough family money to start up my own business, aren't I?'

'Yes, very.'

'And I feel even more lucky that I met Paula. What are the odds against that with us living at opposite ends of the earth?'

'I hope it works out for you. Once I got to know her and realised she didn't want to take away your inheritance and wasn't just using you, I quite liked her.'

'Most people do.' He was silent for a few moments, smiling at some memory or other. 'Anyway, I can sort my things out here while I wait to be allowed to fly again. I'd be on my way to join Paula already but for Laurie, damn her. Have you heard what's happened to her, by the way?'

'Liz told me the authorities have committed her daughter to a psychiatric hospital but it's early days yet. The doctors aren't sure how well they'll be able to stabilise her, because she's been playing around with other drugs.'

'That'd be another benefit of my moving so far away, getting right out of Laurie's reach. Why she took such a fancy to me, I have never understood.'

'You certainly never gave her any encouragement, but

don't underestimate your personal charms.'

He rolled his eyes and stood up. 'Personal, schmersonal! If you're going to say things like that, I'm going to continue sorting out the office. At least the headache has abated somewhat today. I think I'll still take a couple of your magic painkillers, though.'

'Help yourself. I'm going to give the master suite a thorough spring clean and finish removing every trace of Roy's occupancy. I'm really looking forward to Aubrey moving in. I really like him.'

When he gave her a questioning look, she flushed and left hurriedly, saying she had to get on with her day.

Was there an attraction between the two of them already? If so, he hoped it would come to something. His aunt had been on her own for too long.

Later that day, Marian went to answer the front door and found Dan standing there smiling at her smugly, as if sure of his welcome. She didn't really feel like company but held the door open. You couldn't be rude to a neighbour who'd had to drive to get here.

'Do come in. I haven't seen you since the gathering at Liz's house.'

'I've been away in London. I left the party before what I hear were some interesting events and thought I'd see if you knew what's been happening since.'

Oh dear, he would ask that.

He studied her. 'Or have I come at a bad time?'

She was annoyed at herself for showing her distaste for talking about the situation, but he'd find out from someone in the neighbourhood, so it might as well be her. At least she'd be able to tell him the truth. 'I've been rather busy but it's not a bad time because I'm ready for a short break and a cup of tea. Would you like to join me?'

'Love to.'

She led the way into the kitchen and gestured to the table, then got out the fancy teapot.

'I gather Laurie Blythe-Jones doctored your nephew's drink and the person who told me said she's—' He broke off and tapped the side of his forehead in the age-old gesture, which annoyed her.

'Yes. She's in need of care at the moment, got her medicines mixed up.'

'My informant said she spiked your nephew's drink and it affected him so badly he had to be taken to A&E. Has he recovered from her ministrations?'

'He's getting better. They said it'd take a few more days to be fully clear of the effects.'

He studied her face. 'My dear Marian, if you don't want to talk about it, we needn't.'

'I'll give you the potted version then we'll move on to more pleasant topics.'

After she'd finished, he was the one to change the subject and she realised he was now guiding her skilfully towards a description of the new owner. She guessed that was really why he'd come, so said bluntly, 'Why don't you just ask me about Aubrey straight out. I'm a blunt countrywoman, remember?'

'You might be blunt but you're smart and I trust your judgement. Did he seem to like it here?'

'It's a bit early to tell. Why do you ask?'

'I was wondering whether he might be interested in

finding a way to break the entail and then sell all or part of Stovell Abbey and the grounds to my consortium. There. Is that plain enough?'

'It certainly is.'

'He could make a lot of money if he did that.'

'And so could you.'

He inclined his head in agreement and waited.

'I think Aubrey's more interested in coming to live here and I doubt he'd be even remotely interested in making money instead. He sounds to be in comfortable circumstances already. Is that blunt enough for you?'

'Yes. But rather disappointing.'

She shrugged. 'His choice.'

'What about you? Is he keeping you on here?'

'Yes.'

'I'll have to see if I can tempt him.'

She doubted he'd succeed and her expression must have shown that because he changed the subject again. 'Want to come out for a meal tonight?'

'No, thanks. I'm very tired and looking forward to an early night.'

She was glad that Dan left shortly afterwards. She watched him go, thinking that he chatted skilfully even when he was probing for information, but she much preferred a man who was honest and straightforward, a man like the heir.

Oh dear, she'd better be careful.

But when Aubrey rang that evening, it was he who asked questions that kept her on the phone chatting for well over half an hour, which she didn't mind at all. She couldn't help comparing her pleasure in that genuine conversation with her feeling of having to be on guard when talking to Dan.

She'd better watch out. She mustn't let herself show too much interest in the new heir – well, not unless Aubrey showed that he was interested in her.

If he did, she'd be pleased to take things further.

More than pleased, absolutely delighted!

But she was old enough to watch how she went.

It was only after the call ended that she realised she hadn't mentioned Dan's visit and what he wanted.

When Aubrey phoned again the following evening, she told him about Dan's visit and interest in buying the house, trying not to let her biases show.

'You don't sound as if this Dan is a favourite person of yours.'

'He's all right. I knew him when we were both teenagers, but he's grown up to be very business-oriented.'

'I'll take care how I go with him, then. I definitely don't want to sell the house. In fact, I'm looking forward hugely to living there and gradually renovating it, as well as making some improvements.'

'I shouldn't have prejudiced you against him. He's pleasant enough company, but he just – I don't know, seems to be looking for ways to make money all the time.'

'Well, I'm not at all that way inclined. I've learnt after the past year to tread more gently through life. I'm not going to beat about the bush now, either. I wonder if I can move in tomorrow.'

'Of course you can.'

'Good.' He gave one of his delightful chuckles. 'To tell the truth, I thought you wouldn't mind, so I went ahead and booked the removalists. It's not a big load. I've got a few pieces of furniture that I'm fond of and a lot of books. The rest of the furniture can be sold with the cottage.'

'How many books roughly? Shall we need to clear out another room for an extension of the library?'

'No. I'm not in Roy's league for books. I read for pleasure and don't give two hoots whether they're first editions or have marks on the cover, or whatever. I do keep the ones I've enjoyed and may read again. We'll dump the boxes of books in a corner of the library and at a suitable time you can help me sort out Roy's books. Surely they're not all valuable antiques?'

'Heavens, no. He never gave one away but we can do that for him. What time do you think you'll be getting here?'

'Mid-afternoon. It's a small cottage so it won't take all day to move out, and I've booked a cleaning service to go through the place afterwards.'

'Sounds very efficient.'

'Um, you mentioned there being a wine cellar at the abbey. Is there any champagne?'

'Yes.'

'Then could you please put a bottle or two of good stuff to chill and get out two glasses. I feel like celebrating moving in.'

'You don't have to include me in all your meals.'

'Oh, yes I do. Unless you don't want to join me? I don't like eating alone, especially when you'll mostly be doing the cooking. I'm not at all skilful in that area.'

'I don't like eating alone, either, and at the moment Richard is still living here so do you mind if he joins us?

He'll be leaving in a few days.'

'Even better. Invite him to celebrate with us tomorrow night and if he says yes, get out three champagne glasses. See you tomorrow.'

She smiled as she put the phone down. Aubrey always sounded so cheerful.

Even if they only took the occasional meal together, it would brighten her life. She was going to miss Richard greatly.

She went straight down to the cellar and found the champagne, and took up a couple of bottles of white wine while she was at it. Roy hadn't drunk alcohol at all, but she liked the odd glass of wine and from the way Aubrey had talked about celebrating with champagne, she felt sure he would too.

She found herself humming as she worked. Things were looking up.

Chapter Twenty

In Australia, Paula couldn't understand why it was taking her so long to recover from jet lag and she began to wonder if perhaps she really had contracted one of those nasty new viruses on the crowded plane.

She didn't feel up to going to work at the bar and phoned to tell Nick she was badly jet-lagged, then sat out by the canal staring into the distance. She even dozed from time to time, which was unlike her.

After a couple of days like this, in an attempt to stir herself into action, she decided to tidy her drawers upstairs, a job long overdue, and throw away anything that wasn't usable. She could do the job little by little if she got too tired and her possessions certainly needed sorting out. Why had she always been such a hoarder?

It was as she was pulling things out of the bottom drawer in the en-suite bathroom that she paused and stared at the packet of tampons. Then she got up and went to check her bedroom calendar, which she used to keep track of her monthly cycles. She was lucky in that she was very regular but she sometimes got so busy she lost track of the date, so kept a record.

Only, this time her period hadn't happened on its due date. In the confusion and unhappiness of going to the UK, she hadn't even noticed. She stared at the little cross she'd marked on the calendar, astonished that she was well over a week late. She couldn't remember that ever happening before, hadn't been even a day late.

It couldn't be *that* – just couldn't! She'd always been careful that she or her partner used birth control of some sort. And she'd never slept around all that much anyway.

Did you call it sleeping around when you'd fallen in love with a man who seemed to have fallen equally in love with you? She and Richard had only remembered birth control partway through their first encounter in Singapore and had stopped to remedy that. Since it had been so close to her period starting, she hadn't thought there'd been much risk so had forgotten about it.

She'd better check the dates she'd marked again. Had she missed a week in her calculations? She went back to look at her calendar and it said the same thing. Of course it did. Dates didn't change because you wanted them to. She'd been due more than a week ago and nothing had happened.

She sat down abruptly on the bed as she suddenly tied that in with feeling nauseous and a little dizzy the past few mornings.

She couldn't be pregnant, couldn't. Surely it was just the travel and uncertainty upsetting her body.

But what if she was? Her heart began to thump and she had trouble controlling her breathing. She didn't know what she'd do if she had fallen pregnant, but the next step was obviously to find out for sure.

There was only one way to do that: take a test. And she'd do it as soon as possible because she couldn't bear the uncertainty of not knowing.

She definitely wasn't going to her local pharmacy to buy the test because she knew most of the assistants there and they knew her. And she wasn't buying it online and then waiting for it to be delivered. She'd drive to the big shopping centre where she would, hopefully, be just one more anonymous woman passing through.

What's more, she'd buy two tests because if one said she was pregnant it might be faulty, but if two said the same thing, she'd have to believe them.

And then what would she do? She hadn't the faintest idea. It all seemed surreal.

She straightened up and squared her shoulders. She wouldn't go running to Nick, that was sure. Nor could she go running to her doctor for a day-after pill. It was too late for that and would she have done it anyway? She didn't know. The question was irrelevant now.

Surely, surely the test wouldn't turn out positive?

But if it did and she was carrying Richard's baby, she knew one thing. She couldn't in all fairness keep the information from him or do anything at all without consulting him. She'd always prided herself on facing problems squarely.

Stop thinking like that, she told herself. *You haven't even taken the test yet.*

She made sure to grab a shopping bag that zipped up tightly and didn't reveal its contents, then, feeling sick with anxiety – or with something else! – she went out and bought the tests.

After she got home, she unpacked the contents of one packet and suddenly wondered if there were a best time of day to do this. She was ignorant about such matters and didn't even know that, so studied the instructions very carefully then went online to check as well.

To her dismay, they both agreed that testing in the morning was best and more likely to be accurate. That meant she'd have to wait until tomorrow to do it. She didn't think she could bear to wait.

She looked at the open packet and hesitated. No, she was being stupid. She had to do this properly, didn't want to make a mistake and cause trouble for nothing.

Would it cause trouble? Would he be upset? She didn't know him well enough to be certain of that. But she'd wanted to know him better right from the start, she'd felt so attracted to him. It had surprised her how much. And that feeling hadn't gone away.

Richard rang again that evening but she didn't pick up the call. He'd left a message last time that he'd wait for her to phone him but he hadn't waited. He'd phoned again. That meant he was seriously interested in her, surely?

She hadn't replied and was feeling guilty about that. She would probably have picked up the call tonight if it hadn't been for this latest worry. The situation had changed so much, she felt bewildered. First things first: she had to find out what the test said before she spoke to him. She didn't want to blurt out her worries and then find it was all a mistake.

Of course she didn't sleep well, so at two o'clock in the morning she decided to make herself a cup of hot chocolate and stayed downstairs to drink it, finding its warmth comforting. Then she went back up to bed.

The warm drink made no difference whatsoever to her insomnia, nor did it stop her thoughts zipping around inside her head, going over every possibility, as she lay there. How could they reconcile living in two countries so far apart with bringing up a baby? Would Richard move to Australia? She couldn't bear the thought of living anywhere else.

She suddenly remembered what Nick had told her years ago after her holiday in Hong Kong, that she might find it helpful to see a counsellor about her inability to feel comfortable when she was away from this country.

She'd pooh-poohed him on that, but now, after her experience in England, she was beginning to accept that she probably did need that sort of help and wonder where best to find it.

It was impossible to keep from glancing at the bedside clock every few minutes. Four o'clock in the morning. Five past four. Oh, hell! She couldn't bear to wait a minute longer. She gave in to her fears, got up and took out the pregnancy test she'd opened, holding it in a hand that trembled.

'Just do it!' she ordered aloud. After rereading the instructions, she followed them slowly and carefully, then waited impatiently for it to reveal its findings. The five-minute wait it said on the packet seemed like an eternity. She didn't let herself look at the little space where the blue line might or might not appear until she thought five minutes must surely have passed, but only three minutes had gone by. She glanced at the test anyway and of course nothing was showing yet.

'You are definitely a fool, Paula Grey!' she told her anxious face in the bathroom mirror and went back to staring at the little space every few seconds.

'Idiot!' She counted up to twenty before she looked again. Nothing showing yet.

When the timer sounded for five minutes, she looked down and was shocked to see the blue line clearly visible.

She stumbled into the bedroom and plumped down on the bed with one hand flat on her belly, staring down at it. She'd always wanted children, though to have them at some vague time in the future, with a husband there to help bring them up.

The shock slowly gave way to wonderment. A child! She was carrying a child.

Suddenly she *had* to take the second test, just to be utterly certain. It was stupid. They didn't sell faulty tests. But somehow she had to do it again.

'To be sure, to be sure,' she muttered making a pitiful effort at an Irish accent.

So she went through the whole procedure again – with exactly the same results.

She threw the used packets in her wastepaper basket, then pulled one out again to show him when he came to join her – if he came. Then she went back to staring at herself in the mirror. Was there really another life growing inside her?

She tried to think sensibly. What should she do about it next? Actually, that was a no-brainer. She'd tell Richard, of course, and then they would decide together what to do. But how best to tell him?

She was, she realised, terrified in case he rejected her.

But he had a *right* to know. And she didn't think he'd reject her.

What exactly did she want from him? That was easy. Most of all she wanted him to put his arms round her and tell her he loved her and was happy about the baby.

In the end, she tried to pull herself together. She phoned Nick to say she was feeling a little better and was going out for a long, peaceful walk so he wasn't to worry if she didn't answer her phone.

She went for a short walk instead, strolling along to the little park at the end of the street, from which she could look right along their side canal to the main canal. She smiled at a little boat which was turning carefully round at the end. It had a family in it: two parents and two little girls wearing brightly coloured floaties round their upper arms.

Was her baby a boy or a girl? She didn't care. She would welcome either.

Would Richard care whether it was a boy or girl? She didn't think so.

Somehow the day meandered past and it still wouldn't be morning in the UK. That was when Richard usually phoned her. She checked that her phone was switched on, unable to settle to anything except waiting for him to call.

'You stupid woman!' she suddenly shouted. 'Why are you waiting for him to phone? Why does he have to be the one calling? You're a modern, liberated woman, aren't you?' She was acting more like an old-fashioned, unliberated fool, that's what she was doing. She picked up her phone and rang him.

A sleepy voice answered and she realised it was only about four o'clock in the morning there. 'It's me,' she managed in a childish-sounding voice. 'Paula.'

'What? Oh, thank goodness! Are you all right? I've been trying to contact you for days.'

'I know. I was so jet-lagged I couldn't think straight, so I waited. Our relationship is too important to mess things up.'

His voice softened. 'I don't want to mess things up, either. Are you thinking straight now?'

'Yes. Well, sort of. When will you be able to come to Australia?'

'Not for nine more days, according to the doctor, unfortunately.'

She suddenly realised that she couldn't tell him something so important on the phone, she just couldn't. She needed to see his face to be utterly certain of his real feelings. 'Let me know the details of your flight and I'll meet you at Perth airport. I have something important to tell you but I can't talk about it on a phone.'

'That's exactly how I feel. Don't end the call yet. Please don't. Just tell me you aren't going to finish with me.'

'Of course not.'

'Thank goodness. I don't want to lose you. Now tell me how you are. I was so sorry you were upset by what you saw. I was barely conscious by the time you left.'

'I'm OK. I've been doing a lot of thinking about – you know – the future. And I've been worried about you. I can't believe you had to be taken to hospital. You looked sleepy from across the room and she looked triumphant.'

'I was losing consciousness. And she had lost all sense of reason.'

'I shouldn't have run away without speaking to you. I'm really sorry about that.'

'Water under the bridge now. We'll make up for it. I just wish I was allowed to fly now. Two weeks seem to be dragging on for ever. I'd ignore them but I really don't feel quite right.'

'You mustn't take any risks.'

'It's hard to do nothing.'

'You're going to recover fully, though?'

'Of course I am. I feel better each day. I've already resigned from my job at the abbey. I definitely don't want to carry on working here. The new owner is a nice guy but it's his home now, not yours or mine.'

'It never felt like mine.'

'I know, love. You were a fish out of water.'

'What have they done about Laurie?'

He explained, saying sombrely, 'What she did was dangerous, so she can't be left to ricochet around the world like a drunken canon ball.'

There was a silence and she couldn't think of anything else to say. 'Well, I have some stuff to sort out so I'll end this call.'

'I'll phone you tomorrow.'

'No. Don't do that unless there's some other news I need to know.'

The silence continued at the other end and she couldn't bear to put the phone down and worry that she'd upset him.

'Richard? Are you still there?'

'Yes. I'd much rather keep in touch by phone each day, though.'

'I lose my wits on the phone when it comes to important discussions, even when I do it seeing a face. It simply doesn't feel real. Just email or text the details of your flight when you know them and we'll talk properly after you get here. I really do have to go now.'

She ended the call without waiting for him to say goodbye because she was overcome by nausea and also close to weeping. She didn't trust herself not to blurt out her news like a fool. No, she had to see his face when she told him because she wasn't going to let him marry her for the child's sake.

Even speaking to him for a short time had made her realise how much she wanted to be with him. She hoped he felt the same about her.

But when had things ever gone smoothly in her attempts at relationships? Never. And her marriage had been a disaster. She prayed this time things would be as different as they felt with Richard.

Then the nausea took over and she had to run for the nearest sink. That was another reason she'd have trouble talking about something important on the phone; the nausea wasn't just in the mornings. It could hit her at any time, she was finding. So why did they call it morning sickness?

The next subject she'd research on the Internet would be sickness in early pregnancy, she thought as she wiped her mouth. There must be some way to control it.

She'd have to go and see a doctor about that. She hated going to doctors and avoided them if possible, but this time she couldn't sort things out on her own.

Her reflection was scowling at her again from the mirror. It had scowled a lot lately, that reflection had. As Shakespeare had said in *A Midsummer Night's Dream*, 'the course of true love never did run smooth'. She'd studied the play at school and remembered that line, for some weird reason.

She surprised herself by smiling suddenly at the whole situation. Hell of a thing to happen at her age. One night of partial carelessness was all it had taken.

'I'll have to do it,' she said at last. 'I'll go and see a damned doctor about the sickness.'

And she wouldn't tell Nick or anyone else what was going on until she'd told Richard. That was only fair.

Later that evening she was still feeling restless and twitchy, so just because she could, she picked up an ugly little figurine someone had once given her, which she'd always detested, took it outside and set it on the ground between thick sheets of newspaper.

Smiling in anticipation, she went into the garage and found her mallet, then went back and pounded out her frustrations, smashing the stupid little shepherdess to smithereens.

That felt so good.

She hummed happily as she cleared up the mess.

'That's better!' she said and went up to bed, where she slept like a log for ten hours straight for the first time since she'd come home.

The next day, Paula woke up feeling lazy and well rested till she got out of bed. Then the nausea kicked in again.

She couldn't risk going into the bar because if she was sick, Nick would soon guess what was wrong. Instead she lazed around the house and gradually started feeling a little better.

She phoned the medical practice where she'd signed up but had only visited twice and made an appointment to see a doctor.

'Is it urgent?' the receptionist asked.

'No, not really.'

'Would Monday of next week be all right then?'

'Yes.' She scribbled it down on her calendar, annoyed with herself. It was more urgent than that, if only for her peace of mind, and she should have said so. She simply wasn't thinking clearly at the moment.

Chapter Twenty-One

When the doorbell rang a few minutes later, the last person Paula expected it to be was her mother. Her heart sank. At best, their encounters were awkward because they saw one another so rarely and had nothing in common. And she wasn't feeling at all up to it today.

She felt even worse when she saw a taxi pulling out of her drive and realised that her mother was carrying a little overnight case.

'Come in.'

Amanda came into the hall but made no attempt to give her a hug as her stepmother would have done. Oh, she still missed Jenny so much.

'I didn't realise you ever came to Australia.'

'Jean-Pierre and I travel quite a lot.'

Paula frowned. They'd called to see her in England and now here they were in Australia only a few days afterwards. That was unprecedented. Were they following her? If so, why? And it looked as if her mother intended to spend the night here.

What the hell was going on?

'Are you going to keep me standing in the hall, Paula?'

'Oh, sorry. Isn't Jean-Pierre with you?'

'Yes, but he's putting up at the hotel next to the casino tonight. He enjoys an occasional flutter and has arranged a poker game for tonight, but I find it rather boring. I'll be joining him there tomorrow but I thought you and I could enjoy a nice little mother-daughter chat.' She gestured round them. 'You surely have room to put me up for a night or two?'

It was the last thing Paula wanted but good manners had been drummed into her by Jenny, so she said, 'Yes, of course.'

By then her mother had walked across the great room and was looking out at the water. 'Gorgeous position for a house. Do you own it or is it mortgaged?'

Something made her decide not to show that she had any money to spare. 'It's mortgaged up to the hilt to pay for my share of our bar.'

'Oh, yes. Your little business with whatsisname. Surely you can find something more classy to do than serve drinks?' She didn't give Paula time to reply but continued without a break, 'Now, if you'll show me to my room, I'll have a quick shower because I always feel I need one after a plane journey.'

It must be one of the few things they agreed on, Paula thought sourly.

'Then afterwards we can go out and grab something to eat. My treat.'

'No need to go out. I've got plenty of food here.' And she wasn't at all hungry. Could hardly keep anything down. Would she be able to hide that?

She took her mother upstairs, enduring in silence comments on how the stairwell and bannisters could be redone to bring the area up to date. She left her in a bedroom which looked out on the canal and had its own en-suite bathroom. It was already a relief to leave her guest.

As she walked slowly downstairs, she shook her head in puzzlement, still unable to work out what the hell this was about. Her mother was the last person to want girly chats. They probably hadn't seen one another more than half a dozen times since Paula grew up, not even once a year.

It must be to do with the inheritance. What else could it be about? Didn't they know she was no longer the heir?

He was good at winkling out information, so they might. And they must believe they could gain something from her or her mother wouldn't have bothered to visit. Well, if it was money they wanted, they were going to be very disappointed. She had none to spare.

She put on the percolator and set off some coffee, though the smell made her feel even more nauseous, then she paced up and down, waiting for her mother to rejoin her.

As if she didn't have enough to worry about. Now she'd be worrying about the reasons behind this visit.

Aubrey arrived at Stovell Abbey late in the afternoon, followed by a small removal vehicle with two people in it.

He was beaming as he bounced out of his car and hurried across to where Marian was standing by the kitchen door. She couldn't help chuckling as he grabbed her by both hands and whirled her round.

'What's this for?'

'I'm so excited to be here!'

When he didn't let her go, she stayed where she was, enjoying the feel of his left arm round her shoulders.

A man and woman got out of the removal vehicle, smiling at his exuberance.

He looked sideways at her, went a bit red and let go. 'I'm being a fool, aren't I?'

'No. It's great to see someone openly happy. I enjoyed being part of your victory dance.'

He gave her a long, level look. 'Good. And to gild the lily, you're a perfect height for me to hold in my arms.'

It was a moment before she could put words together, because being hugged like that had made her heart beat faster and his words made her feel wanted. It had been a long time since a guy had held her close, especially a guy she liked. And then he'd hinted at – something between them. She'd better not believe in that till it was certain.

The female removalist cleared her throat. 'We need to get on with the unloading, Mr Lloyd.'

'Oh yes, sorry. Just glad to see my friend.'

Marian tried to concentrate on practicalities. 'Um, what sort of furniture have you brought, Aubrey? I wasn't sure whether you'd need a room clearing out to put it in or what?'

'Actually, the most important things I've brought are my own desk and office equipment. I'd like to put them into the estate room and take the present stuff out. Would that be all right? Only, mine are old friends and I've grown used to them.'

'That's not a problem. My nephew's cleared his

personal possessions out of the office and the estate papers are all neatly filed, because he's a neat freak where offices are concerned, so it will be easy enough to transfer the furniture. We can just dump the old one's contents in neat piles on the floor and then put them in your pieces when they're all in place.'

'Good. The rest of the furniture is what I'd call downstairs stuff, items I'm fond of. I'll have to see whether the pieces fit in here as I grow used to the place. They're none of them big because I've been living in a small cottage, so we can move them about later ourselves as needed.'

Her nephew came down the stairs to join them just then. 'Hi, Richard.'

Aubrey studied the younger man's face. 'I hope you're feeling better now.'

'Today I'm feeling absolutely normal for the first time since it happened. It's a wonderful feeling to have a clear brain again, I can tell you. I heard you talking about where to put your furniture. If your removalists can help, we can put the desk and other furniture from the office in the end storage shed. I cleared a lot of my old stuff out of there and it's not needed for anything else at the moment.'

He paused to think for a moment, then added, 'Let's dump your other furniture in the dining room for the time being. No one has used that room for ages and I doubt you're planning to hold any formal dinner parties for a good while.'

Aubrey grimaced. 'If ever. I'm not a formal sort of person. Let's get the furniture brought in then these people can drive home to their families.'

'Would you two like a cup of tea before you go?' Marian asked the removalists.

'I'd kill for one,' the woman said.

'I'll go and put the kettle on. Aubrey, will you bring them to the kitchen when you've finished sorting out the office furniture?'

'Of course.'

When everything had been dealt with and the removalists had drunk their tea, they pocketed some money that Aubrey had slipped them and left with beaming smiles.

He came back to join the others and said firmly, 'Champagne time now. I'm determined to celebrate.'

'I've got everything ready in the old butler's pantry,' Marian said. 'My goodness, Aubrey, you're whizzing round the house like a whirlwind, stirring everything up.'

He looked a bit abashed. 'Am I making a fool of myself, acting like a child at Christmas? I feel so happy to be here.'

Marian took his hand in both hers. 'No. It's not at all foolish. You're reminding us of how good life can be, and how full of pleasant and lively feelings and emotions. Roy liked everything kept quiet, too quiet for me. I can stand a lot of bouncing around to make up for that, believe me, Aubrey. And if you want to sing as well as dance, go ahead and I'll join in if I know the words.'

'It'd be a fun idea but sadly I've not got a good voice, so perhaps we'll stick with the dancing and champagne.' He tugged her into another impromptu twirl round the huge entrance hall that left them both laughing and breathless.

Richard watched them with a smile. 'Carry on, children. I'll open the champagne.'

He poured three glasses and they all drank to a happy life for the new owner of the abbey.

'You know what,' Richard said as he put down his

empty glass, 'it feels different here already. I think you're going to brighten up the old place considerably, Aubrey, and it's needed bringing to life again for as long as I can remember.'

'Wait till my grandchildren arrive. They'll be sliding down bannisters and racing round this hall playing tag.'

'I've slid down those bannisters a few times myself, but only when Roy was out. He didn't even like me coming into this part of the house.'

Marian drank the last of her champagne, then tried and failed to stop Aubrey refilling her glass. She picked it up and moved towards the door. 'I think it's time for a snack or we'll all be getting drunk. Give me a few minutes and I'll have something simple ready.'

'Good. I'm feeling hungry now. Here's to the cook.' Aubrey raised his glass to her.

When she'd gone, Richard said, 'Just to let you know, I'm going to Australia soon and I hope I can rely on you to keep an eye on my aunt. She's been working too hard for her own good in the past few years because she loves this house and Roy was mean about paying for extra help. All he cared about were his books. I was going to gift them to a museum and be done with them.'

Aubrey looked across at the door to the kitchen as if to make sure their companion wasn't within hearing and said softly, 'It'll be my pleasure to lighten Marian's load. We definitely need some more help here. And I hope you don't mind, but I'd like to get to know your aunt better on a personal level. I already feel that's far more important than getting used to the house.'

Richard stared in surprise. 'Really? Well, you couldn't find a nicer person. Good luck. She deserves some happiness.'

Two days later, an official-looking letter was delivered to the abbey by a special courier just as they were sitting down to breakfast. Aubrey had to prove who he was before he could even sign for it, which meant going into the office for his passport.

After the man had handed the letter over, Aubrey studied the sender's address on the envelope and asked if the courier had orders to wait for an answer.

'No, sir. I was told you'd deal with any response yourself.'

Strange that some stranger was making assumptions about how he'd react, when he didn't even recognise the name of the business which had written to him and was sure he hadn't dealt with them before.

Once he'd seen the man drive away, he came back to re-join the others in the office and studied the envelope again. For some reason he felt reluctant to open it, which wasn't like him. He hoped it wasn't bringing bad news.

Still without opening the envelope, he held it out to show Marian and Richard, pointing to the name of the firm in the top left-hand corner. 'Is this legal group anything to do with the Stovells?'

'Never heard of them,' Richard said after a quick glance.

Marian shook her head. 'Neither have I.'

'Hmm. I thought it wasn't one of ours. I've had quite a lot of correspondence with the Stovell lawyers in the last week or two. I wonder what these people want.' Aubrey found a knife and slit open the envelope carefully.

The others kept quiet as he read it, then he read it all over again, whistling softly. 'I didn't expect this from what you've told me about my Australian relative.'

He passed it across to Richard, who read it, gave him a shocked look then said firmly, 'I don't believe it's actually from her. Paula wouldn't do anything like this.'

'It says these lawyers are acting on her behalf,' Aubrey pointed out.

'You haven't met her. She's honest to a fault, blurts things out. She's not at all the sort to sue anyone for a cause as nebulous as "mental distress".'

Marian had also been re-reading it. 'I agree with you. She's very direct, Aubrey. What's more, this is an English firm and she's in Australia, so why would she choose them to represent her?'

'Why indeed?'

'I've got a feeling I've seen this law firm's name before but I can't remember where,' she said slowly. 'It'll come back to me.'

'Apart from anything else, that's a large sum to sue someone for,' Aubrey said. 'It'd have to be covering huge mental distress. How long did she stay here?'

'About a fortnight.'

'And was she extremely distressed about anything?'

'Upset at the thought of coming here and homesick for Australia but I'd not call her distressed. Angry at her life being thrown into chaos would be a more accurate description of her main feelings.' Richard shook his head again. 'The more I think about it and about her, the less I can imagine Paula doing this.'

'I have a friendly lawyer,' Aubrey said. 'I'll run this past him before I respond in any way. He'll probably be able to find out something about these people. But if you do remember where you've seen this law firm's name before, Marian, come and tell me at once, day or night, given our international links.'

He stood up. 'I'll phone my friend straight away.'

He came back ten minutes later. 'Fraser is in court all morning, but his clerk will pass my message on. How annoying!'

'I'm going to phone Paula and ask her what's going on,' Richard said. 'It's a mistake or a scam, it has to be.'

Aubrey grabbed his sleeve to stop him leaving them. 'No. Please don't do that until I've spoken to my friend. We want to be sure of each step we take with such a claim hovering over us.'

'Well, I still don't believe Paula would ever be involved in this sort of thing,' Richard said stubbornly.

'Nor do I,' Marian said.

Aubrey looked from one to the other. 'If you two are sure of that, who else could it be stirring up trouble? Can you even hazard a guess?'

Richard shook his head but Marian looked thoughtful and said, 'Her mother is married to a man I consider a scoundrel. I wonder!'

'Well, I'd be obliged if you'll continue wondering and wait to contact Paula until I've spoken to my lawyer. It'll probably be better if Fraser makes contact for us first.'

Richard and Marian both nodded but with obvious reluctance.

* * *

Paula waited impatiently for her mother to finish her shower and come downstairs again. At one stage, she crept upstairs and listened outside that bedroom.

It sounded as if Amanda was speaking to someone. Was she making a phone call already?

Well, no use standing here. It wasn't possible to hear what was being said because of the running water, but she wished she could. She had never trusted her birth mother, which had always made her feel sad. When she'd told her stepmother that, Jenny had admitted that she didn't trust her husband's first wife either.

Paula had asked why and found out that Amanda had once tried to get money out of him on the threat of taking their daughter away from him.

'Your father only laughed at that. He knew the last thing she wanted was to lumber herself with a child,' Jenny had said. 'But he was careful to keep an eye on you for a while, so he must have thought her capable of kidnapping you. And we moved suddenly a few weeks later, changing our surname till the next move.'

'That must have been when I had to call myself Paula Smithers for a while.'

'Yes.'

Paula banished those memories and glanced at her watch again, wondering whether to phone Richard.

She was also wondering why she had a feeling of something being wrong, a feeling that had started with her mother's arrival?

At last she heard footsteps on the stairs and Amanda strolled into the room. 'Ah, there you are. How about opening a bottle of wine and we'll have our chat?'

You had to humour a guest so Paula took a bottle out of the fridge and two glasses out of the cupboard. Then she remembered suddenly that you weren't supposed to drink alcohol when you were expecting. So she poured a glass of Chablis for her mother then got out a can of lemonade for herself and mixed a large glass of lemon, lime and bitters.

Amanda stared at her. 'Don't leave me to drink on my own.'

'I'm not in the mood. I've had an upset stomach for a couple of days and as I'm still only picking at food, I'll pull something out of the freezer for your evening meal. Would you prefer chili con carne or chicken risotto?'

'I'd prefer us to have a meal at the hotel with Jean-Pierre, which is what I'm planning whether you join us or not. Are you sure you won't change your mind about eating out? My treat.'

The mere thought of a restaurant full of noise and smells of food made Paula feel queasy and she shook her head.

'I'll just have some cheese and biscuits for the time being, then, and perhaps a few olives if you have some,' Amanda said.

While Paula was putting together a plate of nibblies, she thought she heard her mother's voice and peeped round the kitchen units. Yes, Amanda was just putting her phone back into her handbag.

Once they were sitting down, her mother studied her thoughtfully. 'Actually, I have something rather important to tell you.'

'Oh?'

'Jean-Pierre and I were worried about your situation

after the other heir turned up and we contacted a lawyer friend. He said you would have a good case for suing the Stovells about messing you around.' She waited, head on one side. 'You might as well take advantage of the situation, don't you think?'

'Suing? Why would I do that? And on what grounds?'

'For the money, of course. It might even be enough to pay off your mortgage. And you can always work something out to sue for if you have a good lawyer.'

'I'm not into that sort of stuff. And anyway, it'd cost a fortune and more money would probably go to the lawyer than to me in the end. No, definitely not. I was *glad* not to be the heir, anyway.'

'That's irrelevant. You really ought to look after yourself better financially. And if you won't do it for yourself, then maybe you'll do it for me.'

'What do you mean? What's my suing someone got to do with you?'

'Jean-Pierre has had a run of bad luck with the cards lately and we're a bit short of money. Well, a lot short actually.'

Paula suddenly realised this must be the real reason for the visit. She put down her glass and said loudly and clearly, 'No! I'm not doing it.'

Amanda gave her a half-smile. 'It's a bit late to refuse, I'm afraid. We've already put in a claim on your behalf. I told Jean-Pierre you might need a little nudge. You're not good at seizing opportunities.'

'Well, you can un-claim it. Not interested.'

'You'd find it a bit hard to withdraw your accusations now. If you do, the new heir could probably sue you back in return for vexatious activity, or whatever the legal jargon is for it, and then you could lose your share in the bar *and* this house.'

'He can sue away. I'm still not doing it.'

The doorbell rang just then.

Paula stood up and went to answer it, not at all surprised to see Jean-Pierre standing there.

She held the door open. 'Come and join the party, then you can take my mother away again. I'm not feeling well, as it happens, and I really can't cope with guests.'

When she sat down, he sat next to her on the sofa, uncomfortably close, and tried to take her hand. She pulled away and moved to the very end of the sofa, ready to transfer to a nearby chair if he tried that again.

Amanda poured him a glass of wine then sat down again.

Jean-Pierre took a big mouthful of wine and then began to lay out a series of careful reasons for Paula taking legal action, ending with the fact that he had experience of doing this sort of thing, so could help her get a very good deal.

The nausea welled up again and she stared at him through a blur of need that had her jumping up and rushing off to the downstairs cloakroom.

When she came out again, she found the two of them standing in the hall doorway as if they'd been listening to her throw up.

'You should have told me,' her mother said. 'Do I say congratulations or is it an unwanted nuisance?'

Paula clapped her hand over her mouth and pretended she was feeling sick again. 'I can't think straight, let alone talk about it till I'm feeling better. This time of night is the worst of all for throwing up. Please go away and leave me to get over it in private.'

They exchanged glances, then Jean-Pierre said, 'When's the best time to talk?'

She did a quick calculation. 'Late morning.'

'We'll be back then.'

'We do have your best interests in mind,' her mother added.

She forced a burp and rushed off again, listening to a short, sharp argument between them, then she heard her mother go upstairs and come back a few minutes later, her high heels tapping out her anger on the wooden floor of the hall.

Just to add colour, Paula made noises she hoped sounded as if she were being sick again and when she came out of the cloakroom, she saw the distaste on Jean-Pierre's face.

'We'll come back tomorrow morning,' her mother said. 'I'm very determined to help you with this, to make up for the years I was a bit neglectful.'

Paula managed not to tell her to stop lying but decided they'd find a locked door facing them if they did come back and no one answering it. Once they'd gone outside and got into what was presumably a hired car, and a rather shabby one at that, she locked the front door.

She noticed that the little wall cupboard rack of spare keys kept wasn't properly closed. How had that happened? She'd not opened it at all for days.

When she looked inside, she saw an empty hook, the one for the spare front door key. They must have taken it while she was in the cloakroom.

'Oh no, you don't!' she muttered and shot the top and bottom bolts on the door as well. No one was coming into her house unless she wanted them to.

She suddenly wondered how her suing the new heir would benefit them if she was nominally doing the suing. But she really was feeling woozy so in the end she stopped trying to figure out what exactly they might be plotting and instead picked up her phone.

She needed to discuss this with someone else and if the legal stuff was going to be aimed at the new heir, she'd better tell Richard and get him to warn Aubrey Lloyd. And she might as well tell him her news.

But Richard's phone rang and rang, and he didn't pick up her call.

She went upstairs and lay down on the bed. She'd just rest for a while then try again.

Chapter Twenty-Two

When his phone sounded, Richard looked at it and said, 'It's Paula. Shouldn't I answer it?' She'd said she didn't want to talk until she saw him, so this might be important.

Aubrey shook his head. 'Please wait a little longer. I'd rather speak to my lawyer first. He's a very savvy chap and well worth the retainer I pay for his advice.'

'Shouldn't we speak to Paula *before* you talk to him, find out what's going on and ask for his advice once we know that?'

'I've found that doing nothing until I'm sure what would be best is an excellent way of preventing trouble from escalating. And that letter from your friend's lawyer sounds like major trouble could be looming to me. Or do you want to see the Stovell family estate bankrupted by lawsuits?'

Aubrey was speaking more crisply than he ever had before and his advice would make sense if you didn't know Paula. But though Richard didn't take the call, he did know her and didn't believe she would ever try to sue anyone so was trying to work out what *he* thought it best to do.

Richard could see how determined Aubrey was to do it his way and simply said, 'I think I'll go and have a lie-down till you've spoken to your lawyer friend. I thought I was fully better but I'm clearly not.'

He didn't like lying to the two of them but what he really needed was time on his own to think things through.

He went up to his room but couldn't bear to be shut up indoors, so went outside and paced up and down the paved area outside the estate office at the rear of the house.

He was torn between phoning Paula and doing as Aubrey wished and waiting. Oh hell, what was the best thing to do?

When his aunt joined him, he could see she was worried.

'Just when things seem to be going well, this happens,' she said.

'The more I think about it the more sure I am that it isn't something dreamt up by Paula. She's not grasping. On the contrary.'

'But maybe someone is guiding her and she's been tempted.'

'Who would that be? Her friend Nick didn't seem like a litigious type to me, either. In fact, he's like her, frank and open.'

'I've been wondering—' She broke off.

'Go on.'

'It's a wild guess but her mother called in to see her during the period when the lawyers thought she was the heir. If you'd met Amanda, you'd understand that this was unusual. She's never had much to do with her daughter but maybe she's found some way to profit from the mistake about who inherits? Do you suppose she could be behind it?'

He shrugged. 'I don't know the woman so I can't say. We have no way of finding out what's going on unless we contact Paula, and Aubrey is very much against that. However, she'd told me she wasn't going to phone unless there was something important to discuss. And she's just phoned me. So something must have happened.'

'Well, Aubrey's lawyer will be phoning back in an hour or so. Maybe that will give us an idea of what dealing with this threat will involve. You can wait that long to contact her, surely?'

She took his agreement for granted and glanced at her watch. 'I'd better go and put something together for lunch.'

He hadn't contradicted her but when she'd gone, he went back to his bedroom and took out his phone. Paula had sounded distressed when she left her message, which was not at all like her. He was in the wrong place to deal with whatever was wrong. No, he had to speak to her.

But there was no answer when he called her.

'Damn it, I need to make sure she's all right.' And a phone call was an unsatisfactory way of solving a major set of emotional problems anyway.

The decision seemed to make itself all of a sudden. 'I'm not waiting!' He phoned his regular travel agent and was lucky to catch her when she was free to talk.

'Nadia, I need to get on the first flight I can to Perth, Western Australia. It's extremely urgent. I have a friend who isn't well and I need to get to her.'

'Some woman you care about?'

'Very much, yes.'

'About time you found one. I owe you a favour so I'll see what I can do. Stay near a phone. You may have to make a quick decision.'

'I'll be right here.'

A few minutes later, his aunt popped her head round the door. 'Come and have something to eat, then we'll see what Aubrey's lawyer has to say. Unfortunately his clerk has phoned to say he'll be delayed for another hour or two.'

'I'm just waiting for a friend to call me back. I'll be down as soon as I've dealt with it.' Or maybe not, if he was very, very lucky.

His phone rang five minutes later. 'Nadia. Have you been able to achieve any miracles for me?'

'Depends how rich you're feeling. There was a special first-class suite arranged on a direct flight to Perth and the celebrity has had to back out at the last minute, so you can have it at a thousand pounds above the usual business-class rate. My friend is doing this as a special favour to me, only you have to decide within ten minutes, pay immediately and get to Heathrow within three hours.'

It was a no-brainer. He didn't know why he felt so strongly that Paula needed him but he did. 'I'll take it.'

'Give me your credit card details and it's yours. I'll phone back shortly to confirm that.'

He paid a swingeing amount of money, then began slinging clothes into a cabin bag. After receiving Nadia's confirmation call, he phoned for a taxi and went downstairs.

Marian stared at him in amazement as he came into

the kitchen wearing outdoor clothes and carrying a backpack.

'I'm flying to Perth.'

'What about your doctor's orders not to do that yet?'

'To hell with them. I've been feeling OK for the last couple of days and I need to get to Paula ASAP.'

'Is there some problem her end?' his aunt asked.

'I don't know. I just feel as if she needs me. She and I are in the process of getting together and I really care about her.' He glanced at his watch. 'I've already called a taxi.'

While they waited for it to arrive, he looked at his aunt pleadingly. 'I've given her the number of the house phone. If she rings, will you tell her I'm on the way? She's tried to phone me twice, only we can't seem to coincide.' He could send her a text message but would she pick it up. She wasn't fond of modern technology.

'Yes. And Richard – I'm glad you've found someone to love. I've been worried about your lack of a significant other for a while.'

'I've got my fingers crossed for you and your new friend as well.' He saw her blush and chuckled.

The taxi must have been nearby because a horn tooted outside the back door shortly afterwards.

When he'd gone, Marian went to find Aubrey and told him what had happened. 'I'm glad he's found someone. I hope she cares as much about him as he clearly does about her.'

'I hope so too. She must be nice if he's so concerned.'

'Yes, she is.' Marian gave a wry smile. 'She might throw something at us if she were angry, but she's not the devious sort and I don't think she'd try to sue you either. Believe me, when you meet her, you'll agree with me.'

'In that case we should maybe use some delaying tactics, to give Richard time to get to Australia.'

'You trust my opinion about her enough to do that?'

He pulled her to her feet and put his arms round her. 'Yes.'

She gave in to temptation and leant against him and at that exact moment she remembered where she'd heard the name of the lawyers who'd contacted Aubrey about a threat to sue.

She clutched his arm. 'I've remembered! Those lawyers brought a case against a friend of mine, trying to sue her for something. Fortunately, she was able to prove they were wrong, but she found out they specialise in getting money out of people and told everyone she knew to avoid them like the plague. The last name in their company is the same as my mother's maiden name, which is why I remembered it.'

'All the more reason to hold back from taking action till Richard has got to Paula. It might be useful to send him a text telling him about the lawyers.'

She did that immediately, then said, 'Let's go and sit somewhere comfortable. We may be on the phone a lot today if your lawyer friend is any good.'

'Great idea. It's the wrong time of day for a glass of wine, unfortunately. But not the wrong time of day for a cuddle. Would you mind very much if I fell in love with you?'

She gasped and stopped moving. 'So quickly?'

'It was like that with my wife. Two days was all it took

to know I wanted to be with her and I enjoyed every year we spent together.'

'That's a lovely thing to say.'

'You'd have liked her and she'd have liked you. I've got the same feeling about you as I had then so if you think you can reciprocate, then I'll count myself a very lucky guy.'

She smiled and turned slightly to kiss his cheek. 'I've been trying not to count my chickens too soon, but I fancied you the first time I met you, so now you've said that, they're clucking loudly.'

'Some people don't believe in love at first sight.'

'I think it's more like attraction at first sight and if it's mutual, then it can quickly turn into real love. That's how I see it anyway. Let's work on that premise.'

'Delighted to.'

So they sat quietly, hand in hand, waiting for the lawyer's phone call.

It took longer than the clerk had thought it would and as far as Marian was concerned that was a good thing. It took nearly a day to fly to Western Australia, even on a non-stop flight. She hoped Richard had snared a seat on one of those because he might feel all right now, but she was still worried about him and the less time he spent on a plane the better.

It seemed ages till the phone rang and she listened intently to Aubrey talking to his lawyer friend. After a few moments, he held out the phone to her. 'Can you tell Fraser what Paula is like as a person, how likely to sue?'

In the end, she said, 'Look, Fraser, stop considering those two are causing this. I'm sure they're not. Richard is an utterly sane human being and I'd trust him with my life. He would never double-cross anyone or get involved in trying to gain money by false pretences. As for Paula, she's what I think of as very Australian – what do they call it? An ocker Aussie. She's blunt to the point of what some people would think of as rudeness, but it isn't. She simply talks with utter frankness. And unless I'm very much mistaken, she's in love with my nephew, which makes her even less likely to try to cheat him or his closest relatives out of money, don't you think?'

After the call ended, Aubrey smiled at her. 'You certainly leap to the defence of those you care about. I like that. So we'll not answer calls from this Amanda de Vanne or her husband, and I'll refer any lawyers working for them to my own lawyer, who has agreed to take on our case.'

'Why are you so sure there's going to be a case?'

'I've been the target before of spurious attempts to sue me for a variety of reasons.'

'May I ask why?'

He looked a bit embarrassed. 'I'm quite rich. I've not only been lucky with investments but inherited a small fortune from a relative and, sadly, was the recipient of the payout of my wife's life insurance, which she'd insisted we take out. I hope you won't mind?'

'It's you I'm interested in, not your money. I'm not rich. All I own is a small house in the village. But I've dealt with rich people for most of my life, so I'm not awed by wealth.'

'Yes. I guessed you might take such things in your stride. I have a nose for gold diggers. I've been targeted by a few since Sylvia died.'

He came across, took her in his arms and kissed her again, murmuring, 'You're addictive. Now, we're going to have a very interesting set of events, unless I'm very mistaken. In the meantime, I know it's not romantic, but I'm ravenously hungry so could we please get something more substantial to eat?'

'I'm hungry too. Come with me and choose from my offerings. I always keep a large stock of frozen food, mostly stuff I've made myself, so that I don't have to shop or cook every day, and also so that I know I'm not eating harmful chemicals. If you look at the list of ingredients on some prepared foods, it's as long as my arm. I agreed with Roy on that. He was a pure-food fanatic.'

'Excellent. I felt the same when I found I had cancer.' He took her hand and they walked into the large pantry to check out one of the two large freezers and its neatly labelled contents.

Paula woke with a start, hearing the house phone ring from somewhere downstairs. How long had she been asleep? How long had that phone been ringing before it woke her? And why had she left it downstairs. How stupid!

It stopped ringing abruptly and she sat up carefully, pushing the covers aside. The last thing she remembered was lying down on top of the bedcovers for a short rest. She must have pulled up the covers without realising what she was doing and fallen fast asleep.

As she caught sight of the bedside clock, which was a fancy one with the date in one corner as well as the time in big numerals in the centre, she gasped. It couldn't be! Had she really slept for ten hours straight?

She didn't attempt to rush downstairs to check her phone, because she was finding it better to move slowly and carefully after she got up or changed position in the mornings. It paid off this time because though she felt faintly nauseous, she didn't need to actually be sick.

She grimaced. She supposed that was an improvement.

When she'd visited the bathroom, she went downstairs, still moving slowly, and going straight to the kitchen area of the great room. Most of all she was thirsty and, after drinking a glass of water, she put the kettle on, feeling a longing for a cup of tea.

While she waited for the water to boil, she picked up the phone to find out who had been trying to contact her.

It was her mother. Amanda must have noted down the landline phone number while she was here.

Well, Paula wasn't answering that. When it rang again five minutes later, she let it ring out and the answering service pick it up again.

She wished she hadn't told Richard not to get in touch, wanted so much to speak to him properly.

She tried his phone again, but it was switched off completely and all she could do was leave another message to contact her as soon as he could, because she needed to tell him something very urgently.

Or had her mother put him off with this stupid attempt to gain money from the new owner of Stovell Abbey?

The doorbell rang an hour or so later and she went to peer out through the squint to find out who it was.

Her mother and Jean-Pierre. Well, that was easy to deal with. She'd ignore them completely.

After conferring, they drove away again. *Good. And don't come back*, she thought.

She was wondering whether she could ring Richard's aunt and ask her to give him a message. No. She didn't feel close enough to Marian to do that. And anyway, Richard ought to be the first to know about the baby. Only after she'd told him that face to face would she mention the stupid lawsuit.

She smiled fondly. She'd bet he didn't believe she'd set that up, as she wouldn't have believed it if it was him.

It was agony to wait until he got in touch or at least switched his phone on again so she could tell him she needed to see him urgently. She wished he'd hurry up.

Richard woke with a start, unable to work out for a few moments where he was. Then he remembered and stared round. This miniature 'room' was like no aeroplane compartment that he'd been in before. There was actually room for a tall person to lie down comfortably.

As if she'd been waiting for him to wake up, a stewardess peered round the screen that separated him from business-class passengers. 'Ah. I thought I heard something. Now that you're awake, sir, would you like a cup of tea or coffee, or even a glass of wine?'

'I'd kill for a big pot of tea.'

'Which sort do you prefer, sir?'

'I don't care. I'm desperately thirsty. And a big mug would be good, rather than a cup. Use the tea which brews most quickly.'

He got up and used the small bathroom cubicle to one side of his space, then found his bed had been turned back into a genuinely comfortable seat. Within a few minutes he was presented with a large mug of tea.

'That looks great. Thank you. White, no sugar.'

They waited on him attentively, the latest films were

available for him to watch, but all he really wanted was to get to Perth and find Paula.

When they asked whether he wanted to hire a limo to meet him, he realised that if he didn't manage to contact her, he'd have to make his own way to her house so he arranged to have a hire car waiting for him to drive himself instead.

But in spite of the wonderful service and extreme comfort, he was fretting, couldn't wait to get out of the plane and phone her.

He still had a strong sense of unease.

The front doorbell rang again and Paula went to see who it was, sighing when she saw that her mother and Jean-Pierre were back again.

To her amazement, when she didn't open it after three rings of the doorbell, he tried the stolen key again. Thank goodness she'd slid the bolts across the door as well as using the lock last night. The lock might now be allowing the key to turn but the door stayed firmly closed.

What the hell were they intending to do if they'd got inside? Kidnap her? Drug her? Surely not?

She was tempted to shout at them to rack off and leave her alone, but decided not to.

She managed to watch them from upstairs where it was easier to stay hidden.

Jean-Pierre began looking round and testing every window at the front, shaking his head and looking annoyed.

The side gate was also locked but she saw him lean over and pick the fancy number-keyed padlock so that it opened. As he then continued round the side house, peering at the window locks of the granny flat, she decided she needed help and phoned Nick.

'I'll set off straight away,' he said at once, 'and I'll bring Jonno with me. He has a black belt in some sort of martial art. I think you should call the police as well.'

'I don't like to do that. She is my mother.'

'Only in theory, not in practice. She sounds to be a real chancer and if he's into gambling, who knows how far they're prepared to go to get money.'

'You don't think . . . ?' She couldn't even say the words.

He said it for her. 'I doubt they'd kill you, love, but do not take any risks. Phone the police immediately!'

So she did. She felt a fool explaining that two people were trying to break into her house and she was afraid for her safety. She didn't say who they were. She could pretend to be surprised about that later if it came down to them catching the would-be intruders.

'A car is on its way,' the crisp voice said. 'Do you have somewhere safe to take refuge till we get there?'

Her mind was a blank, then she decided the granny flat's big store cupboard would keep them away from her for a while because its door opened inwards and she could block it. She told the person at the other end where she'd be and was asked to stay on the line if she could.

This was ridiculous and, as she barricaded herself in the cupboard, she felt furiously angry to have to act like this in her own home. But she felt distinctly uneasy about why they were trying to break in and wasn't stupid enough to take risks. They must have some plan. What?

She suddenly remembered Richard being drugged at

the party and didn't want that sort of thing to happen to herself. He'd only looked sleepy but had been unable to move properly or defend himself.

As an afterthought, she picked up the baseball bat she'd kept by the side of her bed when she lived in this part of the house 'just in case' and took it into the big cupboard with her.

Just let them try anything! She'd make them sorry.

Chapter Twenty-Three

It seemed to take for ever to get through customs and pick up the hire car, yet Richard had been ushered through in style while most of the other passengers were still queuing to be checked through.

He cut the clerk's explanations about the car short. 'I've driven this model before and I know how to find my way to the freeway and get down to Mandurah. I'm in a big hurry.'

When he got outside, he found a sunny morning, the sort that usually lifted your spirits, but somehow he couldn't feel happy until he made sure Paula was all right. He'd tried again to contact her before he set off but hadn't got through and now he was driving, he couldn't try calling again unless he pulled off the road and stopped.

He concentrated on moving as fast as the speed limit allowed, relieved that the roads were fairly clear now that the morning rush was over.

The sky was bright blue and the air seemed almost to sparkle, which lifted his spirits a little. Somehow the sun seemed brighter and the sky higher above him here in Australia.

* * *

When Nick and Jonno got to Paula's house, they saw a car parked in the drive and a woman standing outside the front door trying to peer in through the stained-glass windows to one side.

She swung round when they pulled into the drive and parked behind her car, then took out her phone, staying in the little porch in front of the door, watching them warily. After a couple of moments, she looked down at the phone in annoyance and took something out of her handbag.

Nick nudged his friend. 'Look at that.'

'It's some sort of handbag weapon, presumably for self-defence, because it's big enough to land a telling blow on an attacker. What does she think we're going to do to her?'

Jonno chuckled in spite of the seriousness of the situation. 'It's stereotyping because you're big and have dark skin. She doesn't know what a great big softie you are.'

Still keeping an eye on them, she tried again to make a phone call but still failed to get through.

Nick was about to ask her what the hell was going on when another car pulled up and a man he recognised got out. He waved to him, smiling. 'Richard, I'm so glad to see you. I didn't know you were back down under. This is my friend Jonno.'

'Hi. Is there any sign of Paula?'

'No. She rang me for help about quarter of an hour ago and said her mother and stepfather were trying to break into the house and she felt threatened. We only arrived here a few minutes ago.'

Jonno gestured towards the front door. 'We found this woman trying to peer in through the hall windows and when she saw us, she threatened us with a small cosh.'

'Paula isn't often afraid,' Nick said in a low voice. 'But she has enough sense to call someone if she needs help, as she has done with a couple of small incidents in our bar.'

The sound of smashing glass from the other side of the house made Richard exchange worried glances with Nick and Jonno. 'I don't like the sounds of that. How about Jonno and I go round to the other side of the house and find out what's going on while you keep an eye on this woman, Nick?'

He waved them off. 'Good idea. Get going. You two are younger than me if there's any violence. This female won't be able to get away from here with us parked behind her car.'

As they ran off, the woman shouted, 'If you lay one finger on me, I'll call the police.'

'I've no desire to lay a finger on you, lady. And I've already called the police,' Nick retorted.

'We don't need them as long as you stay away from me!' But she was looking to one side as if worried and she tried her phone yet again, muttering something that sounded like a curse when she got no response.

Richard and Jonno went round to the gate, where they found that it was swinging open and a dustbin on the other side had been overturned.

This looked like a forced entry and made Richard even more anxious for Paula. When he got to the rear first, he flapped one hand behind him to warn Jonno to keep quiet. They watched a man brush some fragments of glass away from the window frame with a broken-off branch from a large ornamental plant. On the ground nearby was a small statuette, looking the worse for wear.

He edged inside carefully and a couple of minutes later

opened the patio door from inside, presumably in case he needed to escape.

'Well, that'll make it easier for us to get inside,' Richard whispered.

It was Jonno who moved forward first this time, stopping behind the big plant and gesturing to him to wait. They stayed back, more or less out of sight, watching the man, presumably Paula's stepfather, going round the inside, trying the various doors.

When he found the door to the granny flat and realised it was locked, he gave it a hard shake but couldn't manage to pick the lock. Paula must have some fancy locks in place.

As the man threw himself against it, Richard got his phone out and took a photo of him doing that a couple more times. Then he put the phone away and looked at Jonno, who gave a bow and gestured to him to go first.

'You stay out of sight.' Stepping forward to the open door on the canal side, Richard asked in a loud voice, 'Looking for something?'

The man jumped as if he'd had a cattle prod stuck into him, then relaxed a little when he saw only one man. He said with a slight French accent, 'I have a right to be here. My stepdaughter rang to say she had an intruder.'

'Looks more like you're doing the intruding to me.' There was the sound of a siren coming closer and Richard smiled. 'The police have got here more quickly than I'd expected. Tell your story to them. I doubt they'll believe you any more than I do.'

The man tried to run round the house, but Jonno stepped out from behind the shrub and just stood there, towering over him.

Jean-Pierre stopped dead, staring up at him, then sagging because it was obvious who was the stronger.

'Too easy!' Jonno said quietly, then stepped back as a police officer appeared at the corner of the house and demanded that they stop fighting.

'I found this man breaking into my stepdaughter's house,' Jean-Pierre said at once.

Richard leant against the wall and laughed. 'Other way round, officer. This man broke that window. There were three of us at the front of the house when we heard it being smashed, so we came round to see what was going on.'

The officer kept an eye on Jean-Pierre as he said, 'So I gather. We've already spoken to the other man.'

Richard held out his phone. 'I have a photo of this chap trying to break into the granny flat before he saw us.'

'Granny flat? You know the house?'

'Yes. It belongs to my partner, Paula Grey.'

'That's the name of the person who called for help.'

'We hadn't got here then.'

'Let's go and speak to her, check the situation out.'

At the front of the house, they found Amanda arguing with a police officer, insisting she was here to help her daughter, while Nick was standing to one side, arms folded, smiling as if more than a little amused.

'Where is the owner of the house?' one officer asked. 'We spoke to her on the phone on the way here. Is she still hiding?'

'Must be. Can one of you come into the house the back way with me?' Richard led the way via the patio, calling her name.

The officer held up one hand. 'Just a minute!'

They heard a faint sound, which seemed to be coming from inside the granny flat.

'Are you there, Paula?' Richard yelled.

Her voice came faintly. 'Yes. But this stupid cupboard door has got stuck and it won't open.'

'The door to the granny flat is locked,' he told the police officer.

'There should be spare keys in the little cupboard on the wall just inside the front door: you need the one labelled "granny flat store cupboard",' Nick said.

Accompanied by a police officer, Richard went into the hall, saw that the bolts on the front door were still locked and smiled at his companion. 'You might like to let your friends in while I find the key.'

He got the keys out and the officer held out one hand for them. 'I'll do that.'

Once the man had opened the door of the store cupboard, Richard said, 'Let me!' He edged past him, holding his arms wide, and Paula threw herself into them.

'Are you all right, Miss Grey?' the officer asked.

She continued to cling to Richard. 'Yes, but I hate being shut in anywhere.'

'Well, you did the right thing to go into hiding.'

She looked from one man to the other. 'Did you stop them breaking into my house?'

Richard took it upon himself to answer. 'Sort of. Your stepfather smashed one of your patio windows, I'm afraid.'

She stiffened. 'Damn him!'

'Do you know why they were so eager to get inside?'

'I haven't the faintest idea. I think they had some plan

to persuade me to sue the new heir to Stovell Abbey. As if I ever would.'

Richard explained to the police officer, 'That's a house in England belonging to a relative of Paula's.' He turned back to Paula. 'A lawyer contacted Aubrey to say they'd be suing him on your behalf over a day ago, but I knew you wouldn't have done that, and so I told him and Marian before I left England.'

He beamed at her and, heedless of the audience of interested bystanders now watching, he pulled her close and kissed her. 'I'm really glad you're all right, love.'

'He's definitely on her side,' one police officer murmured to the other with a grin.

When Richard drew away, she dragged him back and returned the kiss enthusiastically.

'She definitely likes him too,' the other officer said.

'Aww, sweet!' Nick shared a beaming smile with Jonno.

That broke the spell and everyone except Amanda and Jean-Pierre chuckled.

Afterwards, they had to answer questions and supply information, not to mention turning out their pockets. One of the police officers whistled softly when he pulled a small bottle of pills out of Amanda's handbag.

'This looks to me like a well-known date-rape drug,' he said curtly.

Paula gasped and clutched Richard's arm.

'You'd not remember clearly what you did if you took one of these,' the officer went on. 'I particularly despise crims who resort to using these.'

'We'll take these two down to the police station and charge them,' one of the others said.

'Paula, just tell them I'm your mother and it was a joke,' Amanda pleaded.

'Only it wasn't a joke, was it?' she asked. 'And you knew why it'd be particularly unwise for me to take any pills like that, given my condition.'

The officer looked at her. 'May I ask what condition that is? If you need medical help, we'll send for it straight away.'

Paula looked at Richard ruefully. 'I wanted to tell you this privately: I'm expecting your child.'

He looked at her in shock, then seemed to pull himself together and pulled her into another hug. 'We'll discuss it when we're alone.'

'Your fiancée looks utterly exhausted. I think she'd better have a rest, given the circumstances. Perhaps you two gentlemen could follow us to the police station now to give us further details.'

Nick and Jonno nodded. 'You're my hero!' Nick murmured and Jonno tittered.

'And you two could perhaps come later this afternoon to make a statement? Are you sure you don't need to see a doctor, Miss Grey?'

'I just need a rest.'

When the police had left, Nick said, 'If you want a good glazier, I'll email you the name of one who's been helpful to us at the bar a couple of times.'

'Please do.'

Jonno nudged Nick. 'I think these two would like to be left alone now, don't you? And we have an appointment with the police.'

Nick winked at Paula and waved goodbye.

When they'd gone, she felt suddenly shy. 'How come

you're here, Richard? Not that I'm complaining about you coming to my rescue.'

'I was worried about you. I didn't know why, I was just . . . worried. I also knew you'd not have tried to sue Aubrey and even my aunt said she couldn't imagine you doing it.'

'I definitely wouldn't.'

He brushed her hair tenderly back from her face. 'Is it really true?'

'That I'm pregnant? Yes. Do you mind?'

'I'm delighted. It must be a lively little tadpole to spring to life from that one careless incident.' He pulled her into his arms and dabbed kisses all round her face. 'But – I'm – abso-bloody-lutely – thrilled.'

She dabbed a few kisses back and when he looked down at her stomach, she smiled. 'It won't show for weeks yet.'

'I'll be waiting. There aren't words to describe how utterly delighted I am.'

'You're not just saying that?'

'No, darling. Us creating a child is the icing on the cake of us getting together. How do you feel about it?'

'Overjoyed – well, I was once I got over the initial shock.'

'That settles it. I shall have to make an honest woman of you.'

She gave him a poke in the ribs as he struggled to hide a smile. 'It's me who'll be making an honest man of you, Richard Crawford.'

'When is it due?'

She shrugged. 'I'm not sure exactly. Just work out nine months from Singapore for the time being.'

'Haven't you seen a doctor?'

'Not yet. There hasn't been time. Anyway, I've been too busy being sick.'

'You poor thing. Are you feeling sick now and shouldn't you be lying down after all the excitement?'

'There's a faint residual nausea but it's worst first thing in the morning and it can hit me in the evening too. And no thank you. I've been lying down all night. I'd rather be up and about now. In your arms will do for a start.'

They stared at one another, each beaming, then moved across to the sofa where they sat and cuddled.

When he moved his head slightly away from her, she reached out to brush away a tear from his face. 'Men don't usually cry.'

'Men aren't usually this happy about something. How soon can we get married?'

'As soon as you like, only I'm not wearing one of those stupid white meringue dresses.'

'I can't even begin to imagine you wearing one.'

'And there will be all sorts of decisions to make about where we live and so on.'

He put one finger across her lips. 'Let's not look at the problems yet. Let's just enjoy the thought of being together and creating a family.'

She nestled down against him. 'Yes, let's.'

When he looked down, she seemed to be asleep. She was kidding him, wasn't she? Then he realised she wasn't kidding, she really was asleep. He beamed down at her. He'd tease her for the rest of their lives together about falling asleep on him at such an important moment.

She jerked awake ten minutes later and it took her a few seconds to realise where she was.

He dropped a kiss on her forehead. 'Good timing. My arm was just starting to go numb. How are you feeling?'

'Better for the nap. I keep doing that, falling asleep for a few minutes. Silly, isn't it? But it's very refreshing.'

'You looked adorable and you even have very musical snores.'

'I do not snore!' She sat upright and stretched her arms above her head. 'I'm famished. It's pretty hard to keep anything down when I first wake up but I think I can manage to eat something now.'

'I'll get it for you.'

'No, love, we'll do it together.' She linked her arm in his, reluctant to let go of him, even for the short stroll across to the kitchen.

They had to stop halfway across the room for another kiss.

Epilogue

The plane journey seemed to take as long as ever, but this time Aubrey had his wife of a few months sitting beside him so the time passed more pleasantly than long flights usually did.

He turned to Marian and pointed out of the window. 'Only a few minutes to go now. You can see Perth down there.'

She shuddered. 'I don't like looking down from aeroplanes.'

He chuckled.

'I'm so looking forward to seeing Richard again. It's been nearly a year now. And no, I do not count an image on my phone or computer as seeing him properly. I want to give him a big, long hug.'

When they walked into the airport, Richard ducked under the barrier, grabbed Marian and gave her a twirl, almost bumping into another passenger, but fortunately one who smiled at his excitement.

Aubrey continued to push the luggage trolley forward and went to introduce himself to Paula. 'This is better than faces online,' he said as he gave her a hug.

Paula returned the hug then continued rocking her three-month-old son's pram to and fro, hoping to stop him crying.

Aubrey smiled down at young Hal, who was now wide awake and waving his arms around. 'I love it when they have fat, kissable cheeks.'

The others came up to join Paula and Marian gave her a hug, then brushed a gentle fingertip over the baby's soft cheek. 'He looks just like Richard did at that age.'

Her nephew pulled a face. 'Poor child.'

As they walked to the car, Marian moved closer to Paula and said, 'We're friends now, aren't we?'

'Of course we are.' She reached out to clasp the hand Marian was holding out to her.

When they got back, they showed their guests round and, once Hal had gone down for a nap, were able to catch up with explaining the preparations for the wedding.

'It's taken me long enough to persuade her to tie the knot,' Richard said.

'I'm doing it now, aren't I?'

'Have you got many guests coming?' Marian asked.

'No. Just the people who matter. You two, Nick and Jonno.' Paula went a bit pink. 'I don't like being the focus of a lot of fuss.'

Richard shrugged. 'And I don't care how we do the deed as long as she commits officially to becoming my wife.'

'You said we were all going for a trip down south afterwards,' Marian prompted. 'But you haven't told us why.'

'And I still won't. You'll have to wait and see.'

* * *

Later, Richard managed to spend some quiet time with his aunt, sitting outside by the canal.

'I've never seen you look so happy,' she said.

'I don't think I've ever been this happy. She's such fun to be with, and you never know what she'll come up with next.'

'Yes, and happiness glows in her face as well as yours.'

'I wish we could have come to your wedding, Marian, but by the time she stopped being sick because of the pregnancy, Hal was well on the way and we didn't want to risk anything.'

'Yes. Pity. But these things happen. You told us the wedding isn't going to be traditional or fancy. Is anyone giving her away?'

'Perish the thought. She'd throw a hissy fit if anyone tried to suggest it.'

Marian chuckled. 'So no fancy white dress?'

'She teases me that little Hal is the only one who'll be wearing white. I suspect she'll be wearing a bright red dress, but I've not let her know I caught sight of some red garment being hidden away.'

'She's like a different person from the one who came to the abbey, glowing with life and health. Um, I've been wondering about this surprise you promised us.'

'And you can keep wondering till after the wedding.'

Marian pulled a face. 'Paula's not pregnant again?'

'Heavens no. You'll just have to be patient.'

Three days later, with the visitors recovered from jet lag, a simple ceremony was held out on the patio with a visiting marriage celebrant. Only Nick and Jonno were present as well as Marian and Aubrey.

And the bride's dress was indeed scarlet, a stunning garment rather like something Marilyn Monroe had once worn.

Paula got tears in her eyes as she made her responses, though, and the loving way she looked at Richard made his aunt and Nick shed happy tears too.

The baby slept through it all in his pram.

'There. Done!' Richard said when it was over and the celebrant had completed all the paperwork.

He swung Paula into his arms and circled the patio, humming a waltz. 'Gotcha, Mrs Crawford.'

'I'm not taking your name. I told you that already,' Paula said at once. 'How would you like to be called Mr Grey?'

He laughed. 'I knew that'd get you fired up. Actually I'd not mind doing that if you considered it necessary. It's you I want, darling, not changed names or fuss.'

She tried to speak, wiped away another happy tear and pulled him into a long kiss.

'They're a strange couple,' Aubrey whispered to his wife with a grin. 'But anyone can see the love they have for one another. I hope we look as happy to be together as they do.'

'I certainly feel it.'

'So do I.'

The following day, Richard drove them all 'down south' so that his aunt and Aubrey could see the surprise.

After a couple of hours, he turned off the main road and soon afterwards left the minor road via some dilapidated gates.

He stopped the car a couple of hundred yards away from a colonial-style dwelling with huge verandahs, flourished one hand towards it and said, 'Voilà! This is an old farm homestead, but it'll make a very stylish wedding venue as well as our home once I've finished renovating and extending it.'

Marian looked at Paula. 'I thought you adored your canal house and your bar?'

'I do. We're not selling that house, which we can use on our visits to the metro area, and you two are welcome to use it for holiday stays too. We're letting Jonno buy my share of the bar, though. But I always wished I could afford this sort of place and was planning to save up for a smaller one. Only I never expected to be able to afford it so soon.'

'I'm really happy for you.'

Aubrey nodded. 'I always felt guilty about hiding my existence and letting you take over at Stovell, Richard, but I can see how happy you are now. And my daughter loves managing it. She's even met a new guy there.'

'I'm delighted to hear that.'

Marian joined in. 'And because of that we will be able to take you up on your offer to let us use the canal house from time to time. That is such a wonderful place to live.'

Paula linked her arm in Marian's. 'You'll be very welcome.' She gave Richard a challenging grin and gestured to the baby and pram. 'You're a liberated man, darling. You can push the pram.' She stuck out her tongue at her husband and led the way inside, leaving the men to follow with the baby.

'She's even more fun in person than she was online,' Aubrey said. 'Come on. Let's follow our ladies.'

'I've already followed mine to the ends of the earth,' Richard joked. 'How liberated can a man get?'

'I suspect you'll find out.'

Chuckling, they started to push the pram and the baby woke up to join in the smiles.

Anna Jacobs was born in Lancashire at the beginning of the Second World War. She has lived in different parts of England as well as Australia and has enjoyed setting her modern and historical novels in both countries. She is addicted to telling stories and recently celebrated the publication of her one hundredth novel, as well as sixty years of marriage.

annajacobs.com